Will o' the Wisp

by

Lucy Naylor Kubash

This is a work of fiction. Names, characters, places, and incidents are either the product of the author's imagination or are used fictitiously, and any resemblance to actual persons living or dead, business establishments, events, or locales, is entirely coincidental.

Will o' the Wisp

Cover Art by *Kristian Norris*

The Wild Rose Press, Inc.
PO Box 708
Adams Basin, NY 14410-0708
Visit us at www.thewildrosepress.com

Publishing History
First Yellow Rose Edition, 2019
Print ISBN 978-1-5092-2694-8
Digital ISBN 978-1-5092-2695-5

Published in the United States of America

The man who stepped from inside the truck was definitely not Doc. Tall, with shoulders stretching the faded fabric of his denim shirt and shiny black hair that glistened in the sunlight, he would have towered over Doc's stocky figure. As he started toward the barn, she couldn't see his face, but the easy swagger to his walk, the way he rolled his booted feet from heel to toe, spoke to her of things she thought she had forgotten. Had worked very hard to forget. Feelings she'd buried ten years ago. Uncomfortable, she dropped her gaze to her daughter who had come to stand next to Gypsy.

"Is he Doc's helper, you think?" Lizzie scrunched her nose. "I don't think I know him."

Sudden awareness clutched Allison's heart, giving it an extra beat, as if to prove the man walking toward her was still easy on the eyes but hard on the heart. He'd certainly been hard on hers.

It would stand to reason Doc might call on him to give a hand.

But why does it have to be my barn that needs visiting this morning?

Her heart thumped hard in her chest as Shane McBride came closer, stopped short, and tilted his head back to get a better look at her. For a second, surprise lit his eyes to the color of the sky, then, sticking his hands into his denim pockets, he shook his head. A slow grin touched his mouth. The mouth she remembered so well.

"Allison," he said in his slow, sexy way.

Praise for Lucy Naylor Kubash

"Powerful and fast-paced with an unexpected twist. Beautifully crafted."

~Don Phelan, author and beta reader

Dedication

Dedicated to horse rescuers everywhere,
who risk their hearts and sometimes their souls
saving the horses no one else wants.
May there be a special place in heaven for them.

Chapter 1

Just before sundown, an uneasy stillness crept across the farm and settled like a silent summer mist. Allison sensed it the same time the horses did. They whickered and stamped in their stalls. She paused to brush an arm across her gritty forehead and peer out of the barn to the darkening woods beyond the pasture. Tiny goosebumps prickled the back of her neck. What on earth was out there? Something elusive. Something unseen. Something that had them all definitely spooked. For the third night in a row, she sighed at the prospect of being awake at two a.m.

Reaching to the radio on a shelf near the door, she tuned in a classic country station and cranked the volume up several notches. Willie Nelson crooned a mellow song, and she hummed along. Sometimes music helped soothe the barn inhabitants, but she had a feeling tonight even old Willie would have a hard time calming them.

When she turned to push the wheelbarrow back to the grain bins, she nearly tripped over Pouncer and Priscilla. Tails in the air, the skittish tabbies scrambled away, leaping to their hiding place in the loft.

"Crazy cats," she muttered to herself. Usually the antics of the animal menagerie that lived here didn't bother her in the least, but tonight, her cotton shirt stuck to her sweaty body and her feet ached. Hot, tired, and irritable, she couldn't wait to get into a cool shower.

"Suppose you darlings can let us get some sleep tonight?" She paused at each stall to check the horses one more time. They had gone back to nosing their hay, but a few still swished their tails nervously. "Just let the country music ease you to sleep," she murmured. "Heaven knows we all can use the rest."

She parked the wheelbarrow and pulled a bandanna from her jeans pocket to wipe her face and hands, pausing just outside the tack room to peek in at her daughter. "Ready to go, hon?"

In her excitement about the upcoming horse show on Sunday, Lizzie had promised to have her tack ready to go by tomorrow, and she worked earnestly to clean her show bridle, head bent to the task. Dark braids swung past the thin shoulders.

Her daughter glanced up. "I still have to go over my saddle one more time, Mom. But it's okay. I'll be up to the house in a little bit."

Allison hesitated. As a girl, she had spent countless hours in this barn and had always been perfectly safe. But after the occurrences of the last three nights, she had no intention of leaving Lizzie here alone.

"Let it go 'til tomorrow. I'll help you finish up. We should get some extra winks tonight anyway. Sunday will be a very early day."

"But I just wanted to…"

"No," Allison said firmly. "I'd rather you came up to the house now. Dinner's in the slow cooker and should be ready. You know you need to eat well before a show."

Reluctantly, Lizzie put her cleaning supplies back in her tack box and hung the bridle on a hook. She flipped her braids out of the way while she tidied the little room, leaving Allison to chuckle softly. If only her daughter's bedroom would garner such loving attention. Last time she'd looked, clothes, stuffed animals, and books had been strewn around in disarray.

Before leaving the barn, she called Gypsy to come with them. The Border Collie obeyed, but on the walk up to the house, she, too, glanced anxiously toward the woods, stopping and dropping her head low as they almost reached the front porch. The thick ruff of hair on the neck rose, and a deep growl rumbled in the collie's throat.

A shiver raced down Allison's spine.

"What is it, Mom? Why is Gypsy growling?" Lizzie propped her hands on her skinny hips and frowned. "She's been acting funny all day."

Once again, Allison searched the edge of the woods. So quiet. Not a leaf moved; not a breath stirred. Not even hers. What was out there?

For Lizzie's sake, she tamped down the sudden fear churning in the pit of her stomach. "Maybe there's a storm brewing somewhere. You know animals have a sixth sense that tells them before we ever hear the first roll of thunder. C'mon. Let's get inside and wash up. I don't know about you, but I'm starving."

She ushered her daughter and the reluctant collie into the kitchen and quickly shut and bolted the door. Sagging against the solid oak for a moment, she let out a sigh of relief.

This is crazy.

She'd grown up on this land, her grandparents' farm, and she and Lizzie had lived here alone for nearly three years. She'd never had cause to be afraid…until these past few nights.

The sturdy walls of the farmhouse were secure around them, and the rich scent of simmering stew wafting from the slow cooker reassured her.

While Lizzie went to wash up, Allison stepped into her tiny home office off the kitchen and noticed the flashing red light on the answering machine. She punched the button and listened to the message from her sister-in-law, sighing at Ronnie's ramblings.

Just what I need before dinner.

She deleted the message. Calling Ronnie back could wait until she put something in her stomach.

They were just sitting down to eat when the telephone rang, and she reluctantly answered it.

"How's my single sister-in-law?" Ronnie asked.

"Still single and not looking." Allison stuck the landline phone between her ear and shoulder while she poured glasses of milk.

"I called earlier and left a message, but I guess you didn't get it."

"I had a couple of late lessons today, and we just finished up in the barn." She motioned for Lizzie to say her grace and start eating without her. "Things have been a little hectic around here lately. We're getting ready for a show on Sunday."

"Honestly, Allison, do you still plan on hobbling after horses when you're ninety? Now you've even got Lizzie hooked."

She didn't bother to explain to Ronnie—horse-crazy was a condition you were born with, like a defective gene. She didn't need to teach Lizzie to be a horse-lover. The child had practically been born knowing how to ride. Pony had been her first word.

4

"There are worse things for her to be hooked on." She clutched the phone while glancing out the kitchen window facing the barn. Had she heard a whinny? The barn was closed up tight, but still…

"Allison. Allison, are you even listening?" her sister-in-law nearly shouted in her ear.

"Look, Ronnie, I gotta go. Like I said, Lizzie and I—"

"What about dinner?"

"I have it on the table." *What does she think, I never make dinner?*

"I mean for Saturday night. Didn't you hear me ask you over? Jerry's got this new guy working in his office, and he invited him here. It'll be casual. We'll barbecue."

Allison rolled her eyes. A little paunchy with thinning hair, Jerry Blake was a nice enough guy, but his friends looked too much like him. And Ronnie could be such a pain.

"Does he even like horses? No sense in my meeting him if he doesn't. You know that."

"My brother didn't know a thing about the wretched beasts," her sister-in-law reminded quietly. "You married *him*."

Allison bit her tongue against a sharp retort. The whole Delaney family thought they knew why she'd married Jason. Trouble was, they didn't even know the half of it.

"Since we have to be up by five a.m. Sunday, Saturday night is out of the question. Now, my dinner's getting cold. I'll talk to you later." She hung up before Ronnie could say anymore.

The woman meant well, but her matchmaking

efforts drove Allison nuts. Her sister-in-law figured three years of widowhood was enough and for the last six months had proceeded to trot out every eligible male she could come up with in the hopes she'd find one acceptable. There had been other casual dinner invitations, and Allison had even gone out with one guy twice, but when she canceled a date with him to sit up with a colicky horse, he didn't call again.

Most men just didn't understand. Her daughter and the horses would always come first. That's just the way it was. Jason had never seemed to mind, and she'd loved him for it. She doubted she'd ever find another man so tolerant.

A sharp longing for him tugged at her when she ventured back down to the barn later. Flashlight in hand, a prickle of fear teasing the back of her neck, she hurried to investigate the latest commotion. Right before turning in, she'd heard a few hooves whack against the barn walls and several nervous whinnies echo up the drive. Exhaustion tugged at her, but she had to find out what the heck had the horses so riled up.

She slid the door open. Sensing her presence, the horses whickered and pressed soft noses against their stall doors. She spoke quietly to them, as if to restless children, and began again to check each one, pausing at every stall to stroke a velvet nose or scratch a forehead. There were five boarders right now together with horses that could call Allison's Farm their final home.

In the first stalls stood the black-as-night sisters, Starlight and Stardust, who had come here last summer as a two-year-old and a yearling, neglected, starved, and frightened. Then came Major, a tall sorrel, used up show horse nobody else wanted anymore but who was still a good jumper. Next to him his best buddy Tank, a stocky dun quarter horse, nickered to Melody, a palomino broodmare. Also past her prime, Melody was one of the most gentle of horses for young riders.

I still remember the night I pulled those three from the horse auction.

Duncan, the old gray, had been here for as long as she could remember.

Mystri, her sweet little bay Arab, called softly to her from the stall next to Cayenne, Lizzie's chestnut and white pinto pony. But the newest addition, Pride, was setting up the most ruckus. When she peered into his stall as he turned, she immediately saw the ugly gash on his left shoulder.

How did that happen? And how had she missed it when they came in from the pasture? Maybe when she'd gone to help old Duncan find his stall, and Pride had just rushed into his, eager for his dinner.

She eased the stall door open to avoid spooking the buckskin even more and spoke in her calmest sing-song voice. "Take it easy, big fella. How'd you manage to get this?"

Allison slid a steady hand along his neck before stopping to examine the wound. It had already started to crust over but must be painful. At about three inches long, the cut appeared a little deeper than she cared to tend herself, but she'd treat it until she could get the vet out in the morning. She hated to call old Doc Brewster this late at night.

In the tack room, she gathered antiseptic and gauze to clean the gash and antibiotic ointment for after. Pride stamped one hoof, not happy about standing still while crosstied, so she had to work quickly. The rest of the horses watched, curiosity keeping them quiet for now.

"Too bad you all can't tell me what happened." She glanced down the aisle at the equine faces peering at her from their stalls. "It would help considerably." When it came to the horses' welfare, she never took any chances.

When she'd finished, she put the buckskin back in his stall and cleaned up. What could have happened in the pasture to cause Pride's gash?

First thing in the morning, before turning any of them out, she'd walk the fence line. Right now, she had to get back to the house. She'd left Gypsy with a sleeping Lizzie, but still…

On the path, she darted her gaze to the now pitch-dark woods. Mist crept up the hill, stealing the day's heat, and it should have been a relief. Instead, a chill rippled through her body at the distinct notion something she could not see could definitely see her.

Chapter 2

"It's not Doc's truck." Lizzie watched the black pickup crew cab pull into the drive.

Used to Doc Brewster's ancient red vehicle, Allison observed this strange one as it rolled up to the barn. She'd only gotten the answering machine when she'd called the clinic this morning, and Murray at the feed store had told her last week Doc wasn't feeling well. Had he finally gotten someone to help him out? He'd been the family vet forever, but he was nearing eighty. Well, she just hoped he was okay and that this vet had Doc's way with horses.

Gypsy took off like a bullet, barking at the unfamiliar truck. Allison called her back as the driver parked in the spot closest to the barn.

"Sit. Stay."

The collie took up her place beside her, glancing up as if waiting for an explanation of this new intruder. Allison shielded her eyes against the bright morning and waited, too.

The man who stepped from inside the truck was definitely not Doc. Tall, with shoulders stretching the faded fabric of his denim shirt and shiny black hair that glistened in the sunlight, he would have towered over Doc's stocky figure. As he started toward the barn, she couldn't see his face, but the easy swagger to his walk, the way he rolled his booted feet from heel to toe, spoke to her of things she thought she had forgotten. Had worked very hard to forget. Feelings she'd buried ten years ago. Uncomfortable, she dropped her gaze to her daughter who had come to stand next to Gypsy.

"Is he Doc's helper, you think?" Lizzie scrunched her nose. "I don't think I know him."

Sudden awareness clutched Allison's heart, giving it an extra beat, as if to prove the man walking toward her was still easy on the eyes but hard on the heart. He'd certainly been hard on hers.

It would stand to reason Doc might call on him to give a hand.

But why does it have to be my barn that needs visiting this morning?

Her heart thumped hard in her chest as Shane McBride came closer, stopped short, and tilted his head back to get a better look at her. For a second, surprise lit his eyes to the color of the sky, then, sticking his hands into his denim pockets, he shook his head. A slow grin touched his mouth. The mouth she remembered so well.

"Allison," he said in his slow, sexy way. "I…wasn't sure it was you who called."

Her throat closed up, and she had to clear it twice to speak. "I left the message on the machine. Do I sound so different?" After ten years, she supposed she did. Ten years could rob you of a lot of things, a lot of memories, especially if the memories meant nothing to you.

"Sandy called and gave me the message, so I could come straight out without stopping at the clinic."

Doc's receptionist—efficiency in person.

Allison nodded, words still sticking in her throat. After this many years, how did you talk to your first love? She glanced at her daughter and noticed the curious stares bouncing between them.

"What's your name anyway?" Lizzie piped up.

He looked down and lifted one brow a little, as if surprised at the forthright question. Then he stuck out his hand and politely introduced himself. "Dr. Shane McBride. And you are?"

The small hand fit into his big one. "Lizzie Delaney. And this is my mom. But, I guess you know that."

As he shook her hand, his gaze flicked from her daughter to herself and back again. "Nice to meet you, Lizzie. I hear you've got a horse I need to see. Maybe you can show me the way."

Finding her voice again, Allison stepped aside from the door of the barn. "Go ahead and take him to Pride's stall, honey. I'll be done feeding the others in a minute."

When they walked past, Gypsy looked up at her and whined, as if asking to follow them. Though normally wary of strangers, the collie didn't seem to mind the one walking the aisle of their barn this morning.

"Traitor," she muttered but motioned for her dog to go.

She finished handing out hay and grain to the rest of the horses and filled buckets with water. By the time she made it back to Pride's stall, Shane had gone to his truck for an injection. Outside the stall, Lizzie kept watch over the buckskin, who had calmed down since last night and hungrily pulled breakfast from his hay net.

"The new doc says you did a pretty good job on the

cut." Her daughter hung on the wooden half-door. "It won't need stitches or anything, but he said Pride needs to stay inside today."

Which would go over like a lead balloon when they let the other horses out. But then, considering she still didn't know what had happened to the buckskin, maybe keeping all the horses in today wasn't a bad idea.

"Did he say where Doc Brewster is?" Allison brushed wisps of hay from her T-shirt.

"He's in the hospital. He...he might need an operation." Lizzie jumped down from the door and looked up at her, uncertainty shimmering in her sky-blue eyes. "That's scary, isn't it, Mom?"

Allison nodded and tried to tamp down her own fear for the old man's well-being. "Very scary." She'd known Doc all her life, remembered when he and Pop went fishing together up north, and all the times he came to the barn to treat a sick horse. He and Pop had been the best of buddies. A jolt of fear clutched at her. To think they might lose him, too, was simply unacceptable. "I'm sure he'll have the very best doctors," she tried to reassure them both.

"I hope so." Lizzie leaned against her side. "Doc McBride is here to help out for the summer. He seems really nice."

She smoothed one hand over her daughter's dark braids. "Does he now?"

"Yeah. He just got here in Michigan yesterday. We're his first barn call."

Lucky us.

"What else did he say?" A twinge of guilt for pumping her daughter for information twisted her stomach, but there were some things she had a right to know.

"Mmmmm…" Lizzie twirled one of her braids with her fingers, then shrugged. "He drove here from Wyoming. I guess it's a long way."

Wyoming? Last I heard, he lived in Montana. "Well, good thing he was here to fill in for Doc." She could have called the other vet in the county who treated large animals, but she trusted her horses to Matthew Brewster. Today, she'd have to trust his replacement to treat her animals well, even if she'd learned the hard way not to trust that same man with her heart.

The sound of his boots echoed through the barn but stopped when Priscilla attempted to curl around his ankles. Instead of nudging her aside, he stooped to give the tabby a scratch behind the ears. Allison heard him talking to the feline and swore she could also hear the cat purring. Twenty minutes and he'd already won them all over—dog, cat, horses, her daughter…

When he stood before them again, Lizzie moved aside but stayed to watch what would happen with Pride. Allison clenched her hands at her sides, determined to keep the situation under control.

"I'm going to give the big guy a shot to prevent any infection from setting in. Maybe we best bring him out to the cross ties."

She took Pride's halter from its hook and slipped it over his head, led the buckskin out, and stood by him while Shane gave the injection. When they finished, Pride rubbed his head against her arm.

"Looking for sympathy, huh? Guess you've come to the right place." She rubbed his velvety nose and slipped him a piece of carrot from her pocket. "You know a sucker when you see one don't you?"

"He's a nice-looking fella." Shane came around to face the buckskin. He ran a big hand over the thick neck, pausing to comb out a tangle in the dark mane with his fingers. "Is he yours or a boarder?"

"Oh, he's ours," Lizzie piped in. "Mom bought him at auction last winter. She's training him to be a lesson horse. When we got him, he was really skinny. Mom said someone had neglected him. But she's got him in pretty good shape now." She stood next to Shane and peered up. "You're really tall, aren't you?"

Allison flushed at her daughter's boldness, but what the imp said was true. Even at five foot-nine, she'd always had to look up at Shane. She glanced up at him now, wondering what he thought about the girl with the dark braids and very blue eyes.

A slow grin hitched up one corner of his mouth. "Yeah, I guess I am. Doc used to say I could sprout half a foot overnight."

Those blue eyes grew round. "You knew Doc when you were a kid?"

His gaze lifted to meet Allison's, and at its touch a frisson of awareness rippled down her spine, setting even her fingertips to tingling.

So many years, so many dreams ago.

"I did. I worked in the clinic during summers, and sometimes I went out to the farms with him."

"Is that why you're a vet?"

"Lizzie, enough questions for now." Breaking the sudden reverie that threatened to take her back in time, Allison unhooked Pride from the cross ties and led him back to his stall. None of the horses would be happy cooped up all day, but until she figured out what had happened in her pasture yesterday, they would stay in the barn. She turned up the radio to keep the horses happy.

Outside, Shane packed up his supplies in the covered back of the truck. Lizzie still shadowed him, standing on one sneakered foot and then the other, while she peered at all the wondrous things a vet carried around. Allison had the distinct feeling she needed to squelch this fascination in the bud.

"Why don't you go on up and fix yourself some breakfast, honey?" She nodded to the house. "There's a new box of cereal. I'll be there in a minute."

Reluctant to leave, her daughter scuffed the toe of one sneaker in the dust. "I'll bet you didn't have breakfast yet either. Would you like some coffee?" She gave Shane her squinty look.

Allison could have screamed. She really just wanted to get rid of the man before things got sticky. Before she started to remember too much. "Lizzie, I'm sure the doctor has other calls to make. We're holding him up."

Shane shrugged. "I actually could use the coffee. My next stop is Johnson's hog farm."

A memory popped into her head, of Shane wrinkling his nose at the hogs she'd raised for the fair one summer. She kept them scrupulously clean, but he said they still smelled like hogs. He obviously still would much rather work with horses.

Man and child both looked expectantly at her.

"Come on up to the house," she finally murmured.

They took turns washing up in the downstairs bathroom. Allison poured two mugs of coffee while Lizzie poured juice and cereal then pushed a bowl in front of Shane.

"I hope you like them. They're my favorite."

He nodded, picked up one brightly colored loop with his fingers, and popped it in his mouth. "Love 'em."

His gaze locked with Allison's again. Blue as the morning sky, it sparkled with mischief. She had to turn away when her face grew warm.

So far, practically everything the man said dredged up some forbidden memory. *Sitting on the front porch, eating morning cereal, Shane teasing her, stealing a bite from her. Stealing a kiss.*

Her cheeks burned hotter.

Oh, for heaven's sake!

She downed her juice and coffee while standing at the counter. Lizzie didn't seem to notice the tension simmering in the kitchen. Between gulps of her breakfast, her daughter asked more questions, and patiently, Shane answered them all.

When they'd finished, Allison snatched their dishes and put them in the dishwasher. Now he would leave. Now she could regain some sense of composure and think about what she must do today.

He rose from the table and gave Lizzie's upturned nose a tweak. "Okay, Shortstuff, I really need to get going. Thank you, and your mom, for your hospitality."

For a moment, his gaze traveled around the cozy country kitchen with its blue and white gingham curtains and casual clutter. Did he also remember? The dinners she'd cooked for him and Pop after Grandma Ellie passed. His helping her with dishes while Pop read the newspaper. Sitting on the porch swing later, listening to the whip-poor-will. Watching for the will o' the wisp. Sharing a sweet iced tea…and kisses even sweeter.

Ten years had not diminished those memories, and heat like a shot of noonday sun flowed through her limbs. *Dammit!* After this long, she hated he could still do this to her. And she wouldn't let him.

"Go upstairs and make your bed, Lizzie."

"Ah, Mom!"

"Do it now. We have to go into town today. I have some work to finish up at the store before the weekend."

Dragging her feet, Lizzie made to leave the kitchen but paused in the doorway. "'Bye, Doc. Are you coming back to check on Pride?"

"Maybe. But I'm sure he'll be fine. See you, Shortstuff." He gave her a quick wave.

Allison saw him out to the porch where they stood for a moment staring out over the land that had once produced bushels of apples and peaches and crates of strawberries. She had first met Shane when he'd come to help pick the summer harvest. The orchards were long past their prime now, and the berries had gone wild.

He stuck his hands in his back pockets and cleared his throat. "I…was sorry to hear about Jason. And Pop. Must have been hard on you, losing them so close together."

She lifted her chin and faced him. "It was. But I had a child to take care of, so I had to keep going."

He nodded, a frown creasing his wide brow. "How come you didn't pack up and move down to your parents' place?"

"To a condo in Florida? Not my kind of living.

Besides, where would the horses go?" The horses she'd taken in, the horses nobody else wanted and would no doubt have gone to slaughter. The horses that had always given meaning to her life.

It always came down to that. Even as a child, she'd much preferred living here with her grandparents to traveling with her corporate executive parents whose lives revolved around their work and each other. They were retired now, and while Allison had taken Lizzie to visit them last year, she had no desire to live the country club life her parents did.

She shifted uncomfortably, wishing he would take his leave so she could get on with the day's work. Murray expected her to get the payroll done today…and she still had to check the pasture.

"Well, it looks like you've done all right for yourself with your boarding business and lessons. Doc Brewster told me. Pop would be proud."

When he stepped down from the porch, Gypsy suddenly blocked his path. Hair bristling again, she growled low in her throat.

"Hey, old girl, in case you haven't noticed, I've been here the better part of an hour and you didn't seem to mind. What's up?"

The collie's gaze fixed on the place farther on where the open field met the woods.

"It isn't you." Allison lowered her voice. "They've all been restless lately, and I can't figure out what it is. It's almost spooky, especially with Pride getting hurt yesterday."

Shane stepped back up beside her, and his arm brushed hers. A shiver climbed Allison's backbone. Was it because of the strange disturbances of the past few nights…or the appearance here this morning of the man she never thought to see again? Combined, they were enough to rattle her for sure. She rubbed her arms to drive away the chill.

Shane must have noticed because he offered, "Hey, you know how horses are. They love to kick and bite each other. I'm sure that's what happened."

She glanced up at him, hating the fact she suddenly needed reassurance and it would have to come from, of all people, Shane McBride.

"I think it's more than that. I've just had this weird feeling lately." She regretted the words the moment they left her mouth. He would think her crazy for sure. Allison Delaney going a little nutty living all alone out here with her kid and her horses. "I just mean, I think there might have been someone in the pasture yesterday. Something sent them running scared, and I think that might be how Pride got hurt."

"Well then, maybe we should take a look."

He took the steps two at a time. Before she knew it, they were striding toward the pasture and perhaps whatever had spooked them all these past few nights.

Just as though ten years hadn't stood between them, she walked the fence line beside him and hated to admit she felt suddenly safer. Time had certainly brought to maturity the man who had once been promised in a tall, lanky kid. She knew from Doc that while attending veterinary school, Shane had worked on ranches from Colorado to Montana, and the grueling work had no doubt helped increase the width of those football player shoulders, the strength of the muscles that rippled beneath the denim shirt. She also didn't want to admit the way his body moved alongside hers was still pleasurable. From her fingertips to her toes, notes of awareness played up and down every nerve ending and settled low in her belly.

Well, okay—she was twenty-seven years old and had a perfect right to feel some kind of reaction to a guy as good-looking as Shane. But their history was just too explosive to allow it to go any further. There was too much pain…and too many secrets.

Allison strode a little faster and pulled ahead of him, until he called her back.

"There, look. Tire tracks alongside the fence, and scrambled hoof prints here, as if the horses suddenly took off running. The corral is at least thirty feet from the road. Why would someone drive in here?"

He went closer to inspect the tire tracks, studying them for a few minutes before rejoining her at the fence. "There are two sets. One's pretty wide, but the other's much narrower. Truck and trailer maybe? You can see where they circled around to go back out."

Allison clenched her hands into fists. She had a pretty good idea who the culprits might be but would never mention them to Shane.

After following him back to his truck, she waited impatiently for him to get in.

As if reluctant to leave, he tapped his knuckles on the door handle. "Maybe you should call the sheriff."

"And if my boarders get wind something strange is going on here, I'll end up with an empty barn. I can't afford to lose my customers." She stuck her nervous hands in her back pockets. "You know how quickly things get blown out of proportion in this town."

"But if someone is harassing the horses, you can't afford another injury either. Next time, it could be serious."

He had a point, but it'd been difficult enough to get her business off the ground, and she'd worked hard to earn the confidence and respect of her boarders as well as the parents who brought their children to her for lessons. Yet, all it took was one offhand remark by someone, and it could all go away.

"I'll call him, if you want," he offered.

"No, I can take care of it." Hadn't she taken care of things for some time now? "Thanks anyway. And…thanks…for coming out this morning."

"Just helping out Doc. I owe him." Shane slid into his truck. He paused before starting the engine, his blue eyes deepening to a serious hue. "If you need anything, at any time, you call, understand? I'm staying at Doc's place."

She didn't acknowledge his offer but watched silently while he put the truck into gear and backed away from the barn. When a cold, wet nose inched its way into her hand she jumped a little and looked down to find Gypsy's questioning gaze.

Allison let her hand rest on the collie's head. "Where was he when I did need him?"

****

"Well, hell, some things never change," Shane told himself as he pulled away from Allison's Farm. Pop Tyler had named the place after the granddaughter he'd helped raise. He remembered the old man telling him that.

Since he'd stepped from his truck this morning, he'd had to deal with a multitude of memories and crazy emotions. A couple of miles down the road, he still couldn't sort them out. They ran the gamut from surprise to apprehension to pure pleasure at seeing Allison again.

She didn't look a bit different. Still tall and slim with incredible legs that looked especially good in soft faded jeans, and golden, honey-brown hair falling past her shoulders like silk. Ten years and he hadn't forgotten how the strands drifting across his face always smelled like wildflowers. Of course this morning, she'd tied it back in a haphazard ponytail, and dark smudges had lurked beneath her wide brown eyes, making her appear tired and almost...afraid.

A word he would never connect to Allison. She'd never been afraid of anything. But when he'd known her, she hadn't been a widow with a child to raise and a business to run.

The child. Jason's child.

He'd tried to detect some trace of his best buddy in the skinny, coltish girl, but Lizzie was a miniature of her mother—except of course for the dark hair and blue eyes. A gift from Allison's grandmother, perhaps? When he'd known Ellie and Pop Tyler, they'd both been white-haired.

The closer he got to Johnson's hog farm, Shane had to acknowledge another emotion he thought he'd conquered but now realized ran rampant through his veins. Jealousy. Pure and simple.

He and Jason Delaney had been best friends who'd shared three interests—football, fishing...and Allison. When Shane had admitted to being in love with her, he and Jason had nearly come to blows. He still remembered Doc breaking up the confrontation. Jason had backed off at the time, but in the end, he'd gotten what Shane had wanted more than anything in the world—Allison as his wife, a child with her...and a home.

And even though Jason was dead, Shane knew he could never quite forgive him for what he'd done.

Chapter 3

At Jackson's General Store, Allison settled into her corner of the stuffy office. The air conditioning Murray had installed last year didn't quite extend to the back room, and she had to be content with switching on a small desk fan and letting its feeble breeze blow away the morning's distress. After two unwelcome surprises, she definitely needed a few moments to gather her wits before tackling the store's payroll. While the ancient computer booted up, she rested her elbows on the desk, her forehead in the heels of her hands, and tried to let her mind go blank. It didn't. Instead, in full color, she could still see the man who had changed her life forever ten years ago by leaving her to deal as best she could. And now he was back.

Her jaw clenched. *Just what I need.*

"Murray wants to see you up front when you get a chance and—hey, are you okay?"

She glanced up to see Sylvia standing in the doorway. A frown of concern creased her co-worker's narrow face.

"Yeah, just not handling the heat too well." She pushed away from the desk. "What's Murray want?"

"Not sure, hon, but you ought to talk to him about getting some air pumped in back here. You shouldn't have to work in a sweatshop."

The fact Murray Jackson had spent any money at

all on a computer and air conditioning was a miracle, and she doubted he'd take to the idea of spending more. Pop had called him thrifty. Allison called him a penny pincher. But he'd helped her out when she needed it, offering her this job after Jason's accident. He and his wife, Thelma, were strong shoulders to lean on when the going got tough. So the man was a little tight. He'd been generous the first Christmas after Jason died, when she thought she'd not be able to give her small daughter any gifts. With his extended girth, fake beard, and toys in a sack, he'd made a fine Santa.

Sylvia knew nothing of this, and Allison would never let on Murray Jackson was really a softie at heart. Let her believe the grouchy boss act. It helped keep Sylvia in line.

"Sure you feel all right? If I knew how to use the computer, I'd be glad to help you out."

I'm sure you would, she thought, but simply nodded. Before leaving the office, she minimized the document and switched off the monitor. She found Murray filling the wild bird feed bins. He puffed while getting the last of the cracked corn out of the sack. Without actually offering to help, she just lifted another bag and dumped it in one of the bins.

"You shouldn't be doing that," her boss scolded.

"Neither should you." She opened the sunflower seeds and emptied them into the next bin.

"I didn't hire you to do the heavy work around here."

Allison thought of the fifty-pound bags of horse feed she regularly hauled in the barn. "Maybe you should hire somebody else to do it then." She eyed the heavy-set man, noting the sweat beading on his brow. If he didn't watch out, he'd be sharing a hospital room with Doc. She finished with the birdseed and leaned back against one of the bins. "Sylvia said you wanted to see me. What's up?"

He hitched up his pants beneath his belly and ran a hand through his grizzled hair. "I'm taking off this afternoon to go see Matthew. Then the missus and me are meeting Kate and Rich for dinner. It's Kate's birthday, and she wants us to come and see the room she's fixed for the baby."

Murray and Thelma's only daughter married Rich two years ago, and they were expecting their first child any day now.

"And?" With Murray, there was always an "and."

"I need you to close up the store for me tonight. Sylvia's here 'til six, so you'll only have two hours by yourself. Think you can handle it?"

Of course she could handle it, but it would mean another trip into town when she really needed to get some rest before Lizzie's show.

Oh well, I'll just have to catch up on sleep next week.

Yeah right.

"Okay, but I need to pick up Lizzie from the library and go home and take care of the horses before Sylvia leaves."

She didn't want to come right out and ask it but wondered if Murray trusted the brassy blonde. She certainly didn't, being almost certain the woman had helped herself to a few items in the store since being hired last winter.

"You go on home then when you're done in the office. I'll call Thelma and let her know. She's just so darned excited about this baby. You'd think nobody ever had a grandkid before."

"That's what grandmas are for," Allison teased and went back to her cubbyhole corner.

In spite of the stuffiness and crazy thoughts about the morning running through her head, she managed to get the payroll done and had just shut the computer down when Murray stopped back in the office.

"Thelma says to thank you for helping out," he said gruffly. "She says for you and Lizzie to come for dinner sometime."

She didn't mind accepting their invitation. At Thelma and Murray's dinner there wouldn't be any eligible men invited.

Closing the office door behind her, she followed him to the front of the store, where she told Sylvia to expect her back by six.

"I take it you're not going out to Farmer's Country Club to hear the new band tonight?" Her co-worker checked her lipstick in a small compact. "Pete says they're pretty good. We're going, and we can save you a spot at our table."

"Thanks, but it's a little hard to get a babysitter at such short notice. Anyway, Lizzie is showing this weekend, and we need to get our rest."

"Well, if you change your mind, let me know when you get back. Pete could probably dig up one of his friends. We could make it a foursome."

"Dig up" being the operative words, she thought, escaping into the afternoon's heat. Any friend of Sylvia's boyfriend was *not* someone she wanted to meet.

****

Allison tidied the candy shelf for the third time and checked the clock. Ten more minutes and she could lock the door and turn over the Open sign to Closed. There hadn't been a customer in the store in the last half-hour, but she wouldn't deny Murray any last second sale.

Lizzie sat in the back room, listening to music and reading one of the books she'd checked out of the library earlier that day. Sometimes, she worried the girl was too much of a loner. Miss Smarty Pants made straight A's in school and had a few riding friends, but she never went to the slumber parties other girls her age seemed to enjoy. She preferred to hang out at the barn and enjoyed her weekly trips to the library. Her daughter was a happy child, as far as Allison could tell, but it concerned her that she might end up just like herself—more at home with horses than with people and with a social life that really stunk. She would have to make a more concerted effort this summer to get them involved in a few activities that didn't include horses.

Another check of the clock showed three minutes to eight. Allison headed for the door, but jumped when it suddenly opened. A painful jolt of apprehension gripped her stomach and set her heart to thumping when Duane and Darren Potter—two men she least wanted to see while alone with Lizzie—walked into the store. Truthfully, she never wanted to meet up with them again, but in a town as small as Silver Creek, it was bound to happen sooner or later.

Only why did it have to be now?

Refusing to let the two brothers intimidate her, she straightened her shoulders and lifted her chin. "Store is closing, guys. You'll have to hurry." She continued on to the door, closed it behind them, and turned over the sign.

For a chilling second, Duane brushed his arm against her, and she caught the nauseating smell of liquor and stale cigarette smoke clinging to his clothes. Instinctively, she stepped away, but not before she heard the crude, *"Bitch,"* muttered beneath his breath.

Allison straightened her back and strode to the register. She would not let them rile her, not here, not with Lizzie sitting in the back room.

Please, just stay put until the sleaze balls leave.

They meandered over to the grocery section and took their time picking up a six pack of beer and a couple bags of chips. She kept an eye on them while pretending to busy herself with something behind the counter.

The two men were a few years older than Shane and less than stellar members of the community. As kids, they'd always been in trouble and had ended up dropping out of school. They'd done some prison time for their involvement in a dog-fighting ring and now ran a small car repair shop. They'd never made much of a go of it and didn't seem to care. In the last few years, they'd turned even more strange and reclusive. Survivalist types, Murray called them. Allison had some other names—poachers and animal-abusers being the top two.

They brought their purchases to the register. She had rung them all up and put the items in a bag when Darren pointed a greasy finger to the shelf behind the counter.

"Give us a couple cans of chew."

She suppressed a shudder and tossed the rounds of tobacco into their bag. A filthy habit, and, by the looks of their teeth, one they'd had for a long time. It wasn't the only thing about the Potters that gave her the creeps but more what she knew about them.

Allison caught the sly smirk Duane slid her way and stared back in defiance. The crude comment he had muttered under his breath made her skin crawl, but she refused to let him see her anger…or her fear.

She reached for the money he handed to her, only to have him pull it back.

"Hey, Darren, you wanted some chocolate bars, too, didn't you?" When his brother didn't answer, he gave him a nudge. "Hey, quit gapin', you idiot. Get your candy."

"Think I'd rather look at a real pretty girl, even if she is a…"

Angry tears burning behind her eyes, she reached over the counter, grabbed two candy bars and slammed them down. "Will that be all?" she ground out.

"Now don't go gettin' all testy, Allison." Duane held the money out again. "You know it makes you look ornery, and anyway, what happened to the sweet little woman Jason married?"

"She died when he did," she snapped and snatched the money from his hand.

She had just given Duane his change when Lizzie wandered out of the back room.

"Hey, Mom, isn't it time to go yet? I'm really tired—" She yawned and stretched but stopped short when she saw the Potter brothers.

Her gaze darted from the men to her, and the flicker of fear Allison saw in her daughter's eyes sent her pulse racing.

"Hey, squirt, how's it goin'?" Darren asked.

"Don't call me that!"

To Allison's surprise, Lizzie's chin jutted out, and she glared at Darren.

"Aww, we don't mean no harm." He started toward her, holding out one of the chocolate bars. "Here, have some candy."

"Not from you I don't want any." Lizzie backed away.

"Now you're actin' just like your mom. Think you're better than us?"

Just as Allison was about to fly over the counter and come between the brothers and her daughter, the door opened, and Shane stepped into the store. She gripped the counter edge and bit her lip. He halted when he saw the Potters but said nothing, though a hard expression stole over his face.

"Hi, Doc!" Slipping past Darren and the candy he offered, Lizzie scooted up to Shane's side. "My mom is just getting ready to close up."

"Yeah, I noticed the sign but saw you were still in here. Is there a problem?"

At his presence, a sigh of relief escaped Allison. "No problem." She bagged the candy and held it out to Duane, leveling her gaze at the leader of the two. "They were just leaving."

He gave his brother a shove to take the bag, and they shuffled toward the door. Shane stepped aside to let them by. When they stopped in front of him, Lizzie reached up to grab his hand.

"Didn't know you was back in town, McBride," Duane spoke. "Plannin' on stayin'?"

"For a while."

Narrowed eyes studied him up and down, as if taking an assessment. "Been a long time."

Shane just nodded. For an endless few seconds, tension crackled between them. Then Darren and Duane left the store, and Allison let out a sigh that shook her whole body. She had to clasp her hands behind her to stop their trembling. *Damn.* She hated that she let those two scumbags rattle her so much.

"Would you...p-please lock the door for me?" She tried to keep her voice even, but it trembled a bit.

When he turned the deadbolt, Lizzie, still clinging to his hand, spoke up, "Boy, I'm sure glad you came in when you did. Those guys give me the creeps, and Mom doesn't like them—"

"Never mind, Lizzie." Allison got a hold of herself and turned to cashing out the register. "Go get your things together so we can head for home."

"Will you stay 'til we leave?" Lizzie peered up at Shane for reassurance.

"Sure, Shortstuff. Now, go do what your mom said."

While her daughter went to gather her things, Allison put the cash from the till into a bag and carried it to the small safe, glad she didn't have to take it to the bank tonight. Shane followed her to the back of the store and waited as she locked the office.

When Lizzie joined them, she struggled to slip her backpack over her shoulders. Before she could help, Shane gave her a hand. Her daughter glanced up in surprise and then grinned, showing her crooked front tooth, then seemed to think a moment.

"Hey, guess what? My pony and me are in a horse

show on Sunday. You could come to see us, if you want."

"I'm sure Dr. McBride has things he'd rather do on Sunday," Allison admonished, and then the thoughts ran through her mind. Was he married? Did he have a family? Had they come to Michigan with him?

"Fact is, I'll be at the show. I'm the check-in vet."

Of course you are. Allison turned away and rolled her eyes in exasperation.

They waited by the back door while she checked the front of the store again and turned off the lights; all the while Lizzie chattered on to Shane.

"Then you can see me and Cayenne. He's my pony. He's getting kind of old, but he still wins lots of ribbons. I'm showing him in Western pleasure, halter, and showmanship."

"Then you'll be pretty busy, but I'll stop by and watch," he promised.

Once they were outside, Allison breathed in deeply to steady nerves left raw by a day full of the unexpected. The night air cooled her face and calmed the tension still coiled in the pit of her stomach. She couldn't wait to get home and crawl between the sheets of her bed, put her head on the pillow, and—

"Uh-oh. Looks like we've got a problem, Mom."

Digging in her shoulder bag for her keys, Allison stopped in her tracks, not certain she could take one more thing. "What's wrong now?"

Shane stood beside her aging SUV parked on the street. Staring down at the front tire, he shook his head. "Hope you have a spare, because this one's flatter than flat."

She sagged against the side of her vehicle. "I won't

ask. I won't ask," she murmured, half to herself.

"Ask what?" Lizzie stared at the offending tire.

"What else can go wrong today?" Shane supplied.

Allison saw him watching her, concern darkening his gaze. Did he have a clue the first thing to go wrong was his showing up at her barn? Yet, she *was* thankful he'd been there while the Potter brothers were around. And right now…

"You okay?" he asked.

"I don't have a spare tire." She tried to muster a shrug and couldn't even do that. "I had a flat this past winter and never got it fixed. You're looking at the spare."

He glanced down at the deflated tire and then at Lizzie, who still held his hand. "Well then, how about I take you ladies home, and in the morning, I'll call Ray's Tire Service, see if he can come up with one for you."

Allison shoved herself away from the vehicle. Jason had bought it second-hand for her shortly before he died, and it needed a lot more than just a new tire. She'd been lucky to put brakes on it only last month.

"You don't have to do this," she barely whispered.

Shane shifted his weight to pull the truck keys from his snug jeans pocket. "Yeah, I do."

They didn't talk much on the drive from town. When he stopped his truck in front of her house, Allison quickly stepped out. She started to thank him and drag Lizzie away when she instinctively turned toward the barn and the sound she thought she heard.

Please no. Not again.

She desperately needed to get some sleep tonight, but she'd never catch a wink if she didn't look in on the

34

horses first.

"I have to check on the barn, Lizzie. You go on in the house." She handed her the key.

"But I don't like to go in alone, Mom. I'm coming with you." Her daughter yawned wide and rubbed her eyes.

Normally, Lizzie wouldn't think twice about being alone, but maybe the events of the last few nights had disturbed her, too. Certainly, the appearance of the Potter brothers tonight hadn't helped matters.

Gypsy had risen from the porch, wagging her tail. When she saw Shane, she came down the steps to nuzzle his hand in greeting.

"Honey, here's Gypsy. She'll go in with you." She tried to reassure her daughter.

"How about you and I go do a barn-check, old girl?" He motioned for the collie to follow him to the barn. "Lizzie, you take your mom inside. I think you've both had a long day."

As much as Allison wanted to argue, she was just too tired. She herded Lizzie toward the kitchen door but stopped to toss a glance over her shoulder. On the path to the barn, Gypsy trotted alongside Shane, as if it were the most ordinary thing for her to do. The dog never made friends this easily, but then, maybe her sixth sense told her this man was different. Perhaps she knew.

She shook the crazy thought away, and while Lizzie went upstairs to put on her pajamas, she filled the teakettle and put it on to boil. A hot cup of chamomile tea would hopefully help her relax before crawling into bed.

Please let it be a peaceful night.

****

Shane walked down the center aisle of the barn, stopping at each stall to make sure every horse was settled for the night. He spent an extra few minutes with the buckskin Pride, checking the gash that had brought him here early this morning.

The horse was fine; they all were fine. Too bad he couldn't say the same for himself. One day back in Silver Creek and every emotion he'd ever experienced here had hit him square in the chest. Obligation, jealousy, passion, and now a new one that had assailed him when a child put her hand trustingly in his. Protectiveness, strong and pure.

Strange, but from the moment Lizzie had squinted her blue eyes at him, he'd felt a bond of some sort. A tie, as if he'd always known this girl.

Well, she was Allison's daughter, and at one time he and Allison had shared a bond as strong as the old oak tree that shaded the yard in front of the farmhouse. Had shared a passion, too, as hot as a late July night.

How could she have forgotten and married Jason?

He supposed the same way he had caught a bus to take him a long way away from Silver Creek.

Glancing around the barn one more time, he called to Gypsy, shut off the lights, and closed the door tight behind him.

Going straight home to Doc Brewster's place was probably a good idea, but he needed to tell Allison she could rest easy tonight. Something about her today told him that was important.

He went up to the kitchen door and tapped his knuckles against the wood. When she opened it, he noticed she'd loosened her hair from its ponytail. The

36

color of golden wheat, it fell around her shoulders, and once again he could not help remembering the sweetness of running his fingers through those silken strands.

He swallowed hard. "It's…fine. The barn…is fine," he managed to say.

Gypsy pushed her way past him, shoving him a step closer to Allison. He put out a hand to brace himself on the doorframe and found hers already there. For a second, their fingers touched, and a tightening in his chest…and elsewhere…accompanied the beads of sweat popping out on his upper lip.

Her eyes widened with surprise, as if the zing between them had affected her, too, then she pulled her hand away and retreated into the room, now using both hands to clutch a mug of something steaming.

"Is Lizzie okay?" He stepped back to regain his balance.

"She's…getting ready for bed."

"Then if you're all okay, I'll say goodnight."

"Wait, Doc! I have to show you something."

When he would have escaped, Lizzie's voice stopped him. She clattered down the stairs and into the kitchen. Pink pajamas and bunny slippers made her the picture of innocence, and once again the need to protect rose up, a wave of emotion so strong it nearly sent him reeling.

"See, it's new." She showed him the western hat she carried so lovingly. "Mom bought it for my birthday. I'm going to wear it in the show Sunday. Isn't it great?" She held the cream-colored Stetson up to him.

"You'll look beautiful, Lizzie, and I'll be there to see you and Cayenne," he promised. "Now, you better get some rest."

"Mom said I could have a snack first. Can I have some of Aunt Ronnie's cookies? Do you want some, Doc? They're Snickerdoodles."

"Thanks anyway. I've got some early calls to make tomorrow, and I need to visit Doc Brewster in the hospital, so I think I'll say goodnight." He needed to leave while he still had some sense left in his head.

Chapter 4

In her upstairs bedroom, Allison opened the double windows wider to let in a bit more of the cool night air. She shed her jeans and T-shirt and slipped into a nightshirt with "Save the Wild Horses" emblazoned on the front. Sitting on the edge of the bed for a few moments, she rolled her head back and forth to work out the kinks brought on by stress from the remarkable day. As if enough hadn't happened, with her vehicle in town, she would have to see Shane again to get it back.

Before tucking her daughter into bed, she'd reassured Lizzie the tire would be fixed, and they'd have the vehicle in time to take her and the pony to the show—at the fairgrounds bright and early Sunday morning, where they would again see Shane as check-in vet.

She sighed. Avoiding the man was not an option, so she best figure out how to deal with him and remain sane.

Grabbing a hairbrush from the dresser top, she went to sit in front of the open windows. Using her fingertips, she massaged her scalp first and then slowly, methodically began to pull the brush through the tangled strands. Closing her eyes, she tried to relax but couldn't stop the memories flooding into her mind.

On an evening a week after her grandmother passed away, she had been sitting alone on the front porch, brushing out her hair. Shane had driven up and joined her on the swing. They sat quietly for a while, and then she began to cry. Against his strong, sympathetic shoulder, she spent all the emotions kept bottled up inside, and shed every tear she'd not been able to weep even at Grandma Ellie's funeral. When she finally couldn't cry anymore, he took the brush from her and drew it through her damp hair. Then he kissed her and held her and stayed with her until she slept there in the swing, in the soft summer night.

A sweet memory, and one she would always hold dear, but it didn't take away the pain of the other one, of hearing from her grandfather that Shane had left the state, taking a late bus out of town without any explanation. Leaving a young, vulnerable girl to deal with the secret she was keeping.

Remembering just how alone she'd felt jarred Allison from her contemplative mood. She tossed the brush aside and rested her arms on the windowsill. Staring out into the night, she tried to focus on the front lawn below.

Beyond the circle of the yard light, a half-moon cast a watery glow, and barely-there shadows fell from the old oak and willow tree. Straining to see better, she let her gaze follow the path leading to the barn. There, the moonlight faded beneath a passing cloud, and just past the barn, a shadow moved.

Allison tensed and clutched the edge of the sill. Had she imagined it? Or had something, someone, slipped around the corner of the barn? She kept watching but saw nothing else. The hair at the back of her neck stirred, and a sudden shiver coursed down her spine.

A shotgun sat in the back of the closet in her grandparents' old room. She hated guns, but Jason had made certain she knew how to shoot one, just in case. If anything—anyone—threatened her little family or her horses, she wouldn't hesitate to use it. But for the rest of the hour she sat at the windows, the barn remained quiet, and no more shadows stirred.

****

Allison had just finished with morning lessons when Shane arrived the next day. He waited while she talked to Jenny, the high school girl hired to help out during the summer.

"I have to go into town," she briefly explained to the petite brunette. "Make sure the kids walk the horses before putting them in this front pasture. Then could you stay with Lizzie until I get back? I shouldn't be gone long."

She knew Jenny wouldn't mind. It gave her reason to stay around the horses longer, but the girl glanced curiously at the tall, dark-haired man leaning against his pickup.

"I've never seen him before, but he's pretty cute for an older guy. Who is he?"

Allison had to laugh to herself. Did Shane know he was now considered an "older" guy? "Shane McBride. He's the new vet helping out Doc Brewster."

Jenny studied him a moment longer while he talked to Gypsy, who leaned against his knee as he scratched behind her ears. "Is he a friend of yours?" she finally asked.

Allison dug around in her purse to make sure she had her checkbook. Shane her friend? At one time, he'd been that...and so much more. But now? "We knew each other from high school."

"Well, I think you ought to date him. I mean, he's really hot."

He looked up to see what was keeping them, and she caught Jenny waving. She slipped on her sunglasses. "I'll let him know that."

Shane hid his own dilemma behind dark glasses when Allison hopped into the cab of his truck. He had something to tell her, something he didn't like to think about, and she would like even less. He'd found it out shortly after he had her vehicle towed to the tire shop this morning. Ray himself called with the disturbing message, and now he had to find a way to tell her.

He waited until they were a few miles from town, gripped the steering wheel with one hand, and reached over with the other to touch her arm. She seemed pensive, staring out the window at the farmers' fields slipping by, and jumped at the contact.

"Before we get to the tire shop, there's something you should know. Ray called me about the flat you had."

She stared at him now, her chin lifting a bit. "Is there a problem?"

He returned his gaze to the road, wishing he could say no, but she had to know the truth. "It wasn't just a nail in the tire."

"So, what then? I don't remember running over anything that might have—"

"You didn't run over anything." He glanced over at her, gauging how she would take what he had to tell her. "The tire was cut."

She didn't say anything, and before he focused his attention back on driving, he caught a glimpse of her frown, as if she was trying to absorb what his disturbing words meant.

After a few moments, she finally said, "Cut? As in, something cut my tire?"

"Yeah, that's how it appears."

"Well, that's strange." She turned in the truck seat, and the confusion in her voice reached out to him. "How could it happen?"

He hated giving Allison something else to worry about, but she had to know. "I stopped by the tire shop and had a look myself. The tire wasn't just cut—more like slashed."

"What are you saying?" Her voice rose to a higher octave. "Someone did it on purpose?"

He wanted to spare her this, she'd already been through enough, but there was no getting around it.

Shane nodded. "If it wasn't so dark last night, we probably would have noticed." Sudden tension filled the cab of the pickup. He switched the air-conditioning to high.

"But I…don't understand. Who would want to slash my tire?"

He heard the tremor hidden in her words and tried to reassure her. "Kids playing pranks? Friday nights can get pretty boring around here when you're fifteen." His own background was not without its secrets. He knew how stupid and reckless kids could be, but he didn't think that was the case right now.

"I don't know of any kids around here who would do such a thing, and I know a lot of them. I work with the Young Riders program and give lessons to at least twenty. I can't think of any kids who would do this to me."

Unfortunately, he could think of two adults. In fact, in his mind, after the little incident in the store, they were most certainly to blame. If he had the chance, he would make sure they never bothered Allison again. He just didn't want her to know.

"I suppose it's possible they weren't from around here." Her sighed echoed in the truck cab. "There are a lot of out-of-towners staying at the lake every summer, and some get kind of rowdy. Maybe one of them did it. I guess I need to notify the police."

"I took care of it. Thought I'd save you the hassle."

She opened her mouth as if to protest but then just said, "Thank you. I appreciate it," and turned back to staring out the window.

He had to wonder—did she struggle more to comprehend this latest incident, or the fact she had truly thanked Shane McBride for anything?

Allison was thankful they didn't talk anymore until they reached Ray's Tire Shop. She paid for the new tire and met Shane back outside, where he stood talking to Harry near O'Malley's Bar and Grill. Harry had owned the bar forever and lived above the establishment. When he wasn't working, he sat and watched the town of Silver Creek go by. He knew just about everybody, and if somebody wasn't a local, he knew that, too.

The wiry Irishman nodded to Allison. "Shane here says you had a bit of a mishap with your vehicle."

I guess it isn't enough Shane and Ray know my business, now Harry does, too. She waved away his comment with a brief, "It's taken care of."

"I asked him if he's noticed anybody hanging around the street at night. He said he's always out late."

The bar owner grinned at this. "I am. Haven't seen

anything lately, but I'll keep an eye out. You okay?" He squinted at Allison.

She'd only had coffee for breakfast, and her head buzzed. She really just wanted to get home. "I'm…fine. I'm going to start back now."

"Wait up a sec."

Shane put out his hand to keep her from leaving. Where his fingers rested on her wrist, a tingle like a static shock jolted her, but for some reason, she couldn't pull away.

He clapped the Irishman on the shoulder with his free hand. "Good to see you, man. You'll remember what we talked about."

"Sure enough, and hey, stop by soon. I'll buy you a burger and a beer."

Allison watched the old man hobble down the street before turning back to Shane. "What was that all about?" He still held her wrist, and as if he just realized it, his hand slid down to meet hers, lingered a second too long, and then fell away.

"Nothing important." He checked his phone for messages. "Are you in a hurry to get back?"

Yes—she really needed to get away from him. Needed to…but wanted to? She wasn't sure.

"Jenny is with Lizzie, and we've got to get ready for tomorrow."

"Okay. Just wondered if you could spare an hour or so."

Hope lurked in his blue eyes, and she remembered how darn persuasive he could be. One way he hadn't changed much.

Shane started toward their vehicles parked next to the shop. "I'm heading up to see Matthew. Just thought you might go with me. We don't need to stay long, but he's scheduled for surgery on Monday. He doesn't have much family, and I want to let him know not to worry about the clinic. It's just…" He stopped walking.

She took the extra step to stand in front of him and glanced up. A strange emotion, one she swore resembled something between fear and dread, darkened his expression. "Just what?"

He shook his head and ran a hand around the back of his neck. "I hate hospitals. I haven't been inside one since, well, for a really long time. I honestly don't know if I can go in, but I want to see Doc before he goes under the knife."

She tried hard not to see the silent plea in his eyes. *After all he did for me since yesterday, I suppose I can do this. Anyway, it's more for Doc Brewster.*

The older man only had a niece who lived in Illinois and probably wouldn't be here for the surgery.

She dropped her gaze. "I'll go with you, but I need to call Jenny and let her know." Problem was, the phone she pulled from her purse was totally out of juice.

Without a word, he handed her his.

****

Matthew Brewster lay pale and shrunken against the hospital sheets. It shocked Allison when they walked into his room. She was used to Doc's ruddy appearance and no-nonsense attitude. To see him lying so helpless with monitors surrounding him and an IV running from his arm gave her a moment of alarm.

So much like when Grandma Ellie was in the hospital.

Much as she did then, she straightened her

shoulders and went forward, Shane trailing at her heels. Doc's eyes were closed. She called to him softly and touched one gnarled hand. He woke with a start and took a moment to focus on them. When he would have struggled to sit up, she shook her head.

"No, don't. It's okay." She patted his hand in reassurance. "We just wanted to see how you're doing."

Her heart ached for a man who was so normally active and busy, who worked from early morning until often late at night, and who knew more residents of the county than maybe even the sheriff. That he was rendered so incapacitated had to be very difficult for him.

He managed a smile for her then glanced to Shane behind her. A light of instant affection shone in the older man's eyes. "Hey there," he murmured. "Sandy told me you were here."

"Came as soon as I could. Are you doing okay? Do you need anything?"

Matthew jerked his head toward the medical paraphernalia. "Only to get rid of all this, but it ain't gonna happen anytime soon. I'm getting cut on Monday." He motioned to his chest. "The old ticker needs some repair."

Shane came closer to the bed. He pressed his lips together, as if holding back a sudden rush of emotion, but kept his voice even when he spoke. "Well, I'm here as long as you need me. Everything at the clinic is under control."

His mentor relaxed, a little more at ease as his gaze came back to rest on Allison. "How about you, missy? Everything all right at your barn?"

She would never mention the strange goings on to

Doc. "We're fine, busy with summer lessons. Lizzie is going to show tomorrow."

Matthew lifted one shaggy eyebrow. "So...how'd you two manage to come in together?"

She glanced at Shane, but he avoided her eyes and just shrugged. "We just happened along at the same time."

After a moment, Doc motioned to his water cup. "Hey, missy, could you do me a favor? See if one of those nurses' aides can give you some fresh ice water. Everyone's busy this morning."

Happy to do anything to help ease his discomfort—and the awkward tension—Allison snatched up the foam cup and disappeared down the hall.

Shane noted Matthew waited until she was out of earshot before he beckoned him closer to his bedside.

"We got some talkin' to do, and I hoped we'd have more time. Since we don't, I'm just gonna lay it out straight to you now."

The man could always see through him, knew when he wasn't telling the whole truth. From the young teenage boy he'd taken in years ago to the young man he'd sent away on the bus, Matthew had been able to read what was going on in Shane's head. No doubt he still could. But what on earth did he want to tell him? He wished it could wait 'til after Monday, but he sensed the urgency in Doc's demeanor and kept silent.

"This business of mine, it's pretty serious. They've told me what my chances are of not comin' through."

The thought of his mentor actually dying dropped like a rock in his gut. He swallowed hard and cleared his throat. "What're you talking about? Of course you'll come through."

Matthew silenced him with a chop of his hand. "Just listen. If I don't make it, I need for you to know everything is in order. I've provided for my niece and her family, so there should be no problem with them, and there's something for Sandy, too, for all her years of working for me. But the clinic here is yours, to do with what you think is best. You want to close it down, sell it, and head back to Wyoming, it's your choice and your right. You've more than kept your end of the bargain we made back when I first took you in by stayin' in school and making something of yourself. I've only got one more request to make, and I want your word you'll do it. It'll make it a lot easier for me to face what's comin' my way."

Stunned by the longest speech he'd ever heard Matthew Brewster make, Shane shook his head in bewilderment. He scrubbed a hand over his face and forced himself to keep cool. "Sure, sure. You know I'll do it, but what's this all about? Talking like you won't be here—"

"And I might not. Might as well face it. All I want is to know you've come clean with Allison. You need to tell that gal what really happened ten years ago. She needs to know why you left here like you did. Things have changed, and it's important now she knows the truth."

He wanted to agree, but saying this and actually doing it were two different things. "I know she needs to know. It's just…maybe it doesn't even matter to her anymore." *Maybe it never did.* "Could be she would just rather I went back to where I came from when this is all over."

"Well, you don't know until you've talked with

her, do you? So, just promise this old man you'll do it, talk with her. Get everything out in the open."

He might have protested more, but Allison came back into the room, and Matthew clammed up. Shane moved away so she could put the new water cup on the bedside table. Standing in the corner, he forced himself to come to grips with what Doc had told him.

Matthew reached a shaky hand for the water, and she helped him get a drink. "I made sure there's plenty of ice in it. Anything else I can do?"

"You know, missy, you make a pretty good nurse." He winked at her. "Maybe you ought to change jobs."

She set down the cup and fussed a moment longer, plumping his pillows and helping him settle back. "I think I'm better at nursing ornery horses than ornery men," she teased but patted his arm before moving away.

In spite of his fear for Doc's well-being, watching Allison talk with the old man gave Shane a moment of sweet pleasure. She had always been the nurturing type. He remembered how she'd help care for her ill grandmother. She hadn't lost her touch. It was one of the things he'd loved about her, maybe one of the things he still did.

Outside the hospital, he walked slowly next to her back to his truck, thinking about what Doc had asked of him. He didn't know if he could do it, explain it all to Allison. It would involve bringing up his past and talking about things still painful for him to even think about.

Even more painful would be finding out she didn't care and never had. If she had, she would never have married Jason.

"It's hard seeing Doc like that," she spoke first. "He's always been such a strong person, and now here he is facing surgery. I wish he had more family to be here for him."

"He's got us, and Sandy. I'll come back up Monday as soon as I'm done with the clinic."

He unlocked the passenger side door and opened it for her. Afternoon heat blasted out, and she hesitated before climbing inside the cab. This might be the moment to say something to the effect they had to talk, but when he opened his mouth, he couldn't find the words.

Allison stared at the middle of his chest and then up at his face, and for a brief, crazy moment, it was all he could do not to throw abandon to the wind and kiss her right then and there. Trouble was, she'd probably slug him, and she'd have the perfect right.

He turned on his heel and went around to his side of the truck. For the ride back to Silver Creek, he cranked the radio up and let the music fill the silence between them.

Chapter 5

Allison sat in the grandstand of the county fairgrounds and watched Lizzie and seven other youngsters put their ponies through their paces in the show ring. It had been a hectic morning, but they'd made it in plenty of time for the nine o'clock halter class.

She fixed her gaze on her daughter who stood so straight beside the little pinto. With the cream-colored Stetson perched above her single, long braid and the home-sewn, fringed turquoise shirt tucked into her trim jeans, Lizzie was a perfect little cowgirl. It made Allison proud to see her guide Cayenne through his paces, reminding her so much of herself at that age. Her parents could never understand the fascination with the whole horse scene, but Grandma Ellie and Pop had always sat right here, in this same grandstand, more than happy to cheer her on. They'd never missed a show.

Now, she was left to sit alone and watch the child who had brought meaning back into her life when all had seemed lost.

"She's a natural, just like her mother, but why doesn't it surprise me?"

Shane eased himself down on the bleacher beside her. She was suddenly aware of him in more ways than she wanted to admit. The sight of his long, denim-covered legs stretched out beside hers, the touch of his arm as it brushed against her shoulder, and the fresh, clean scent of the shaving cream he had used this morning all ganged up on her senses, making her head swim.

She scooted over an inch or two, but it wasn't nearly enough space to escape the powerful feelings that suddenly set her body humming. With every bit of common sense she possessed, she tried not to look at Shane, but then found she had to, just to try and prove to herself there were no feelings left for this man. She proved nothing, except his smile could still make her heart beat like a trip hammer, and even shadowed by a straw cowboy hat this morning, his eyes were still as blue as the summer sky. Other details kept her mesmerized for a moment, like the fact his once crooked tooth was straight now, and tiny weather lines crinkled the corners of his eyes. Ten years had put a few miles on him, but he was still awfully darn handsome.

The wink he sent her way gave Allison's heart another jolt, and she flicked her gaze away, just in time to see her daughter go past. She gave a little wave, to let her know she was watching.

Shane waved, too. "Lizzie and Cayenne are quite a pair. She's trained him well."

"He was already a kid-safe pony when I bought him. Lizzie used to toddle alongside of him when she was learning to walk. She started riding shortly after." She wasn't sure why she needed to tell him all this, except in her heart, she knew he deserved to know the truth.

There was just no easy way to do that.

"She was up at five a.m., so worried we wouldn't get here in time." She didn't mention she'd been up an hour before that, thinking about Matthew Brewster in the hospital, the slashed tire, and the prints by the pasture, but mostly about how she was going to cope with Shane McBride being back in town.

"Did you get your check-in duties done?" She decided to try and keep their conversation on an impersonal level.

He leaned back on the bleacher, propping his elbows on the seat behind them. "Yep, everything went off without a hitch. Entrants all had their papers in order and ponies all in good condition. I have the feeling most of these kids have a good instructor giving them lessons, but I suspect they don't realize how lucky they are to have such a pretty one."

Her cheeks flushed with heat, and her toes tingled.
Is he actually flirting with me?

She didn't know and refused to acknowledge the remark. Fortunately, luck saved her from having to do so. Unfortunately, it came in the form of her meddling sister-in-law.

"Hi, Allison, honey. Thought I'd come on out and watch my niece." Ronnie trotted up in her backless sandals, sat down beside Allison, and shaded her eyes against the morning sun while she looked out into the arena. "How is Lizzie doing? Is she feeling all right?"

Ronnie didn't bother to face her but just kept staring out into the ring. In her hot pink capris and flowered halter-top, she was hardly dressed for a horse show, but the fact she was here at all surprised Allison. She was pretty certain her sister-in-law hated horses.

"Lizzie is fine. Why wouldn't she be?"

"Oh, nothing. I just thought she looked a little peaked when I saw her at the library the other day. Are you sure she's eating right? She's so thin."

Ever since Jason died, his sister seemed certain Allison couldn't cope with being a single mother. Sometimes the over-interest in *her* daughter's welfare struck a nerve.

"Lizzie and her appetite are just fine. I ought to know since I made her a stack of pancakes this morning, and she polished it off no problem."

Ronnie dropped her hand from her forehead and brought her attention back to the bleachers. Her green eyes reminded Allison of Jason's, except they were more catlike.

"I'm just trying to help, hon." Her voice dripped with syrup. "In fact, I wish you would let Jerry and me do more. You know he worships Lizzie like she was his own."

Try as she might, Allison could not appreciate their concern, but she didn't have to worry as Ronnie's attention suddenly shifted with recognition to the person sitting on the other side of Allison.

"My goodness, can that be Shane McBride?" She sat a little straighter and pushed her shoulders back, the action lifting full breasts higher in the flower-printed halter.

"Hey, Ronnie," he murmured and nodded but gave her no attention.

"Jerry said he'd heard you were in town. You do know I married Jerry Blake. He was two years ahead of me in school. He served very proudly in the navy before we got hitched. What on earth brings you back to Silver Creek?"

The woman could certainly run on. A nerve twitched in his jaw telling Allison he didn't want to talk to her.

"Just helping out a friend."

"I remember what a good time we all had together. It's certainly been a long time, but I guess not much has changed, huh?"

He lifted his head a little now and gave Ronnie the once over, his eyes glittering from beneath the straw hat. "Some things have. Some haven't."

"Well, it was nice of you to come by and see Lizzie. Isn't she just the cutest thing? Jason would be bustin' his buttons right now. I just wish my brother was still here." She dabbed at her eyes with a fuschia-lacquored fingertip.

"I guess we all wish that," Allison said, forcing her jaw not to clench. "But we're here now, and it's what matters most. Now watch, they're getting ready to judge."

The kids had lined up their ponies, and she focused all her attention on her little cowgirl and the red and white pinto.

By the time the two walked out of the ring, Lizzie carried a second-place ribbon, and Allison hurried over.

"Good job, Lizzie. You both did very fine out there." She ached to give her a big hug, but her daughter was getting to the age where she hated public displays of affection. There would be time later to show her how proud she was of her.

Ronnie had no such qualms. She pushed her way in and hugged her niece, practically knocking her hat off. "Well, weren't you just fantastic? You really should have gotten first place, but what do those old judges know. You were super, honey."

Allison sighed at her sister-in-law's exuberance.

Lizzie grabbed at her hat and tolerated her aunt's affection. Her face lit up when she saw Shane. "Hey, Doc, did you see me? How'd we look?"

He reached past Ronnie and settled the hat back over her French braid. "Pretty darn good, Shortstuff, pretty darn good."

Her daughter's face lit up, his compliment apparently packing more punch than either Ronnie or her remarks. A sudden twinge of jealousy bit at Allison…as well as remorse.

"Okay, let's walk Cayenne back to the trailer." She threw off those feelings and took charge. "You have an hour 'til your next class, so you both have time to cool off."

The day had turned exceedingly warm, adding to her need to get away from these two people who could make her even hotter. Ronnie, because she was such a pain in the butt. Shane because…because he was Shane, and he could still make her hot in ways she didn't even want to think about.

"Come with us," Lizzie invited the other adults. "Mom brought a big cooler with lemonade and sandwiches." She held the pony's reins with one hand and with the other reached out to Shane. With only a second's hesitation, he took the small hand and walked with her to the trailer.

Ronnie followed behind, but Allison waited and watched the small scene of her baby girl placing her trust in someone other than herself.

How am I going to cope with this?

She sighed and blew a few stray wisps of hair away

from her face. The day was still young, but already it drained her to think she had to spend several more hours at the fairgrounds.

While Lizzie handed out PB and J sandwiches and Ronnie poured lemonade, Allison brushed the pony down. Grooming her horses had always helped her deal with frustration and soothe herself. Feeling a horse's warm skin beneath her hands, combing out a tangled mane, listening to him just breathe—it was somehow a balm to her soul, and even the seasoned pony seemed to know she enjoyed caring for him. He turned to nuzzle the pocket of her jeans for the treat he knew would follow. When she'd finished brushing him, she slipped him one of the small carrots she'd taken from the cooler.

"Aren't you eating?" Shane stood just behind her, drinking lemonade from a paper cup.

"I'll wait 'til later when we get home." Allison put the grooming tools back in a plastic tote and glanced over to where Lizzie and Ronnie sat on folding lawn chairs, chatting and munching sandwiches and oatmeal cookies. She turned and shoved the box back in the trailer a little harder than necessary.

"Take it easy, Allison. Ronnie is not worth getting worked up over." He took a step closer, reached around her, and stuck a cup in her hand. "Here, heed your own advice, take a break and cool off."

She had no choice but to take the lemonade from him, but he didn't move. He just stood there, right behind her, and she swore she could feel his heart thumping against her back. Her own heart began to match its beat. Then he touched her hair and moved it over her shoulder, off her neck. In a sudden flashback, she remembered how he had liked to kiss her there.

Allison stepped away, fighting the urge to flee from her own feelings.

"Something wrong?"

She could never tell him the truth and just shook her head. "I just wish Ronnie wouldn't be so pushy where Lizzie is concerned. She acts like *she's* her mother instead of me."

"She and Jerry don't have any kids?"

Allison stared into the lemonade. "I think she miscarried a couple of times, and then they finally gave up. I feel sorry for her. I know it must've been very hard, but sometimes she just annoys me."

"Yeah, she was always that way."

There was something odd in his voice. What was it about Ronnie that annoyed *him*?

Whatever it was, it didn't keep him from acting as a buffer between Allison and her sister-in-law as he sat in the bleachers with them for the rest of the afternoon, watching Lizzie's classes. Ronnie asked a million questions and hung on every word Shane said, suddenly interested in every detail about the subject of horse shows and judging. While he explained the difference between halter class and showmanship, her sister-in-law listened raptly, her hand resting lightly on his knee.

The day grew hotter, and Ronnie continued to chatter until Allison was pretty sure she couldn't stand one more minute of it. She had just turned to say something when Shane grasped her elbow and steered her away. He didn't stop walking until they reached the old apple tree behind the grandstand, well out of Lizzie and Ronnie's hearing.

"What are you doing?" Allison pulled away from

him.

"Trying to keep you from telling Ronnie to can it."

"I would have done no such thing!" She tugged at her collar and took off her hat to fan her face. *At least not in those words.*

"I don't know. I just thought you needed a break. Can't say I blame you. Maybe I needed to get away from her babble myself."

Startled, she met his gaze, and when he winked at her, she couldn't help but start to laugh. He joined her, and it released the tension that had steadily built since he'd sat side by side with her on the bleachers.

When their laughter faded, she sank to the ground and sat cross-legged in the grass beneath the tree. Shane sat, too, his knee almost touching hers. Suddenly, it was like they were back in high school and taking a break after working in Pop's orchard. How many times had they sat like this—just talking—before friendship turned to something else?

Was it possible to have a friendship again?

"Ronnie always did like to talk a lot." He glanced behind him as if to make sure she hadn't followed. "I guess that hasn't changed."

"I'm surprised you remember. It's been a long time since you've been around her." Allison leaned back on her hands and watched him pluck a blade of grass. "Or did she always rub you the wrong way?"

He toyed with the blade, splitting it to make a whistle and blowing through it a few times before answering, "Actually, she tried to rub me the *right* way every time I went to Jason's house."

When it dawned on her what he meant, she sat up straight. "You mean…she hit on you?"

"Tried."

"Did Jason know?"

"Nah, I never told him. I just told Ronnie to lay off. Not long after it didn't matter…Jason and I didn't hang together anymore."

Thanks to us.

She glanced down, letting her hair fall forward to hide the warmth on her cheeks. Even after she and Jason married, she'd still regretted causing the rift in his and Shane's friendship.

"But hey, it was all a long time ago. We need to get over it." His voice was low, and his hand gentle as he brushed her curtain of hair aside and lifted her chin so she had to look at him. "Since I may be here for a while, we have to get over our past. We have to move on."

I thought that's what I did. But for her it was different. She had so much more at stake. She tried to speak but Shane hushed her.

"It's okay. I can accept you loved Jason, and I'm glad you had him when I had to go."

But why *did you go?* She still didn't know the answer, and until she did, she couldn't find her way to tell him the truth he deserved to hear.

"I better get back to Lizzie."

Allison pulled her face away but not before he traced a finger along her cheekbone, and she quivered at his touch as she quickly stood to leave.

Shane let Allison get ahead of him while he dealt with far too many memories, of the first time he'd ever touched her, in Pop's orchard, when they both grabbed the same bushel of apples and brushed hands. The first time he'd kissed her, in the swing on the front porch of her grandparents' farmhouse, and the fire that had burned in him then. The physical ache of staying away from her, once he'd known the sweetness of her love. He could never forget any of it, not now, not ever.

He watched Lizzie's last class from the far end of the arena and waved when she took first place, but he didn't venture close again. Before he went to pack up his truck to go home, he saw Allison give Lizzie a hug, and he knew he'd lied this afternoon.

The past might be in the past, but he still hated the fact she'd been Jason's wife.

Chapter 6

By Monday afternoon, Allison had almost, but not quite, forgotten about the strange incidents of the week before. The last two nights had been quiet, and while busy with lessons and running errands, she'd let thoughts of them slip to the back of her mind. She'd put the horses in the pasture closest to the barn, certain they were safe in broad daylight. Yet, she decided to bring them in early when she finished the last lesson of the day. There certainly was no sense in pressing her luck, and after the busy weekend, she was more than glad to get the chores done early. Collapsing in her recliner with a tall glass of iced tea held a great deal of appeal.

It was harder to convince Lizzie she shouldn't stay outside and watch for the lights that sometimes rose from the marshland this time of year.

"How come we can't?" she grumbled and hung back when Allison called her inside after dinner. "I bet this is a perfect night. I remember when Pop and me use to watch for it. He called it will-o-the-wisp. Do you remember?"

"I do." Allison paused, thinking about the wetland her grandfather had worked with the conservation department to protect, so that waterfowl had a place to land.

She, too, remembered sitting with Pop when she was a little girl, watching for the lights to rise up and dance across that marsh. She'd called them fairy lights. Elusive wisps of fairy dust. Entrancing, but try to touch them, try to hold them, and they were gone.

"I remember we made up stories about what they were. Pop told me they were the ghosts of folks who once lived here. Grandma Ellie said they were the spirits of children who ran away instead of listening to their parents, and they might snatch up children who stayed out after dark."

Lizzie rolled her eyes. "Oh, Mom, don't be silly."

But, Allison grinned as her daughter followed her inside the house without further argument.

She made popcorn and had just settled down with Lizzie to watch a movie when Gypsy rose from her spot by the kitchen door and woofed a warning. Holding her breath, she set down the bowl. *Not the horses. Not tonight.*

No worry about that. Headlights lit up the drive as a vehicle approached the house.

"Who do you suppose it is?" Her daughter knelt on the arm of the sofa and peeked out through the filmy curtains of the French doors.

"I don't know." Allison went through the archway into the kitchen and turned on the porch light. She also checked to make sure the deadbolt was secure. Gypsy sidled next to her and growled low in her throat.

"Mom, I think it's Doc McBride's truck," Lizzie whispered. "Yep, it's him getting out. Why do you think he's here?"

A sinking feeling hit her stomach, as if she instinctively knew something was wrong. She didn't give Shane a chance to knock before she opened the door. His face was pale and drawn, and his normally broad shoulders slumped with fatigue. She could always read his moods, and right now, he was teetering on the brink of a meltdown.

She didn't wait for him to speak but reached out and took his arm, drawing him into the kitchen. "You better sit down." She pulled out a chair and pushed him onto it. He didn't protest but sat, leaned back, and just closed his eyes for a moment.

"Mom," Lizzie spoke from the archway.

Allison put her finger to her lips, then motioned to the coffeemaker. "Could you make some coffee, honey?"

Shane shook his head soundly. "No, I've had enough coffee today to float a ship. What I could use is a stiff drink."

Hmmm. She went to the cupboard where Pop had always kept his "for medicinal purposes only" blackberry brandy. It was still there, and she poured three fingers into a glass and set it in front of him. He downed it in one gulp, and she poured again. This time, he took it slower. When it was gone, he waved away anymore.

She recapped the bottle but left it on the counter. When Lizzie still watched with wide-eyed curiosity, Allison went and turned her back toward the living room. "How about you take Gypsy and finish watching the movie. I'm going to stay with Doctor McBride for a while."

Her daughter glanced back to the man sitting at their kitchen table. He'd propped his elbows in front of him and put his face in his hands. "Is he okay, Mom? He looks a little sick."

"I guess I'm going to find out, but you go on now.

Take Gypsy with you."

When Lizzie went back to her movie, Allison returned to the table, took the chair across from Shane, and pulled his hands away from his face. A bit of color had returned to his cheeks, but his eyes still burned with unshed emotions. "Is it Matthew? I heard from Murray he came through the surgery all right. Did something happen after?"

He ran one hand through his hair, spiking it up. "He's in a coma." His voice shook with raw pain. "He was fine, coming around after the surgery, and then…don't know what the hell happened. They kicked me out of ICU. Murray had gone home, and I stuck around until…they finally told me Matthew had slipped into a coma. It's not good, and I don't…there's nothing they can do but…wait." His voice broke this time, and he leaned forward, putting his head down in his arms.

Allison could only imagine how hard this was for him. Matthew Brewster had been like a father to the sixteen-year-old boy who'd showed up one summer to work on the farms. He'd given him a place to live and told him to go back to school. And she'd heard he'd helped pay for the college education that had led Shane to also become a vet. Now Matthew was clinging to life, and the reality he might die was obviously too much for him to handle…at least alone.

Was that why he'd come here?

Against all her better judgment, Allison stood next to him and put her arms around his slumped shoulders. "I'm so sorry. Doc means a lot to many people, but I know how much he means to you."

His body lost some of its tension, and he turned into her embrace. He buried his face in her breasts, and her heart lodged in her throat. This was dangerous territory. A million taunting memories threatened to come flooding back, but how could she push him away when he so obviously needed someone right now?

Maybe he sensed the danger, too, because he set her away from him and got up to pace around the kitchen. "It's more than you even know. The truth is, I probably owe Matthew Brewster my life."

"How is that?" She watched him circle the table for the second time.

"For one thing, when I finished working on the farm the summer I first came here, I was going back home, to Detroit, and I probably would have gone back to being a punk kid."

"You?" She almost snorted. "A punk kid? I hardly think—"

"You don't know what I was." He stopped and turned to her, his brows low and jaw tight. "You haven't a clue."

She supposed she didn't. Shane had never talked much about his life before Silver Creek. And she'd never asked. She wasn't sure she wanted to know now.

"I guess I don't, but you know what? It's not the time for me to find out. Not tonight." Allison took his arm and led him toward the living room. "Right now, I think you should go sit with Lizzie. She's watching a movie about a girl and a horse. I'm going to make you something to eat, since I'm sure you haven't had a thing all day."

Surprisingly, he didn't argue with her but went to sit in her recliner. She made tomato soup and a grilled cheese because it had been one of his favorite meals. He ate every bit, and when she went to clear the dishes away, he grabbed her hand and held it for a long few moments. Allison saw Lizzie's eyebrows shoot up an inch, and she quickly pulled her hand back and returned to the kitchen to wash up.

How on earth would she deal with this situation? She could hardly tell Shane, in his current state of mind, to go home alone to Doc's house at the clinic, but what would Lizzie think if he stayed here?

The matter was settled for her when she found him sound asleep in the recliner, Gypsy stretched out on the floor alongside, and Lizzie dozing on the sofa. She pulled an afghan from the back of the couch and tossed it over him. Her daughter she roused to usher up to bed.

At the stairway, Lizzie glanced up, her blue eyes droopy. "Doc's so sad, Mom. Please don't send him away. Don't make him go where there's nobody home. It's so much harder when you're sad and all by yourself."

She stroked her daughter's dark hair and pressed a kiss atop her head. She was so wise, her precious nine-year old, and so attuned to other people's feelings. "I know. He can stay here tonight. I hardly think I could wake him anyway."

Something, however, woke Allison a few hours later. She groaned and pulled the sheet over her head, trying to shut out whatever had broken through the deep sleep she'd fallen into seconds after crawling into bed. But as sometimes happened when she slept so sound, she was now wide-awake with little hope of returning to sleep. The bedside clock read three-thirty. A long ways until dawn, and she'd left the book she was reading downstairs.

She threw back the sheet and sat up. A night breeze

from the open window sent a shiver running over her arms, so she pulled her pink terry bathrobe over the tank top and sleep pants she wore and went barefoot to the hallway.

First, she checked on Lizzie. Her baby slept blissfully, arm around the bedraggled teddy bear Jason had bought the day she was born.

If only I could be so carefree.

Halfway down the stairs, she remembered about Shane. But he wasn't in the recliner anymore. She glanced around the darkened living room. Had he gone back to Matthew's?

Then she saw him, standing by the French doors, peering out into the night. He'd taken off his denim shirt, and his white T-shirt gleamed in the dark. His jeans rode low on his hips and his belt hung loose. Even across the room, Allison was mightily aware of his presence, and she considered retreating back up the stairs before he saw her.

All chance of that dissolved when Gypsy thumped her tail on the floor. He turned, and his gaze rested on her where she stood in the stairway. "Did it wake you, too?"

"What?" She tried desperately to keep her wits about her.

"The noise outside."

In an instant, she crossed to the French doors. "Is it the horses? Are they spooked?" She hadn't heard them and leaned past Shane to peer out into the darkness.

"I don't think so. Sounded like…something else.'"

"Well, whatever the something is, it better get away from my barn."

Her indignation brought a soft chuckle from him.

"Or you might go out there in your jammies and chase it away?"

Standing just inches from him, in said jammies and bare feet, she shivered and tried to move back an inch, but the sofa trapped her.

"I can go have a look, so you'll rest easy." His voice murmured low, and her breath caught in her throat. The problem was, she would never rest easy with him standing so damn close to her, but suddenly, she didn't want him going out there, either...to face whatever prowled in the night.

"You got a flashlight?" he asked.

"No, I mean yes. I mean, don't. Don't go out there." She touched his arm to keep him from moving away.

"I'm sure it's nothing, but I know it'll make you feel better if I at least check the barn."

"It won't make me feel better, and there is something out there."

"Then I should—"

"No, you shouldn't."

For the first time she could ever remember, she was actually putting someone besides her daughter before the horses, was actually afraid if Shane went out into the night something dreadful might happen to him. The thought sent a lightning jolt shooting through her veins. But was it from the fear...or because the heat from Shane's body radiated over her skin like a hot summer sun? Biting her lip, she dared to glance up at him.

Chapter 7

What was going on in Allison's mind?

There was only one thing going on in his, and it had nothing at all to do with whatever danger lurked outside. The danger for him dwelled all inside, right here, with this woman. The one who stood just inches away and who could still, even after all these years, turn him inside out.

He had every good reason not to care, and every good reason to turn away, but he couldn't seem to do that right now. Any more than he could stop himself from taking her hand and drawing her closer to him.

There had never been any doubt in his mind being with Allison was the best thing that had ever happened to him. There was no doubt now. He slid his hands through her hair, framed her face, and tipped it up to meet his.

Kissing her had come as naturally to him as breathing. It still did. Her mouth tasted the same, too, sweet like the wild honey from the bees in Pop's orchard. Intoxicating as summer wine and as irresistible as a soft pink blossom. He groaned softly and took everything her kiss had to offer.

If Allison had ever imagined she would kiss Shane again in this lifetime, she would have imagined it this way. So sweet she wanted to die, so hard she tasted the need and the loneliness that bubbled up in both of them.

A sigh escaped her, and only drew him closer, and then he slipped the robe from her shoulders. He kissed her there and in the curve of her neck. When her knees buckled, he caught her and lifted her as if she was a wisp of marshland mist, a will-o-the-wisp.

When he sank onto the sofa, cradling her, she curled into his lap, put her arms around his neck, and kissed him again with all the heart of the young girl who'd first fallen in love with Shane McBride.

Back then, neither of them had much sense when it came to each other. She knew they didn't have much now. His hands were in her hair, skimming down her back, up her sides, cupping the fullness of her breasts, and then rested on her hips, pressing her to him and leaving no doubt he wanted her as much as she did him. It had always been this way, from the first time they'd spread a blanket in the back of his truck to the last time she'd met him on a hot summer night by the lake. The night before he'd left town.

This couldn't happen now. She couldn't lose control, couldn't be the foolish girl she'd been so many years ago. Someone had to stop the madness...

It took every ounce of strength Allison had to forget the kisses and remember instead the pain that enveloped her life when she found out Shane had left, leaving her to deal with the hurt and the shame.

Tears she'd not shed for a very long time suddenly welled up and made it easier to pull away. She placed her hand over his mouth and used her other to push herself from his lap. "I can't do this. We can't. Not with Lizzie upstairs, not like this."

He didn't argue with her but leaned his head on the back of the sofa and took several deep breaths. She could see his pulse thrumming in his throat. It was a long time before it eased and he spoke.

"I'm sorry. I should have known better than to come here tonight. I have no right."

The trouble was he did, and sooner or later he had to know. But where did she start?

He didn't move but just turned his head to rest his gaze on her. "There are some things I need to tell you. Things I should have told you long ago. Maybe it would have all been different for us."

Still shaky with emotions so close to the surface, she shivered. He reached for the afghan and draped it around her but kept some distance between them.

"Whatever it is, you don't have to tell me." *I'm not sure I want to hear.*

"Well, it's like this…I promised Matthew I would, and if the worst happens, I want to know I kept my promise."

Moving a little farther away on the sofa, Allison tucked her feet up under her on the cushion. Clutching the afghan around her shoulders, she prepared for whatever he had to say.

Shane sat up straight but didn't face her. "It goes back to my life before Silver Creek. My parents never married. They were just kids themselves when they had me. My grandmother pretty much raised me. She died when I was twelve. The last place I saw her alive was in the hospital. Neither of my parents were interested in giving me a home, and I went into the foster care system. I did okay, but when I was fifteen, I got into some trouble with the law. It was stupid kid stuff, but I was on probation for a year." He stopped a moment, as if remembering that difficult time still caused him pain.

"When I got done with that, I went to court and got myself declared an emancipated minor. Some older guys I'd met told me about working on the farms here. It sounded a heck of a lot better than staying in the city and maybe getting into more trouble. With twenty-five dollars in my pocket, I took the bus here, and I answered the first ad I saw in the local paper for a farm worker. Pop's ad. I was scared as heck, and I'm sure it showed. Plus, I wasn't what you'd call the best dressed young man back then."

She gave him a rueful smile. "You were a little rough around the edges when you first showed up here. Pop thought you were just a bum."

"I'm sure he did. Your grandparents didn't really want me here with a pretty granddaughter to worry about, but I promised them I'd work hard, so they took a chance and hired me. Pop even convinced Doc to give me a room. Doc's the one talked me into going back to school. Promised me I could live with him and work in the clinic, as long as I stayed in school and didn't get into more trouble. It sounded more than fair to me. So I made good grades, and I worked hard for Matthew. Jason and I became good friends, and he talked me into going out for football. It was the best time of my life. I finally felt like I belonged somewhere. Jase and I sure had a hell of a good time. The following summer I worked for Pop, again…" He paused a moment as he studied her. "Then you and I started dating…and everything changed."

She remembered so well how the friendship had gone south, but maybe it was even more than she knew. "What happened?" she dared to ask.

"One day, Jack Delaney showed up at practice.

He'd decided I was the reason Jason wasn't getting enough playing time. He had a go-round with the coach. It turned into quite a yelling match, and then Jack came after me."

Stunned at this revelation, she leaned forward on the sofa. "Did he…get rough with you?"

"If you call grabbing my jersey and slamming me against the goalpost getting rough, then I guess he did. Coach pulled him off, but not before Jack called me a few choice names and said he'd make sure I didn't play the rest of the season."

"They threatened you? Why didn't you tell anybody? Pop would have stopped them."

He shook his head. "I didn't want anybody to think I was causing trouble. You…you can't imagine how it was for a kid who'd already been to court and on probation, who would have done *anything* not to have it happen again."

She lifted her hands in confusion. "But you didn't do anything wrong. They did!"

"That's how you see it now, but trust me, it wouldn't have taken much. The sheriff and Jack Delaney were good friends, and all Jack would have had to do was tell him to send me packing, and I would have been back in court on some trumped-up charge in a heartbeat."

A long sigh escaped her. "Pop wouldn't have let that happen. Neither would Doc."

"Well, they'd been good to me, and I wasn't about to drag them into the mess." He raked back his hair with his fingers. "They didn't need the hassle."

"So instead, you sat it out on the bench the rest of the season." Her heart broke that he'd thought he'd been alone in all this.

"Pretty much. I guess the coach figured his job was on the line, so he told everyone I was being disciplined. For arguing with him or some such crap."

Her chest tightened for the singled out, lost boy he'd been. "They had no right to do that to you. You should have done something."

Shane shrugged. "What? Should have done what? You don't know the rest of it."

Maybe it's finally time for the truth to come out. She touched his shoulder. "Then tell me. Tell me what I don't know."

He studied her for a moment, as if weighing what he needed to say. Leaning forward, he rested his elbows on his knees and looked down at the worn gray carpet. "Early that next summer, not long after graduation, Matthew and I took care of some abandoned dogs we were pretty sure had been used for fighting. You know, like bait. It was heinous, the worst thing I'd ever seen. Sheriff didn't seem to know who the dogs belonged to, and he didn't seem real interested in finding out. Claimed he didn't have the manpower to spare. The thing is, I did know. I'd heard talk, and I went snooping on my own. It was a stupid thing to do. I could have gotten myself killed, but I couldn't just not do anything."

A memory came back to her, of folks talking and rumors floating around town, but she never suspected Shane was involved. "What…did you find?"

He pressed his lips together for a second, as if holding back a rush of emotion, and his eyes darkened to a midnight hue.

"A dog-fighting ring the Potter brothers had going

with their cousins. I told the sheriff everything I knew, and he actually believed me. A week later arrests were made."

"I remember that, and I was glad they all got busted. They were always jerks. Pop even said he sure wasn't surprised the Potter brothers were involved in it. But you should have told me what you were doing."

His tense gaze settled on her face. "And put you all at risk? I told you what I did was crazy—and a few days after the arrests, I started getting threatening phone calls from a few other cousins in the next county. They didn't take it kindly I'd ratted on Duane and Darren. I ignored it for a while…until one night somebody shot out the back window of my truck."

"You told me a semi kicked up a rock and hit it." His admission struck a note of some new emotion in her heart. Anger? Frustration? She couldn't name it, but it seeped into her voice. "Why did you lie?" She glared at him, demanding an answer. "Tell me, Shane, why did you lie?"

He ran a nervous hand around the back of his neck and winced. "I didn't want you to know anything. Those guys were no one to fool with. That's why Matthew told me to get on the bus and get out of town for a few weeks—and not to tell anyone where I was going. He had some friends out west he arranged for me to stay with until the whole thing died down. So I went."

"Without a word of explanation to *me*." Bitterness black and cold crept in, and she wanted him to feel the pain she'd known. "How do you think I felt? When Pop said you were gone, I…I wanted to die."

"I had every intention of coming back for you, but

I found a job, and Matthew told me I should just stay there, get into college."

He reached for her, taking her hand, but unlike moments ago, she refused his touch, snatching her hand away.

"I was going to send for you," he insisted. "But then I heard…about you and Jason getting married. I was ready to come back and find out what the hell had happened, but the Potters were going to trial and things were stirred up again. Matthew and the sheriff both warned me to stay put, and I guess with you married to the guy I thought was once my friend, what reason did I have to come back?"

Allison jerked her face away, the tears she'd struggled to contain spilling over. *You had a reason. You just didn't know, and that's my fault. But you didn't suffer the way I did at the separation.*

She heard him get up and walk across the room.

"It's nice you have all these, you know? Nice Lizzie knows who her family is. Family is important to a kid."

She sniffed and glanced over to see him studying the display of photographs arranged on the bureau covered with Grandma Ellie's hand-tatted lace scarf. They were all familiar to her. In one photo, Jason sat with his family by the lake. They were all smiling, and he had a football in his hands. The next was a family photo of Jason, her, and Lizzie when she'd been a small baby. There was one of her parents, another of Pop and Grandma Ellie, a recent one of just Lizzie by herself.

Along with sad regret for all the years she and Shane had lost, a sudden realization welled up. Family was something Shane had missed as a kid. At least she'd had her grandparents, but who did he have after his grandmother died? Was there anyone to comfort him?

She couldn't help feeling sorry for the boy who had been so alone, and a fresh onslaught of hot tears streamed down her face. Swiping at them with the heels of her hands, Allison dragged the afghan along as she went to stand next to him. "Have your parents ever…"

He stuck his hands in the front pockets of his jeans, but kept his gaze on the photos. "Nope. My mother has been in and out of rehab since she was sixteen. Last I heard she was living in a halfway house. My dad, I don't even know if he's alive."

She slipped her arm through his and laid her head against his shoulder. "I'm sorry for what you went through here. I wish I'd known."

He put his arm around her and drew her closer, and this time she let him.

Against her hair he murmured, "Would it have changed anything?"

"I…don't know. Maybe."

Would it have? After all this time, it was hard to know, and the hurt from his leaving still lingered inside.

"Just tell me this. Did they treat you okay—Jason and his family? I mean besides Ronnie and her act."

She sighed. "Jason and I were okay. His parents…we never talked much. I know they blamed me for him not going to college on his football scholarship. After he died, they moved away. They remember Lizzie on her birthday and Christmas, but they haven't seen her in almost three years."

He shook his head and gave a short, bitter laugh. "So, I guess she doesn't have much family after all."

"She has *me*." Allison stepped back from him. "I will do anything to make her happy, to give her a good life. *Anything.* I guess it has to be enough." But was it? She did the best she could, but maybe that wasn't enough. Maybe her choice to remain here was a selfish one after all.

"Why did you do it? Why did you marry Jason? I think I have the right to know."

It was the one thing she had prayed he wouldn't ask, but the time had come for all truths to be told, no matter the consequences.

Allison drew the afghan tighter around her shoulders, perhaps to ward off whatever emotions the honesty would finally cost her, and raised her chin. "I married Jason because I was going to have a baby, and I was scared, and I didn't want to hurt my grandfather or go live with my parents…or give my baby away."

As if she'd burned him, he jerked two steps away, his eyes glittering with shards of pain. "You and Jason were…involved? Even before I left?"

She wanted to slap him silly. Instead, she snatched the picture from the bureau, the one of Lizzie in her favorite red sweater with her dark hair loose around her shoulders, and shoved it in front of him. "Take a good look. Take a good, *long* look. Tell me what you see."

He took the photo from her and in puzzlement quietly studied the picture of a smiling Lizzie. Her heart beat a painful rhythm, and she bit her lip as he took in the school picture of the beautiful little girl with shiny dark hair and sparkling blue eyes and a crooked front tooth…

Just like his.

Realization visibly crept over him, and his hands

shook as he clutched the picture tighter. In her heart, Allison had known this moment would arrive one day, and she'd always wondered how he would react. Now the time was here, she waited and held her breath to hear the first words he would say.

His fingers touched the child's image, tracing her exuberant smile. Was he trying to absorb the truth suddenly becoming crystal clear? The truth he'd not been able to see before this very minute?

"Do kids—" His voice faltered, and he took a deep breath, letting it out slowly. "Do they make fun of her tooth?"

"Sometimes." *Often.*

"Kids called me snaggle-tooth. I finally had it fixed a couple of years ago,"

"I'm saving for braces."

"I see."

"Do you? What do *you* see? Jason's red hair and green eyes?" She bit her lip and choked back any more words.

Chapter 8

No, he did not. Shane saw his child. *His and Allison's* child. A child he had not known existed for nearly ten years.

Ten years!

Like he'd been sucker-punched, his stomach clenched, and he stared at her, his vision blurring. "When did you know?" he finally asked. "B-before I left?"

"I had just found out for sure. I...I went to a drugstore three towns over to buy a test. I was so afraid someone would recognize me and tell Pop."

Still holding the photo of Lizzie, his Lizzie, his *daughter*, Shane wandered back to the living room and sat down on the sofa. Shaking his head, he struggled to accept the truth, to understand why he was just finding this out *now*.

"You should have told me. I would never have left you. We would have gotten married. I would have raised my daughter."

She followed him. "I was seventeen years old, scared and confused with no clue how to really handle the situation. I wanted to tell you! I tried, that night before you left, when we met at the lake, but you wouldn't listen. You only had one thing on *your* mind."

He understood her sarcasm, because yeah, he remembered. Remembered being scared someone from the Potter clan was lurking nearby, waiting to take a potshot at him. Remembered just wanting to hold Allison, because he knew it would be a long time before he held her again. It had turned out to be a lot longer than either one of them had ever imagined.

"I remember you wanted to talk, and I wanted to do anything but, because I knew we were going to be separated. I wanted to tell you I was leaving, but I couldn't risk your safety. I didn't *want* to leave you. Can you forgive me because I did?"

She dropped the afghan from her shoulders and crouched in front of him, putting her hands over his so they both held the picture of their daughter. "I guess I've made my own mistakes. Maybe I need forgiving as much as you do." She rubbed his hands, her skin cold against his. "In my heart, I know you would have stayed, if I'd had a chance to tell you, but maybe it wasn't meant to be. Maybe something awful would have happened. I couldn't have stood that."

Early dawn crept through the farmhouse, and her chilled hands trembled over his. Soon the sun would come up, making things much clearer than in the dark hours of the night, but for right now, Allison needed warming.

Shane set the picture aside and eased her up to sit by him. He pulled the afghan from the floor and wrapped it around her while she rested her head on his shoulder, and he snuggled her into the curve of his arm. The wildflower scent of her hair drifted over him, and the feel of her body, like a familiar drug, lulled his senses. Dear God, he never wanted to be free from this feeling again.

After a while, she relaxed against him, and soon

her breathing became soft and even. Leaning back into the sofa, he held her close and protected, something he had not done when he should have ten years ago. Until the sky began to lighten, he just let her sleep while he thought about all the years and all the time he had missed with Allison…and their daughter.

****

O'Malley's Bar and Grill wasn't much different from what he remembered. Shane gave a cursory glance at the five o'clock crowd before finding an empty seat at the bar and ordering whatever was on tap. The last time he'd been in O'Malley's, he hadn't been old enough to drink. Well, at least not legally. Matthew had bought him a meal here the night before he'd boarded the bus for Wyoming. Sitting in a booth in the far corner, they'd discussed the plan—how Shane would take the first bus out the following morning, where he would have to change buses, and what to do once he reached Cheyenne. He'd listened, while he ate like a man taking his last meal. Then he'd gone to see Allison.

How differently things might have all turned out if she'd only told him. If only he'd let her.

Regrets are of little use. Something his grandmother used to say. *It's what you do going forward that matters.*

How would they go forward from here? What she'd told him in the wee hours of the morning still had him rocking in his boots, and he hadn't a clue how to deal with it. One minute, he was mad as hell she'd kept him from being a father to his child for *nine* years. The next, he wanted to kick himself for being such an ass and not coming back even after she'd married Jason. But none of that did a lick of good in figuring out how to come to terms with the situation. Hell, he didn't even know if she would let him be a father now. Didn't even begin to know how they'd explain this all to Lizzie.

He'd left Allison's house while she still slept on the sofa, and there'd been a full day of farm calls plus a few hours at the clinic. He still had to go back and check on a dog the local rescue group had brought in with a broken leg.

He'd sandwiched in a trip to the hospital, where he found Matthew still in ICU. Seeing the old man in such sad shape gave him a shot of reality, not unlike the last time he'd visited his grandmother, the night before she passed away. His life had changed then, and not for the good, but meeting Doc had kept him from going down many bad roads. In truth, he owed Matthew Brewster his life.

What would happen, how would he handle it, if his mentor didn't recover?

According to the nurse, it was still watch and wait, but waiting was not something he did easily, patience definitely not one of his virtues.

Yet, wait was about all he could do right now. That, and drink his beer.

Harry set the amber mug down in front of him. He quickly lifted it and took a long, slow drink.

The wiry Irishman watched him with a careful eye. "Looks like you've had a long day. Being one of the big animal vets in the county isn't easy. No wonder Doc Brewster wore his ticker out. Heard any more how he's doing?"

Shane wiped the foam from his upper lip and thought about draining the rest of the mug in one gulp. He set it back down instead. "I stopped at the hospital, but there's been no change. Sandy said his niece is on her way here tomorrow."

"Yeah, I'm sure she wants to be around if the old guy croaks. I don't recall she's ever come back since they moved out of state, but let somebody look like they're dyin' and the family hightails it back in a jiffy."

"Well, let's hope it doesn't come to that," a red-haired waitress commented as she picked up her order. "We shouldn't give up on Doc just yet. He's a tough old bird."

Very true.

A farmer a few barstools down spoke up. "Even if he does pull through, who knows if he'll be able to keep working. We still might have to find us another vet. The one from South County sure can't cover all this territory. Good thing we haven't needed anybody this week."

"Somebody's supposed to cover for Doc, but I haven't heard who and sure ain't seen him yet," another gruff voice added.

Glancing sideways, Shane recognized Big Bob Anderson and Ruben Tucker in their coveralls. Their sons, Tim and Lucas, had played football when he and Jason did, and Big Bob had been a cohort of Jack Delaney's. Apparently, he didn't know Shane was covering for Doc Brewster, or realize it was him sitting five seats down. He hoped Harry didn't share that bit of news right now.

The possibility disappeared when someone called for a refill, and Harry limped away. Tilting his hat down to shadow his face, Shane tipped back another gulp of beer. The last thing he wanted right now was to deal with any of these local yokels. He should probably just finish his beer and leave.

He'd taken the last swig when Harry came back, towel slung over his stooped shoulder, a twinkle in his Irish eyes. As if he'd sensed Shane's discomfort, he jerked his head toward the back of the bar. "Booth just emptied out. Go on back, and I'll bring you that burger I promised."

He hesitated only briefly. Might as well take Harry up on his offer, otherwise dinner would be the can of ravioli he'd seen in Doc's cupboard.

Shane walked to the rear of the place, and slid into the booth, glad it took him away from the rest of the crowd. The burger arrived, delivered by Harry himself. He plunked it and a basket of fries before him, adding a ketchup bottle he snagged from another table.

"Thanks. Smells really good, too, or maybe I'm just starving."

The Irishman beamed. "We been voted 'best bar burgers in town' two years in a row," he bragged. "You go on and enjoy, but before you leave, I got something to tell you, something about what maybe happened to Allison's car the other night."

He furrowed his brows in concern. What did the old bartender know? Were Allison and Lizzie in any danger?

The idea set his pulse to thumping. Whatever it was, he needed to find out. He paused before he whacked the ketchup bottle over his fries. "Whatever you know, I'd like to hear it."

"Be back in a couple minutes. You eat up."

He did, while keeping a wary watch on the rest of the bar patrons. Many of them he didn't recognize at all, a few brought back memories of his life here in

Silver Creek ten years ago. The people who'd brought their pets into the clinic the last few days were all new to him and had been pleasant enough to deal with, but that wasn't the case with the likes of Big Bob and Ruben. From the sound of it, they were still a couple of loudmouths whose opinions were the only ones that mattered. He wondered what Tim and Lucas were up to. Had they gone into farming, too? Or found a different life far from Silver Creek?

He just finished eating when Harry found a moment to slide into the seat across from him. "Feel better now?"

Shane nodded. "Yep, best burger I've had in a long time." He wadded up his napkin and tossed it into the empty basket. "Now, you had something to tell me?" He folded his arms on the table and leaned in closer.

The Irishman glanced behind him to make sure no one was within earshot. "Remember you asked me to let you know if I recalled seeing anyone hanging around on the street the other night, when Allison's tire went flat?"

"I did. Did you see something?"

"Not outside, but must have been around half past nine they came in here, the Potter brothers. They'd already had more than a few and were in their usual rowdy mood. They weren't too happy when I refused to serve them. I don't need the sheriff comin' down on my establishment for serving someone who's already intoxicated."

Where's Harry going with this story? "Did they leave then?" he prompted.

"Not right off. They sat back here and played the video game 'til I guess they ran out of money. Then one of their cousins came in and joined them."

"Was it Red?" Shane remembered him well. He was pretty sure he'd been the one who shot the window out on his truck.

The gray head nodded. "They carried on, getting louder and obnoxious, and I finally told Mike, my bouncer, to get 'em out of here."

"Excuse me, Harry, but what has this to do with Allison?" Fatigue from the long day, and worry over what he'd learned from her, started to tug at him, leaving him suddenly impatient.

"I'm gettin' to it," the old man insisted and grabbed the empty burger basket. "Just before Mike showed 'em the door, I think I heard one of 'em, mention her name. Something about 'had it coming to her' or 'she deserved it.' Didn't think much of it at the time, but then after we talked, it came back to me."

Yeah, he could picture the Potters, acting like the scumbags they were. For them to say Allison's name, let alone threaten her, made him burn inside.

He plucked a toothpick from a holder on the table and stuck it in his mouth, flipping it to the corner. "What do you suppose they meant? What would she deserve?"

Harry shrugged, then turned when he heard his name called from the bar. "Be there in a minute," he snapped. To Shane he added, "I don't know, but could be they'd messed with her vehicle. Think you ought to tell her? It's a little scary, her living out there all alone with her little girl." The Irishman got up when the waitress yelled his name again. "I just thought you should know."

Shane nodded his appreciation and motioned for

him to go take care of his customers. He watched the old guy hobble off, wondering why the Potters would have it in for Allison? She was afraid of them; he'd sensed it in the store last week.

He took the toothpick from his mouth and snapped it in two, thinking how he'd like to do the same to those two creeps. What had been going on here before he'd driven back into the life he was sure he'd left behind?

Chapter 9

Allison checked the saddle girth one more time before leading the bay Arab mare from the barn. She and Mystri hadn't been for a ride in a long time. She didn't have any lessons scheduled for today, but a storm front was predicted to roll in later in the afternoon, so this morning seemed a perfect time to take a short trip through the old apple orchard.

Lizzie was spending the day with Ronnie, shopping and going to lunch. It was good for her daughter to get out and do the things most girls liked to do, and if she hoped for her to be well-rounded, it had to start somewhere. Lizzie and Ronnie got along well, so she figured it was time to allow her sister-in-law more time in their lives. She'd even conceded, after her daughter's big blue eyes glistened with excitement, for them to take Gypsy to the Pet Palace this morning for a much needed bath and grooming.

I just hope it's a step in the right direction.

She let out a long breath, matching the one Mystri expelled when she poked her belly to tighten the girth. "We both need to get out of the pasture for a while." She rubbed the mare's neck before pulling herself onto the English saddle. "I think we're getting a little stale."

For about two seconds, she debated the wisdom of riding out alone, but she simply had to do something to get her mind off Shane and all the problems he'd presented. Riding had always been a way for her to chill out.

She reined Mystri toward the path leading away from the barn, and soon came to the orchard that had once helped provide a living for her grandparents. As a child, she'd spent hours out here with them, working side by side. She'd never really minded the work. Pop and Grandma Ellie had provided a lonely child with a stable home, and any time she'd spent with them had been treasured. Some days, she still missed them so much.

A sweet breeze played with Mystri's dark mane and whispered against the leaves of the apple trees. It was quiet here and soothing. After the last week with its rush of worry, confusion, and resurrected feelings, Allison was grateful for a short spate of peace and quiet. She sighed and relaxed in the saddle, letting the mare follow the familiar path.

Half an hour later they reached the creek where it wound through the property, and she pulled the bay Arab up to rest for a minute on its mossy bank. She dismounted and let Mystri have a drink, then found a stone to sit on and, holding the reins loosely, watched the mare nip at a patch of clover. As the day grew warmer, the humidity pressed in even here near the woods. The rich scent of old trees and ferns made the air thick, and the promise of rain seemed more eminent. But for a brief time, she enjoyed the mellowness that crept through her in this peaceful spot.

Just a little over forty-eight hours ago, she'd told Shane Lizzie was his daughter, and she'd not heard from him. Since she'd awoken on the couch and found him gone, she'd mulled over and over again in her mind whether telling him was the right decision. Whether opening that Pandora's Box the right thing to do. But how could she have kept it from him any longer?

Except, now she would also have to tell Lizzie the truth, and that frightened her more than anything else. How did you tell a child the man she'd called Daddy, the man who'd rocked her as a baby, tucked her into bed at night, read stories to her, and whose grave she still visited every Father's Day was not really the man responsible for her life?

Allison closed her eyes and tried to let the doubt and uncertainty flow out of her. Grandma Ellie would have told her to pray about it, but for a long time now, prayer hadn't been a big part of her life. Yet, maybe asking her grandmother for help on figuring this thing out was a way of praying.

You don't know Lizzie, but I wish you could have. I wish she could have known you. She's my life, Grandma Ellie, so how do I hurt her this way? How do I tell her the truth?

In the woods, a mourning dove cooed and its mate answered. Songbirds twittered in tune. An insect buzzed loudly, joined briefly by a chorus. And then suddenly they stopped, and all turned still.

She opened her eyes. Mystri lifted her head and twitched her ears, her nose quivering. "What is it, girl? What's wrong?"

The mare whickered and jerked against the reins, almost pulling them from her hand.

Allison jumped to her feet and tightened her grip. "Whoa, it's okay. It's nothing."

She tried to soothe the mare but saw the whites of Mystri's eyes as she tossed her head again. Speaking softly, she drew the horse closer, hoping to calm her so she could get back in the saddle. It took a minute or two, but she finally did and shortened the reins.

"All right then, let's just stay cool," she murmured. "No need to get upset."

Mystri quieted, but her ears still flicked back and forth, as if the mare heard something she did not.

Allison glanced quickly about, searching for whatever might have spooked the bay. She saw nothing, heard nothing, and yet, whatever lurked in the woods had them both spooked now. Turning Mystri around, she did not have to kick her into a gallop toward home.

****

After knocking at the farmhouse door and getting no reply, Shane walked through the barn looking for Allison. Her vehicle was parked in the driveway, so she had to be here somewhere, didn't she?

When the feed room provided nothing, he stopped by the tack room and peered inside. Bridles hung neatly from their pegs on the wall and saddles sat on their wooden blocks. Except one block was empty.

Could she be out riding? Where's Lizzie?

Strange…even the dog was missing.

On the drive here, he'd noticed dark clouds piling up in the sky. Surely they wouldn't have gone out riding with a storm moving in. Allison had too much sense.

For about five seconds, he stood staring at the empty saddle block, then he turned on his heel and went back outside. The sky had grown darker in just those minutes, and a flicker of lightning pierced the purple clouds. A few seconds later, a rumble of thunder rolled across the land, and on a sudden gust of wind, a curtain of rain swept in from the west.

Just as he stepped back into the shelter of the barn, he heard the pound of hoofbeats echo from the direction of the woods moments before Allison and the mare made a beeline from the old orchard.

Even from here, he could tell something had spooked the mare, and the horse had every intention of streaking into the barn and heading right to her stall and safety. Briefly, he debated trying to halt the frightened horse, but it might just make matters worse, causing her to rear—Allison could be thrown and badly injured. He would have to let her handle the situation. He just hoped she could stay aboard in that damn English saddle.

He waved an arm to let them know he was there. Allison appeared to attempt to bring the mare up before they reached the barn, but the wind-driven rain hampered any control she might have. With her feet firm in the stirrups, she pulled back on the reins; the mare slowed just a bit, but enough to keep them from careening past him.

"Whoa—whoa, take it easy, girl." He kept his voice low but stern and stepped toward them, putting out his hand, palm upward. As the mare started to veer to the right, he feared Allison would go flying, but she managed to keep her seat and once more pulled back on the reins. This time, the mare slowed to a canter and then finally a trot, snorting and tossing her head in the rain. When Allison brought her back around to the door of the barn, the mare walked in and stopped, her sides heaving and flecked with foam. Breathing as hard as the horse, Allison slid from the saddle but kept a tight hold of the reins. With her free hand, she slicked her wet hair back from her face and leaned against the bay's neck.

Shane could hear her murmuring to the animal as he followed them in and slid the door closed. Standing behind Allison, he held himself back from touching her trembling shoulders. After they'd stilled some he asked, "Are you all right?"

She took a moment to compose herself before stepping back from the horse. "Yeah, I'm…okay. But I have to rub Mystri down and walk her…cool her off."

"Here, let me." He ignored her protests and took the reins from her hand. "You get yourself dried off. I'll walk her. Mystri is it?"

Hearing her name, the mare nickered and rubbed her head against his arm, as if she hadn't just made a wild run from the woods back to the barn. "You've got yourself into quite a state," he spoke to the bay Arab as he led her down the center of the barn. "Not sure what you and your mistress were up to but doesn't look good."

He unsaddled the mare, grabbed several old towels from the tack room and rubbed her down, then walked her until she dried. Once she was safe in her stall, he went back to Allison who sat on a feed bin, toweling her own hair and wearing a strange expression. He noticed her hands shook, and he went over to take the towel from her and began to rub the darkened, gold-brown tresses.

"That was a crazy ride. Do you usually go out when there's a storm coming?" he couldn't stop himself from asking.

"It wasn't storming when we left. We just went through the orchard to the creek."

"Something obviously spooked your horse pretty

bad. Just the thunder?"

She shivered and gave pause. "I'm not sure. She was acting weird right before the lightning started."

He stopped rubbing her hair. "Weird. Like how?"

"Like…she heard something…something I didn't." She clasped her hands together as if to ward off another tremor.

"Animals always know when a storm's coming," he sought to reassure her. "She probably sensed it then."

"Maybe." Allison chewed her bottom lip then turned to lift her gaze to meet his. "Why are you here?"

Because what you told me rocked my world, he wanted to say. *Because we have to talk. I have questions only you can answer.* But now wasn't the time. "Just checking to make sure you and Lizzie were okay. No more flat tires?"

She glared. "We're fine. We've been fine for the past nine years. Why would we need you to check up on us now?"

He held up his hand without the towel. "Now don't go getting your dander up. By your admittance, things are going a little haywire around here lately. Horses restless at night, the buckskin's injury, and someone did slash your tire. Would it be reason enough for someone who cares about you to ask if things are okay?"

Allison's eyes had flecks of gold that burned bright when she was angry. How well he remembered. They fairly glittered now as her chin jutted up in defiance.

"I don't need anybody watching out for me. I can take care of us just fine."

"Yeah, well, I'm not so sure. Especially when you go out riding when a storm's brewing and—"

She snatched the towel from his hand. "I told you.

97

There was no storm when we left. If there was, I wouldn't have taken my horse out. I'm not a child."

"But you're the mother of *my* child. That changes things." He didn't mean to broach the subject like this, in anger and resentment, but it had to be hashed out sometime…and soon.

Shane stepped away from her fiery gold gaze, and tried to figure out how to tell her knowing Lizzie was his daughter changed everything.

Saying nothing, she left the feed room. He followed while she checked on Mystri and found the mare content and dozing in her stall. "Thank you, for walking her. I was afraid…she might be hurt." She hesitated a moment before turning to walk down the main aisle of the barn.

He noticed she was limping and caught up with her. "I think it's you who's hurt. What happened out there?"

"It's nothing. We brushed up against a tree in the orchard is all."

But after a few more steps he caught her grimace and noted the ragged tear in her jeans where she rubbed her leg.

Shane went to the door and opened it a bit to peer out. "The storm's passed. Let's go up to the house, and I'll take a look."

"It's not necessary." She started to limp outside.

"Maybe not, but I think it's a good idea. And while I'm not a people doctor, I am a vet, and that's a medical degree. So don't argue." When he took her elbow, she leaned on him a little and let him help her up the path to the house. Once inside, he noticed she was shivering. The temperature had dropped during the storm, and she was still soaking wet. "Go change, but I still want to see the damage you did."

Offering no protest, she disappeared upstairs while Shane filled the kettle and put it to boil. If he remembered right, Grandma Ellie had kept a first aid kit in the downstairs bathroom. In the medicine cabinet, he found it, cotton balls, peroxide, and antibiotic cream and took those plus a few other items he might need back to the kitchen. He was filling two mugs with hot water and instant coffee when Allison returned, dressed in baggy sweatpants and white T-shirt, her damp hair pulled into the familiar ponytail. He motioned for her to sit, then, after fixing her coffee the way she'd always liked it—one spoonful of sugar and a dash of milk—he brought both mugs to the table.

"Drink up. You look like you're still chilled to the bone."

"You're just full of orders today, aren't you?" she murmured but sipped at the hot brew.

After drinking the coffee in silence for a few minutes, Shane scooted his chair up to hers. "Let's see the damages."

He waited for her to tug the sweatpants halfway up her thigh. Just as he'd figured, several abrasions had already turned a deep purple, and a long scratch slashed across them. He laid his fingers gently on the bruises; the heat of the wound seeping through to him.

"Nice of Mystri to run you into a tree while on your wild ride," he mused. "Lucky it didn't break your leg."

"She was just scared."

"So you said, but you don't know of what?" He doused the cotton in peroxide and stroked it over the scratch.

Allison flinched before explaining, "The storm came in sooner than expected. But she had spooked before we heard it coming. I had to calm her down enough to get in the saddle." She paused a moment while he cleaned the scratch and then put a cool cloth over the largest darkening bruise. "We were just sitting by the creek, and everything was fine...until it wasn't. Even the birds stopped singing."

When she shivered, Shane didn't think it was from the cold this time. His gaze met hers, and her eyes no longer held their fiery hue but had turned the soft golden-brown that always made him melt inside. He averted his gaze back to her bruised leg, but it didn't help squelch the sudden flare of heat creeping up his neck. Allison had shapely legs, to be sure, and it was hard not to remember running his hands up their curves and having them wrapped around him...

He cleared his throat and got up to rinse out the washcloth in cool water again. "It would be wise if you took it easy the rest of the day and kept your leg elevated." This time, when he stood by the table, he handed the cloth to Allison. "Leave that on it for an hour maybe."

"But I have work to do and dinner to make for Lizzie. She'll be home in a few hours. Ronnie thought by around three."

"She's with Ronnie?" He frowned. "I thought you two weren't so friendly."

"Well we're not, but she wanted to take Lizzie shopping and to a movie. Then they're picking Gypsy up from the groomer. I think it's a good idea for Lizzie to do a few girly things I haven't the time to do. And

Ronnie is her aunt, after all."

Not really. Which brought him to the real reason he had stopped to see Allison today. He took the empty mugs to the sink and rinsed them. Outside the window, the blue sky was clear of thunderheads. If only the storm clouds in their lives could clear so quickly. "When will you tell her?" he finally asked.

When she didn't answer, he swiveled around to find her hobbling toward the living room. Not willing to give up, he followed, waiting until she settled in the recliner and propped her leg on the footrest. Shane sat across from her, on the sofa, where he had kissed her for the first time in nearly ten years.

He shook the thought away and insisted, "We have to tell her. She has the right to know the truth."

"She does, but I'll decide when the time is right. It's…not going to be easy, you know. She loved Jason. He was a good father."

Maybe so, but he took something from me I can never get back. He glowered. "But he wasn't her real one. That would be me." Pain crossed Allison's face, this time not from the bruises, but from the hard truth. Yet he couldn't let up. "It won't be easy to explain to Lizzie, but waiting isn't going to change anything. She needs to know. *I* need for her to know."

"I just need some time. The past few days have been crazy. The problems I've had here…you coming back. It's a lot to deal with. Just…give me a little time to figure out how to do this." She leaned her head back and closed her eyes, as if by not looking at him she could make him go away. But this time, he wasn't running.

He wanted to say it was hard for him, too, but truth

was he hadn't been the one to deal with an unplanned pregnancy ten years ago. Hadn't married out of necessity and then had to raise a child alone. All of this Allison had done, and all because of him. The least he could do now was give her the space she needed to come to terms with their past...and to share the truth of it with their daughter.

Pushing himself from the sofa, he went to touch her arm. "I have to head back to the clinic for a few hours. You need to take it easy, and I'll come back and help you with the chores." He hushed her instant protest. "Don't say no. Let's just call a truce for now, until we both figure out how to do this."

With one finger, he traced her cheek, stopping the slow progress of a single tear slipping down her face. Allison's tears had always been his undoing, and it took everything he had not to gather her up as he had in years past...and the other night...but who knew where that would lead? He couldn't take the chance. Her sigh followed him as he walked away to let himself out.

Chapter 10

The Silver Creek Cemetery lay peaceful in the late afternoon sunlight. A few songbirds twittered softly overhead, but otherwise, no sounds broke the silence of the last resting place for the town's former residents.

Shane hesitated as he approached the gravesite. While he tossed a small football back and forth in his hands—the kind cheerleaders often flung into the stands at high school games—his thoughts raced back to those summer practices when he and Jason had run and sweated and joked together. They'd been so young then, so full of life, and so unaware of what life had in store for them. After the coach let them go for the day, he and Jase would often run down to the creek, strip to their shorts, and dive in. He still remembered the cold water, how they'd howled and laughed and carried on. What he wouldn't give to relive just one of those golden afternoons.

The elderly caretaker had pointed out the Delaney plot and babbled on about who was buried there. A set of great-grandparents, a great-uncle who'd died in Vietnam, a baby who'd been stillborn…and one young man who'd not made it to his twenty-fifth birthday.

Taking a deep breath, Shane walked over to the headstone with his best buddy's name engraved on it.

Seeing it hit him like a ton of bricks. He ran his hand around the back of his neck and had to look away a moment. Up until now, it hadn't seemed real that the friend he'd known so long ago was really gone forever. This made it real and final, yet it was what he needed to set the past right. After what Allison had told him, he could no longer feel the bitter resentment toward Jason. Because Jason had done the right thing. The manly thing. He'd taken care of Shane's responsibility, and he'd done it out of love.

He hunkered down on one knee and studied the etching for a moment. Touching the cool stone, he let his fingers trace over the two dates. Jason's birthday had been a week after his. They'd celebrated together by going to a rock concert and driven home singing like fools at the top of their lungs. A month later Shane asked Allison to the homecoming dance. It was the beginning of the end.

Resting his hand on the soft green grass below the headstone, he bowed his head for a long moment. "Thanks, buddy, for taking care of them." His voice came out gruff and full of emotion. "There's no way I can ever repay you but just to say, thanks." Dropping the football by the stone, right next to a vase of wilted flowers, he put his hands on his knee and pushed himself up, and then had to swallow hard to get rid of the lump in his throat. The best way to remember Jason Delaney was to remember the good times. Now, it was up to him, Shane McBride, to do the right thing.

It didn't mean Allison would have him. She'd suffered her own pain these past ten years, and he wouldn't blame her for telling him to take a hike. But he had to at least try.

Turning, he strode away toward his truck, planning to go back to the farm tonight. They'd talk, and maybe, just maybe, he'd convince her they could make a family—he and Allison and their daughter. It was still the one thing he wanted more than anything else in the world.

****

Allison awoke to the kitchen door opening and Lizzy calling out, "Hi, Mom, we're home." She struggled to sit up in the recliner just as the munchkin bounced into the living room, shopping bags swinging in her hands, followed by a newly brushed and shampooed Gypsy and a worn-out Ronnie. Before she could speak, her daughter rushed to her side. "Mom! Are you sick? Were you sleeping?"

"I'm fine," she assured them. "I just needed a quick nap. I guess I didn't sleep very well last night." She tried not to wince when she stood. The bruises really hurt now. "Did you have fun?" A glance to Ronnie met with an equally puzzled frown. "How was the movie?"

"Okay, but are you sure you're all right?" The forgotten shopping bags were tossed on the floor. "You don't look good."

She smoothed her daughter's hair and gave her a hug. "Yes, I'm fine, silly. What did you and Aunt Ronnie buy today? Let's get something to drink and you can show me." In the kitchen, she poured the lemonade while Lizzie showed off several new summer outfits.

Amazing she's suddenly willing to wear something besides jeans and horsey T-shirts.

"Very nice. Why don't you go hang them up and then come down for a snack?" When her excited daughter left the room, Allison swallowed her prideful nature and smiled at Ronnie. "Thanks for taking her today."

"Well, you know I'm happy to have Lizzie anytime."

She glanced around the kitchen Allison hadn't bothered to tidy up after breakfast this morning. Her sister-in-law was always assessing the housekeeping skills that weren't up to her standards, but to her credit she didn't comment right now.

The contemptuous gaze, however, focused back on her. "I've certainly never known you to take a nap. Are you feeling all right? If you don't, I can certainly take Lizzie home with me for the night."

"It's not necessary. I just…had a little run in with a tree this morning while riding and scraped my leg up." A second later, she mentally kicked herself for letting that slip. Her sister-in-law didn't need to know about the riding mishap. All she would do was harp about it. "But it'll be fine," she quickly added.

Ronnie sighed disgustedly. "Now, that's not the smartest thing to do is it, go riding by yourself? What if you'd fallen and gotten seriously hurt? No one would have known where to find you."

"I had my cell phone in my pocket." She hadn't.

"What if you were knocked unconscious?"

"But I wasn't, and I've ridden this farm all my life. I'm very careful." Although careful didn't help much when your horse got spooked by something unseen. She still wondered what had sent Mystri into flight, not that she was about to mention that.

"So was my brother, very careful, and it didn't stop something unexpected from happening to him."

"Please, Ronnie, don't…" The last thing she wanted to talk about was the accident that took Jason's life.

"Which brings me to something I've wanted to discuss with you." Her sister-in-law inspected her bright green fingernails for a few seconds. "What would happen to Lizzie if you were taken ill or, God forbid, something worse. Do you have anyone designated as her legal guardian?"

Bile rose in Allison's throat. Of course Ronnie would think she should designate them, and perhaps a week ago, as much as she hated to admit it, they would have been a logical choice. But things had changed in a matter of a few days, and she wasn't ready to explain any of it to her. "I don't think now is a good time."

"When then? You've got to show responsibility where your child is concerned. You've got to—"

Allison cut her off with a quick shake of her head when Lizzie came skipping back into the room and went right to the refrigerator.

"What's there to eat, Mom? And what's for din tonight?" As if she sensed the tension in the air, her big blue eyes flicked between them. "Is something wrong?"

Allison rose from the table and went to her daughter's side. "Not a thing, but there's fruit salad left from last night. You may have some now, and we'll just grill hot dogs for dinner. Sound okay?"

An astute child, there was never any pulling the wool over Lizzie's eyes, but she fixed her snack without further questions. A few minutes later, thankfully, Ronnie left, but with a promise they'd go to an art exhibit the following week.

Shane called at five to say he was running late after several emergencies at the clinic. Allison assured him she was fine, and she and Lizzie could handle feeding the horses.

"I'm bringing pizza for dinner," he insisted. "Should be there by seven."

Allison agreed, only because it would leave them just enough time to make the quick visit she had decided was necessary before she could tell Lizzie the truth.

****

A chill in the air had followed the storm. Allison tugged on a flannel shirt and followed alongside Lizzie as the sun slipped behind the tall pine trees guarding the cemetery. A light breeze sighed softly through the boughs, an infinitely lonely sound for an infinitely lonely place.

At first, they'd come here every day, then every week. Now she had to stop and think, when was the last time they'd visited Jason other than Father's Day? Her life had become so busy in the past year or two, what with work and the horses and Lizzie's activities. It wasn't that she didn't think of Jason anymore; she just needed to keep moving forward. Keep putting one foot in front of the other to make sure her daughter had every opportunity. A chance to make something of herself. A chance for a good life. Things were going pretty well, up until Shane McBride came back into their lives. Now, she had to change the life she'd made for them, tell Lizzie the truth. The truth that the man she'd believed was her father was not really her father at all.

Her daughter knelt down by Jason's headstone and with her small hands lifted the vase with the wilted flowers. "Well, these are all done for. Do you think Aunt Ronnie left them?"

"Probably." Ronnie often visited her only brother's grave. "Why don't you go ahead and put your flowers in it. She won't mind."

Allison wrapped her arms around herself while Lizzie arranged the small bouquet she had picked from her garden. She took a few minutes to fix the flowers just so before putting them back by the headstone and brushing away some dry leaves blown across the grave.

"Mom, look! Who do you suppose left this?" Lizzie turned to her and held out a miniature football. "Do you think some kid dropped it?"

Her breath caught in her throat as she stepped forward and put out her hand to take the ball. Turning it over, she saw a date written on it, a date from nearly eleven years ago. The last season Shane and Jason had been teammates. Allison smiled to herself and gave the football back to Lizzie. "It stays here, honey."

"But where did it come from?"

"I'll tell you later." She urged her daughter to put it back, then held out her hand. "Come on. I have something very important to tell you, but let's go home first."

When they arrived at the farm, Shane sat waiting for them on the porch. Allison wasn't sure she wanted to talk to Lizzie with him present, but maybe it was for the best. After all, what she had to tell her daughter did involve him.

Chapter 11

Crumpled napkins, paper plates, and an empty pizza box lay strewn across the kitchen table. The sun had long set behind the old apple orchard and only a splash of scarlet shone through the kitchen window. A few minutes had passed since she'd dropped the bombshell, and Lizzie hadn't spoken a word. Allison knotted her hands together as she peered at her daughter's face. "Do you understand what I just told you?"

The small bow lips screwed up, and she wiggled in her chair. "I think I do. You said my daddy wasn't my real daddy. Is that right?"

Allison nodded then glanced to Shane for some idea of what to say next, but he didn't seem to have a clue, either. Well, she really couldn't blame him. He was still coming to terms with the truth himself. "I know this is hard for you to accept, and if you have any questions, you may certainly ask them." Silence. Was it better to let it sink in? Encourage her to talk? It nearly broke her heart to see the confusion clouding her baby girl's eyes. "So, do you? Have any questions?"

Averting her gaze, Lizzie stared out the kitchen window. "Why did he pretend?"

"Pretend?"

"That he was my daddy, if he really wasn't." She turned back, and her deep blue eyes begged for an honest answer. "Why would he do that?"

She weighed her words. "Because he loved you, very much, and because your real father couldn't be here to help take care of you."

"Who is my real father?"

The question that would change everything. Allison flicked her gaze to Shane. This was his to answer. His place to tell his daughter the truth. He had wanted this, but would he do it, or would he once again leave them to their own devices? Run back west where he'd made his life?

Much like Lizzie, he shifted uncomfortably in his chair as he fidgeted with a napkin. Then his shoulders squared, and he drew himself up to face the music. "I am, Lizzie. I'm your real father."

Her brows drew together in a frown, and she studied the man who was suddenly more than just the new doc who took care of the horses. Allison supposed if they'd told her the moon really was made of green cheese she could have more easily believed it.

"But…didn't you know about me?"

"Not 'til I came back here, to Michigan."

A moment of silence passed. "If you had…would you have loved me?"

He passed a hand over his eyes, but Allison saw the glimmer in them.

"Very much, Shortstuff, very much." His voice held a slight tremor.

It was a lot for a child of nine to digest, even one as astute as Lizzie. Allison was proud of how she was handling herself as she seemed to roll all of this around in her mind.

Her brave daughter stood. "I'd like to go to my

room now, if it's okay. I'm so tired."

Allison stood and hugged her close for a moment, stroking her hand over her baby girl's dark braids. Lizzie didn't resist, but her little body remained stiff.

Does she hate me?

In a low voice she said, "Sure, honey. Get ready for bed, and I'll come up in a little while to tuck you in."

After Lizzie left the kitchen, Allison sagged into a chair and put her head down on the table, exhausted and wondering about the next step in this hard left turn her life had taken.

When Shane placed his hand on her back, making a pattern of warm circles between her shoulders, the last strength she'd mustered today slipped away, and a wealth of tears welled up and spilled over. She tried to cover them, but she'd never been any good at hiding her emotions from this man. Why should now be any different?

"Hey, it's okay. Lizzie's a strong kid. I think she'll be fine with all this. It'll just take some time."

"But how can you be so sure?" She swiped at her eyes and jumped up to find a box of tissue. "This is a life-changing event! Everything she's ever known has suddenly been turned on its head. Don't you think she's confused? Don't you think—"

"What I think is that Lizzie is resilient. She's our child, how could she not be? Sure she's confused, but she'll figure it out. Let's give her some credit."

Allison clutched a handful of tissues from the counter. "You always were the confident one in this equation. I've always had a hard time being certain...of anything."

The bruises on her leg started to throb, and any

confidence she'd mustered in order to tell Lizzie the truth drained away. She squeezed her eyes shut to hold back the emotions.

She knew when he came closer, because every nerve ending in her body went on high alert, tingling like tiny shocks. In the next moment, his strong arms drew her to him, and she didn't resist, needing comfort and support and knowing there was no one else to give it. Even after all this time, Shane still knew her best.

"Do you think she hates me?" she asked against his shoulder. "Do you think things will ever be okay again?"

He tucked her head beneath his chin. "How could she hate you? You're the world's best mom. Now me she might hate. *I'm* the one who left. I'm the one who hasn't been a parent." He sighed deeply. "How do I explain that to her?"

She couldn't stop from leaning into him or from feeling the way she had ten years ago, before life handed them problems they'd been too young to handle. Problems they still didn't know how to handle.

"Like you said, it will take time, and we'll just have to figure it out…as we go along. That is…" She hesitated, afraid to assume too much.

"That is if I'm around, to be a father?" he supplied.

Keeping her hands splayed against his chest, Allison pushed herself away and forced herself to meet his gaze. "I can't imagine you haven't made a life somewhere…in Wyoming. After all these years, there must be someone…else."

His eyes darkened to a stormy hue. "There isn't. There was, for a time, but it didn't work out."

The thought of Shane with someone else suddenly

slid a poker through her heart, and a thousand questions popped into her mind. Who was she? Was she pretty? Smart? And why didn't it work out?

She tried to step back from him, but his arms tightened, and he wouldn't let her go.

"I won't pretend I didn't try to get over you. I had to after I heard you married Jason, but no one else ever meant what you did to me. What you still mean to me. I guess the question is, do I still mean anything to you? Other than as Lizzie's father."

A hard question to answer, one that twisted the poker in her heart 'til it jabbed all the tender places in her body. How to answer? How did she explain all the tumultuous emotions spilling through her mind? The conflict that still kept her from giving up to the way her body reacted to Shane's. He was right, of course. They still had to mean something to each other. Staying together just for Lizzie's sake wouldn't be enough, and yet the truth was probably the best. Even if the truth cost her his staying here. "I don't know, but I'd like to find out." Her voice faltered. "And not only for Lizzie's sake, but for both of ours."

With his thumb, he wiped the leftover tears from her cheek. "It will take some learning, but I want to find out, too. I want to be Lizzie's dad, in more than just name, and maybe for us to be…a family."

She rested her cheek against his hand and a powerful sense of awareness thrummed between them.

There was a time in her life when Shane's kiss could work magic, heal a hurt, soften a loss, and take her away from whatever troubled her. Could it do that now? Erase the emptiness that had filled her when she'd found out he left? Fill her now with hope for a future together?

When he leaned down, she automatically lifted her face to meet him. She gave herself up to the fire that had always flared between them, and relished the feel of his mouth on hers and the ease with which her body remembered. While he explored the curve of her back, she slid her hands up the hard muscles of his arms and then wrapped them around his neck. With a sigh, she leaned into the length of his body.

"How I've missed you, Allie," he murmured against her lips. "How I've missed this."

Just as he pulled her up closer and her bones began to melt, a noise from outside the house broke through and pulled her back from the brink.

A slam of hooves against a stall, a loud whinny, and then another. Followed by Lizzie's footsteps overhead as she clattered down the stairs, Gypsy close on her heels.

"Mom! Mom, there's something wrong! I hear the horses! What's after them?"

Before the two burst into the kitchen, Allison broke away from Shane's embrace and flew to the window. He followed her, resting his hands on her shoulders as she strained to see what was happening outside. Summer darkness had fallen, and the shadows of the trees loomed across the yard. She could see nothing, but something was out there, something determined to frighten the horses and make her crazy. Gypsy ran around the kitchen barking, while Shane tried to quiet the frantic dog. In two seconds, Lizzie stood beside her, and small fingers clutched her arm. "What's wrong with them, Mommy? We need to go out there! We need to go now!"

Still drained from the close encounter with Shane, Allison gathered her wits and tried to calm not only herself but her totally frazzled daughter. "Yes, I know, but I need to go out there, not you." She held her back from rushing to the door.

"You always say that!" Lizzie pulled away and ran to put on her boots. "What if my pony is in trouble? He might need me!"

"Listen to your mom, Lizzie." Shane stepped in and put his hand on their daughter's shoulder. "How about you both stay here, and I'll go out to the barn."

Her blue eyes flashed, and in a way totally unlike her, she stamped her foot. "No! Just because you say you're my father doesn't mean you can tell me what to do now. I want to see my pony!"

"Lizzie!" Allison sharpened her tone. "Doc McBride's right. You need to stay here." She pushed her to sit at the table and then, not listening to Shane either, yanked open the kitchen door, shoving the dog back with her knee. "Keep Gypsy with you and lock the door after us. Don't come out and don't open it for anyone but me. Understand?"

Lizzie appeared to listen but it didn't mean she would obey, especially if it concerned the horses. Shane must have figured that out, because when she made to get up again, he pointed one finger toward her and the chair. "Sit down and stay here, Shortstuff. I'm not kidding."

Another loud whinny echoed in the night, and Allison bolted across the porch, leaving him to shut the door tight. Halfway to the barn, he caught up with her. Before either of them could speak again, the sound of an engine starting caught their attention, and she got a glimpse of a vehicle pulling away from the far end of the pasture, the same place where they'd seen the tire tracks a few days ago.

Shane sprinted down to the end of the drive while she slid the door of the barn open. When he joined her a few minutes later, she was checking every horse in its stall.

"It got too far away to get the license number." He walked down one side of the aisle to help make sure none of the horses had been harmed.

She paused at Starlight's stall. The filly was agitated, tossing her head and pawing her bedding. Allison lifted the latch and went inside, hoping to calm her. Speaking softly, she reached out to stroke the satiny neck. "Shhh, it's okay. Nothing will hurt you." She ran her hands over the filly's back and then glanced down at her slender legs. Thank goodness there didn't appear to be any injuries that had escaped her, like with Pride, but something definitely had Starlight spooked.

"Is she okay?" Shane stood outside the stall and peered in. "The others seem all right, just nervous."

After a few moments of massaging the filly's withers, Allison slipped back out and set the latch firmly. "I think these two were making the most noise. When Starlight first came here last year, with her sister Stardust, they were both a wreck. Scared, starved, and wild. They'd had little handling. They still frighten easily." She moved over to Stardust's stall and went inside to check her. She was the older and quieter of the two, but even her eyes were wide and fearful. Allison calmed her with the same gentle massage, and after a few moments, the filly whickered and nuzzled her pocket for a treat.

"Nothing for you tonight," she murmured as the velvet nose tickled her hand. Satisfied the filly was all right, Allison joined Shane. Sighing, she latched the stall and leaned against the knotty pine boards.

He moved closer to her. "Who do you think it was in the car, and why are they frightening the horses?"

Do I dare tell him? About what happened here last winter? Taking a deep breath and letting it out slowly, she steeled herself and said, "The Potter brothers."

Chapter 12

"Scaring your horses, slashing your tire—what do they have against you?"

Allison swallowed hard. "My tire? You think they did that, too?" It was probably true, but explaining it all to Shane wasn't something she wanted to do.

"I have reason to believe they did, but why? I know they still have it in for me, but what did *you* ever do to them?"

His gaze burned intensely, the way it always had when he was dead serious about something. Could she risk letting someone else know about the silent deal she'd struck with Duane and Darren in February, the day she'd seen them hunting in her woods? The deal had sickened her to make, but she'd had no other choice.

Grasping Shane by the sleeve of his denim shirt, she drew him over to Pride's stall. The gash was healing nicely, and the buckskin watched them curiously, nudging at her over the top of his stall. "It all started with him." She scratched Pride's forehead for a moment. "But let's get back inside before Lizzie decides to come down here."

On the way out, she peeked in Cayenne's stall. The pony lay curled in the far corner, apparently unconcerned about the fuss the other horses had made.

At least I can reassure Lizzie he's all right.

She turned out the light, and quickly made her way up to the house with Shane alongside. By now, the abrasions on her leg throbbed worse, and she hated that she had to hold onto his arm.

Once she convinced Lizzie her pony was fine, her baby girl went reluctantly off to bed again but threw curious glances Shane's way. Thank goodness he only nodded and said nothing more to her. Allison could only hope he knew there was time to help their daughter come to terms with what she'd learned, and to eventually accept him as an authority figure. But they'd all had enough excitement for this night.

Sitting on the porch a little while later, Allison twisted her hands nervously together, deciding how to tell Shane about what happened in the past year. "One day last fall, I was driving past the Potter's farm, and I saw this horse stuck in a small pen. I couldn't imagine why they had a horse—they've only ever had a few chickens—and I was pretty sure they didn't have a clue how to take care of him." *And I was right.* "He was okay then, but over the next month, I purposely drove by their place, just to see if he was all right. He didn't have any shelter, and with winter coming on, I was worried. I called the county animal control and asked them to check on him. They said they did and everything seemed fine."

"Even though the horse had no shelter?"

"They told Duane he had to provide some kind of shelter, and the next time I drove by, there was a flimsy lean-to slapped up in the pen." She knew he would understand how much this had upset her. "I asked Doc Brewster if he'd treated the horse at all. He hadn't but said he'd stop by their place. Then the weather got bad,

and Doc got sick with bronchitis. So…I went there."
She cringed and waited for his reaction.

"Alone?" At her nod, he rubbed two fingers
between his eyes and shook his head. "That was
stupid."

So much for understanding. In despair, she threw
her hands up in the air and glared at him. "Well, it
wasn't like I had anyone to go with me, and this horse
needed help! By then, his ribs were showing, and he
was lame with an infected hoof. I *told* Duane he needed
to let me have him, and I even offered to buy Pride, but
he refused."

The day of the confrontation leapt sharp and clear
in her mind. Remembering the cold wind that blew, and
the sad shape Pride was in by then still gave her chills.
She'd been so desperate to save him, she'd actually
shouted at the two brothers, who'd only laughed at her.

Shane leaned back in the swing and shook his head
in disbelief. "What the hell were they doing with a
horse anyway?"

"I asked myself the same thing." She lifted her
hands, palms out in confusion. "I heard they'd done
some work on a car, and the guy didn't have the money
to pay them. So he gave them Pride."

He snorted. "So, what did they plan to do with
him?"

A shudder rippled over her. "How should I know?
But in the shape he was in, no one would have bought
him. He wasn't going to make it through the winter, so
I…took him."

Shane tipped his head as if to see her face better.
"Wait a minute. You…*took* their horse? Without their
permission?"

"If I'd have waited for that, Pride would be dead." In her mind, that was the finality of it.

"How did you...?"

Recalling the incident was difficult even this many months later. She wrapped her arms around herself to stave off the memory of that dark, drizzly night and the sick horse he'd been. "While Lizzie was at a movie with Ronnie, I went there with my trailer. Duane and Darren are never home on a Friday night, so I loaded up Pride and brought him here. I told Lizzie I got him at an auction. I kept him in the barn for a while, he was so thin anyway, and only Doc knew I had him, because he had to come over and treat his hoof. But he wouldn't tell. Doc knows what a bunch of scum those two are." The swing swayed as Shane moved to face her, his knee brushing hers. In spite of his questioning her judgment, she had to squelch a rush of emotion that set her skin to tingling.

"Didn't they suspect before now that you have him?"

Which is the whole issue. "They've known, since the day I caught them poaching deer in my woods. It was a nice day, so I'd put the horses out, including Pride, and then I heard gunshots. Hunting season was long over, so I went down to the end of the pasture to make sure the horses were okay. I saw Darren and Duane's car there, hidden in the trees. I waited until they came packing the deer out."

"Why didn't you just call the sheriff?" He lifted her hair off her shoulder and tucked it back. "Instead of trying to handle it yourself."

"Because I was pretty sure they'd seen their horse." She heaved a heavy sigh. "They could have turned me in."

"As you could have turned them in for poaching," he pointed out the obvious.

She nodded and absently rubbed her leg. "We all had something to hide, but I had Lizzie to think about."

"What happened then?"

Their smirks turned my stomach. "They saw me watching…and eyed Pride where he grazed in the pasture. Then they tossed the deer in the back of their vehicle, got in, and left…and I let them go."

"And you've been afraid of them ever since." He traced one finger along her cheek. "That's no way to live."

She met the gaze of his summer blue eyes and tried to make him understand. "And yet, just as with you, I had no choice."

When he nodded in agreement, she let him draw her into the curve of his shoulder, and for a while the slow movement of the swing and Shane's warmth pushed away the memory of the hard decision she'd made.

A short time later, Allison left the swing to check on Lizzie. Shane stood and stretched. It might be best if he went home now, but reluctance to leave her alone nudged him to follow her inside. While she went upstairs, he put his phone number in the contacts of her cell phone, the old flip kind that didn't require a code to unlock it.

When she came back into the kitchen, he noticed the dusty shadows lurking beneath her golden brown eyes, and the way she limped over to the sink made his heart flip over. For the first time, it truly sank in just what she'd been through, and how she'd managed to stay strong all these years.

"Will you be all right?" he asked. She didn't reply, so he insisted, "Promise to call me if you hear anything else." He handed her the phone.

"We're fine." She took it but lifted her chin. "As we were fine all the years you weren't here."

The comment hurt, mostly because it was true. Yet, he couldn't help but worry now that he *was* here. "Maybe you should re-think talking to the sheriff, about what's going on. For Lizzie's and your own safety. The Potters couldn't be trusted ten years ago, and they can't be trusted now."

She shook her head. "The problem is, I have no proof...and they do." For a moment, she turned to him and put her head against his shoulder. "And tonight, I'm really tired. Can we just let it go for now?"

Shane held her close and didn't ask for anymore. He couldn't blame her independence, and he couldn't expect her to want to talk further about the two men who had caused both of them a lifetime of grief. But as sure as night followed day, he would make sure the Potter brothers didn't bother her again.

****

With a full morning of emergency surgeries at the clinic and the afternoon busy with farm calls, Shane didn't have a chance to call Allison until after six the next day. Then he worried when she didn't answer and decided to drive to the farm right away. After the things she'd told him, who knew what might be wrong?

Maybe she left her phone in the house, or forgot to plug it in. Or maybe the old thing just quit working.

But he had another reason for going there, and they mewed in the basket Sandy had prepared before she left early to visit Matthew. He covered the tiny kittens with a square of soft pink flannel, and as he hoisted the basket under his arm, he hoped Allison wouldn't mind the surprise.

Just as he was ready to lock up, the office phone rang. For a second, he debated letting the call go to the answering machine, but knowing it could be another client with an injured pet or a farmer with a sick cow, he set down the basket and hurried back inside. Pressing the button for line one, he opened his mouth to speak, but Sandy's voice cut him short.

"I'm…so glad…I caught you," she sputtered, breathless. "I left my phone in the car because it doesn't work up here anyway, and I couldn't remember your cell number."

In that instant, his stomach lurched up to meet his throat, and he had to swallow hard. *Had Doc taken a turn for the worse?*

"Sandy, what is it?" He gripped the receiver tight in his hand and steadied himself to take bad news.

"He's awake! Oh my, he's sitting up and acting ornery just like the old Matthew. They said it happened right before I got here. He just…woke up."

Shane let out a long sigh of relief and had to press two fingers to his eyes to hold back the sudden rush of emotion flooding him.

"Dr. McBride…Shane?" Her voice was tearful. "Are you okay?"

He still couldn't trust his own for a couple of seconds. Finally, he managed to get past the lump in his throat. "Yeah, Sandy, I couldn't be better. That's…just the best news you could have given me."

"I know how it is with you two." She stopped, and

the distinct sound of her blowing her nose came through the line. "You're the closest he's got to having a son."

And he's the only father I've ever known. I owe him so much. "Is he…in any pain? Can he talk?"

Sandy laughed. "Well, you know he doesn't say a whole lot anyway, but he asked for something to drink, and he's complaining about the IV."

He could picture that, and the thought made him grin. "I'll be up as soon as I can, but I have to see Allison first."

"That's okay. Why don't you wait 'til tomorrow? His niece just got here, and they're limiting his visitors to two at a time. You go on and see Allison. She needs you, too."

Bless Sandy. Not only was she efficient, she was also perceptive and a hopeless romantic.

"Then tell Doc I'll be there tomorrow around noon. Give him…give him my best." That's all he could manage at the moment. If he said anymore, he would lose it for sure.

On the way to Allison's Farm, Shane whistled while the warm breeze from the open window of his truck blew in his face. He couldn't wait to share that Matthew was out of the coma. Knowing how close they'd come to losing the old man, it was truly the best news he'd heard all week.

The kittens' plaintive mewing drew his attention to the basket on the truck seat. He darted them a quick glance. The pink flannel blanket tucked over the top of it moved, and a tiny bobble-headed kitten poked his nose out, followed by scrabbling paws as he was joined by his two siblings. Shane chuckled and focused back on the road. Taking one hand from the steering wheel, he gently pushed them back into the basket with one finger. "Hang on guys. We'll be there in a few minutes." They clutched at his finger with pointy claws and nosed about, searching for their mother with eyes barely opened. *Poor little critters.*

When he turned into Allison's drive, he saw her at the far end of the pasture, standing at the fence and looking off toward the woods. Her hair, free from its usual ponytail, drifted about her shoulders. It appeared she'd already brought the horses in for the night, so why was she out there?

He parked by the barn and scooped up the basket of kittens. First, he would find Lizzie, then he'd go see what had Allison so disturbed.

His daughter was in the barn with her pony, brushing him and singing along with the radio.

My daughter.

The realization struck him and sent a jolt of joy as well as apprehension surging through him. Holding the basket of kittens, he stopped to listen to her voice, and his heart filled with pride. It was sweet and clear and reminded him of his grandmother, who had loved to sing. He still missed the woman who had tried her hardest to give him a normal life for as long as she could. What would she have thought about Lizzie? *If she had lived longer, there wouldn't be a girl with long, dark braids singing to her pony right now.* His life—all of their lives—would have been so different.

He cleared his throat, which drew Lizzie's attention.

She gave him a half-smile. "Hi. Mom's outside somewhere."

"Yeah, I know. I saw her when I drove in." Tucking the basket under one arm, he went over and stroked the pony's neck. For such an old fella, he was in good shape, thanks to Lizzie's attention. "I…wanted to talk to you first."

"Why me?" She didn't look at him now and kept brushing.

"I have a favor to ask. You see, someone brought a mother cat and kittens into the clinic today. The mother is quite young and sick, and she can't take care of her babies anymore. I'm so busy taking care of Doc Brewster's patients, I can't care for them properly."

When the kittens mewed plaintively, Lizzie stuck her head around the pony and spied the basket. The blanket moved again as the kittens tried to climb out. He lifted it to reveal the three furry babies.

"Oh my gosh, they are so tiny!" She put the brush down and came to take the basket from him. "How old are they?"

"Maybe ten days? The people who brought the mother cat in found her and the kittens under their porch. As you can see, their eyes haven't been open long."

Lizzie lifted one of the babies and cuddled her close. The kitten nosed at her cheek, searching for its dinner. "They're hungry, I'll bet. Do you have a bottle?"

Shane quickly produced the kitten bottle from his shirt pocket. "Sandy fixed a few of these, and I have some cans of kitten milk in the truck. Do you think you can feed them until they're old enough to eat regular food? If it's okay with your mom."

His little girl grinned. "Sure. She won't mind. I'll

just keep them in my room for now." She let the kitten nuzzle against her.

While Shane wasn't sure Allison would love the idea, he didn't think she'd protest too much. He'd once watched her feed some orphaned baby birds until they could fly. And though he could have sent the kittens to the local shelter, bringing them here had suddenly seemed a good way to bridge the gap between Lizzie and himself.

The two kittens left in the basket mewed loudly now, and Lizzie put the one she'd been holding back. "Just let me finish with Cayenne and get him in his stall. Then I'll take them up to the house."

He waited, watching how gentle she was with the pony, so much like her mother in her ways. Was a relationship possible between them? Would she accept him as her father? At this moment, he could only hope.

When Cayenne was happily munching from his hay net, his daughter took the basket and bottle from him. "Come on little ones," she murmured to the mewing babies. "Lizzie's going to take care of you now. Don't you worry."

Just as they left the barn, she turned to him, her brows scrunched into a frown. "I'm kind of confused, you know."

He tipped his head in question. "About what?"

"What I should call you now. I'm not sure I can call you Dad, because, you know, I always thought my dad was…my dad."

He shoved his hands into his jeans pockets and considered this. "Then how about you just call me Shane, until, you know, you might feel different."

"It's okay with you?" Her voice still sounded

uncertain, but her big blue eyes met his, and their sweetness melted away his own concerns.

"Sure, as long as I can still call you Shortstuff." He winked at her, and she winked back her approval. "You go ahead, and I'll come up in a bit to tell you some things you need to know about taking care of the kittens. After I talk to your mom."

She gave him that Lizzie smile, with her nose wrinkling and eyes sparkling. When she started for the house, he watched her go, proud she had worked through this without acting out.

With a sigh of relief, he set off for the pasture. When he reached Allison, she didn't even notice until Gypsy gave a soft woof and came running from where she'd been sniffing along the fence.

"Hey, old girl." He ruffled the collie's ears. "What are you two up to?" Gypsy licked at his hands, then took off to run around the empty pasture. He leaned one arm along the top fence rail and tried to see what had her attention. "What's up? Someone around again?"

"Not someone." Allison motioned to the ground. "But maybe something."

He followed her gaze to a single, large paw print left in the dirt just inside the fence. At the sight of it, a jolt of surprise rocketed through him. What the hell was this? Crouching down to study it, he thought about prints he'd seen like this elsewhere, and how the sight of them had sent goosebumps prickling up his backbone. He looked about in the dirt for any others, but if there'd been more prints, they'd been obliterated by the horses' scrambling hooves.

"What...what do you suppose it is?" She kept her voice low. "Coyote? We had a pack a few summers ago, but I thought they'd moved on."

He reached beneath the fence rail and laid his own hand beside the print. It easily matched his palm. "Not coyote," he said. "The claws are sheathed." He raised his gaze in time to see her shudder as she glanced about the wide, empty pasture. His own throat tightened when he considered the possibility.

"What then? Bobcat? I've heard a few were spotted by the river."

Shane straightened up. "Maybe." He scanned the pasture again, then glanced off toward the woods, and finally settled on Allison. Did he dare say what was in his mind? He didn't want to frighten her, but this was serious business. Better he told her. "I've seen prints like this, but not here."

"Where?" She rubbed her arms. "Where did you see them?"

He glanced away for a moment, squinting into the sun where it slipped behind the trees. "In a canyon, in Wyoming. Where I was hiking."

"Did…did you see what made them?"

Remembering that day sent a shiver prickling up the back of his neck. "No, but I was pretty sure it saw me."

He faced her again, but Allison had turned toward the house.

"Maybe we should check on Lizzie," he heard her murmur.

Before he followed, Shane pulled out his phone and took a quick picture of the print. Would it be enough to convince the local conservation officer something unusual was stalking Allison's Farm?

Chapter 13

Once in the house, they didn't mention the paw print in front of Lizzie, but Shane did tell them about Matthew coming out of the coma. Thank goodness—and the news appeared to give Allison something to smile about, too.

On her way into the kitchen, she stopped and gave him a quick hug. "I know how much old Doc means to you, to many of us. I'm sure you feel so much better. I just don't know what we'd do without him around here."

Did she know her hug made him feel better, too? He managed to sneak in a quick kiss when Lizzie wasn't watching. Tasting Allison's lips, even briefly, sent a triple surge of pleasure rippling through him that blocked out the other worries.

Shane then showed Lizzie the best way to care for the kittens and gave her written instructions of a feeding schedule. Allison cuddled them along with their daughter, as he knew she would. Watching them together on the sofa, both sitting cross-legged and giving each kitten its bottle and rubbing tummies afterward, he knew he'd done the right thing tonight.

When Allison announced bedtime, Lizzie tucked the kittens into their basket and gathered it up. "Can they sleep in my room? Please, Mom?"

"Yes they may, but you'll have to wake for their

middle of the night feeding. Go ahead, and I'll fix some more bottles."

As Lizzie made her way upstairs, a rush of some unique emotion filled Shane's chest. Was this what it felt like to be a new father? He hugged the feeling close.

"I'm going to the kitchen, would you like anything?" Allison had the kitten bottles in her hands as fatigue settled on her face.

He followed. "I hope you don't mind I brought the kittens here. I thought it might be something Lizzie and I could talk about, until we figure out this father-daughter thing."

She put the bottles in the sink. "Seriously, did you ever know me to turn away an animal? And she's just like me, so of course it's fine. She'll be an attentive little mama to them." She lined up the extra clean bottles he had brought, opened a can of the kitten milk, and proceeded to fill the little containers.

Shane came up behind her. "You're right. She is just like you. In every good way." He wanted to hold Allison close and offer any support he could, but was hesitant to touch her. Her unspoken worry over the paw print would make her much too vulnerable, and he refused to take advantage.

As if reading his thoughts, she paused in filling the bottles, and a sudden shiver rippled over her slender shoulders. "What is out there?" Quiet fear rimmed her words. "As if the Potters aren't enough of a problem, now this. I'm afraid to let the horses out in the pasture anymore, but what can I tell my boarders? I have kids coming for lessons in the morning. I can't risk their safety, but I can't lose my business either. What am I going to do?"

He gently grasped her shoulders and turned her to face him, knowing he had to tread lightly. "I think we should start by contacting the authorities. The sheriff's department and the local conservation officer. We have to know what we're up against before we can figure out what to do about it."

"We?" The question in her eyes went beyond whatever doubt she had about his concern and straight to the truth. The truth of how long he would be here and a part of their lives.

"I'm here to help you. For better or worse, I'm part of yours and Lizzie's life. I know you're not sure you want to believe me, but you two are more important to me than anything else right now, and *your safety* means everything. Please know that."

"I want to believe it. I do believe it. But what happens if I report the Potters are harassing me, and they say I stole their horse? As for the poaching, it's my word against theirs, and—"

He touched her mouth with his fingers, then lightly kissed it. "Okay, we won't report the Potters, but the paw print is another matter. If it's what I'm thinking, we have to know for sure."

She placed her hands against his chest and put some distance between them. "And what are you thinking?"

He let her go and paced back and forth a moment, rubbing his chin as he contemplated the notion playing in his mind. "I'm remembering an incident early in the summer before I left. Doc and I went to a farm probably ten miles from here because a horse had been injured. There were bite marks on the neck and scratches on its back. Very unusual, Doc had noted, and he didn't agree with the official report."

"What did the report say?"

"The easy answer was coyotes, and while they don't often go after prey as large as a horse, it has happened. They just don't jump on its back." He felt her gaze on him and hated to speak the word that would frighten her more, but better she knew.

"Then…what does?" Allison's voice trembled.

"Cats. Big cats." He swung around to face her and found her face pale as summer mist.

"Wh-what are you saying?"

"I'm saying the paw print in the pasture is like the ones I saw in that canyon. My guess would be a cougar."

"But how? There are no…"

"Cougars in this part of Michigan," he finished for her. "I know. Same thing we were told that summer, but Doc was convinced no coyotes injured that horse."

Her chest rose with a deep breath. "Do you think that's how Pride was hurt? Whatever left the print tried to…bring him down?"

The shudder of her shoulders and tremor in her voice drew him to her side. He rubbed his hands down her arms and kept them against her chilled skin until it warmed a little. "I don't know, but until we do, I'd keep all the horses close to the barn."

"I will."

When she broke away, she tightened caps on the bottles, and put them away in the fridge. As she closed the door, he noticed her wince and rub at her leg.

"How are the bruises?" he dared to ask.

She shrugged. "They're going away. Just still sting

135

a little now and then."

"You should let me check them, see if they're healing properly."

She rubbed her hands down the worn jeans fitting snugly against her legs. "I can hardly pull these up like sweatpants."

"Then drop them." Her eyes grew wide, and he couldn't help but grin. "Nothing I haven't seen before, you know, but I promise to only look at the bruises."

Cheeks flaming, she unzipped her jeans and pulled them down just enough to show the abrasions, now turning a nice shade of pale blue and purple with a little green around the edges. Shane crouched to inspect them, touching her skin ever so gently, fighting the strong temptation to press a kiss there and run his hands along the curve of her thigh. But a promise was a promise.

He stood and glanced away while she pulled her jeans up. "If you think it's come back around, you have to tell me."

"I will, but can we just let it go for now?"

He suddenly ached to hold her close and make them both forget about their problems, but for now, he couldn't ask that of Allison. He couldn't expect her to just pick up where they'd left off ten years ago, but he was determined she wouldn't shut him out. Not anymore.

Chapter 14

At the feed store the next day, Allison was in the office finishing up payroll when Murray poked his head in the doorway.

"Just thought I'd let you know, Katie had her baby last night. Eight and a half pound boy." His face lit with pride. "She already sent us pictures. Thelma's got them on her phone. He's a fine-looking boy, too, with lots of hair, just like his mama."

"Well that's wonderful, and congratulations to you and Thelma. I know you've looked forward to this little one's arrival." She tried to imagine the often cranky Murray as a doting grandpa. Knowing how kind he was to Lizzie, she didn't doubt he'd spoil the kid. "Please give Katie and her hubby my best, too."

He nodded, and a red flush crept up his neck. Good old Murray, embarrassed at his own reaction to having a new little grandson. She had to smile, then wondered if it was a good time to bring up the subject flitting about in her mind. *Now's as good a time as any.* Before he could leave, she closed the desk drawer and slipped the key into her jeans pocket. "Say, Murray?"

"Yeah?"

She swallowed hard before she lost her nerve. Lying to him went against the grain with her, but telling him the truth? This was better. "I was going through some old newspaper clippings couple of nights ago, just stuff I found in the attic. Pop must have saved them. You remember how he always cut out stuff from the *Silver Creek News*." *At least that's true.* "Anyway, I found a few articles from back about the time Jason and I were in high school, the summer folks thought they saw a big cat around here. I just wondered—do you think there was ever any truth to it?" She didn't know if there was anything in the paper about the incident, but it was worth a shot to get more information on what Shane had told her.

Murray turned from the doorway, his shaggy eyebrows crooked together in a frown. "Now don't go starting that crazy rumor again. You let some hare-brained numbskulls like the Potter boys hear it and they'll be out in the woods, using it as an excuse to shoot up the place. I know some folks swore back then they spotted one, but I never saw any proof of it myself."

"Yeah, probably just a hoax or something." No way would she mention the "proof" might very well exist in *her* pasture. As for the Potter brothers getting wind of it, she had no intention of letting that happen.

****

Later that afternoon, Allison finished up in the barn and made sure to close it up tight against whatever prowled about in the hours of darkness—whatever had left the chilling paw print in the pasture.

An hour later, she'd fed the last kitten and tucked all three back into their basket. The babies snuggled in together, and she hoped they would take a long nap, at least until Lizzie got home from shopping with Ronnie and could take over their feedings again.

"Sleep tight, sweeties." She carried them into the

living room and put the basket in a corner warmed by the last of the day's sunshine. "Keep an eye on them," she bade Gypsy, who whined softly and laid down not far away, her white muzzle resting on her forepaws. The collie had adopted the kittens and would come to get Lizzie or Allison when they stirred, which would probably happen in another hour. *Just enough time to jump in the shower and wash away the day's stress.*

Once hot water streamed on her head, lessening the tension that had strained her neck and shoulder muscles all day, she relaxed a bit. Yet, she couldn't stop thinking about the last conversation she'd had with Shane…and the way he'd touched her as he inspected the fading bruise on her leg. The way she'd wanted to gasp at the sudden heat that had traveled from his gentle fingers to the very core of her being. *Damn that man!* Why did he still manage to have so much control over her? Why did she have to melt whenever he came near? Why inside was she still the seventeen-year-old girl who'd loved him so desperately?

She glanced down at the bruise. It was fading away into a paler shade of green and would soon disappear. He wouldn't need to demand to check it out again. Just as he would no doubt leave as soon as Doc got back on his feet. Except, what would happen if Doc didn't get back on his feet? While Sandy reported he could now sit in a chair, he still had a very long road to recovery. How long could Shane stay here to keep the practice going? What about his life back in Wyoming? What would he do about Lizzie?

Too many questions were giving her a headache. She dumped wildflower-scented shampoo in her palm and lathered up her hair to massage it away.

Once wrapped in her bathrobe, hair in a turban, she wandered into her bedroom and sat on the edge of the bed. Towel drying her hair, she yawned. Was there time to take a nap? Ronnie had said she and Lizzie would have dinner at Johnny's Drive-In, so she didn't need to worry about having anything ready to eat. A half an hour of rest was probably what she needed to curb the last of the lingering headache, so she curled up on top of the coverlet.

****

Shane pulled up to another farmhouse that had, in more ways than one, seen better days. Plastic still covered the downstairs windows, probably in an effort to keep out the cold this past winter, but now it shredded in the summer heat. The porch steps sagged, and ancient cedar bushes on either side sprouted wildly out of control. Past the house, a slanting-sideways barn and chicken coop sank into the landscape, as if wanting to hide their sad state of disrepair. A few scrawny, red hens pecked in the overgrown yard. They were the only sign of life in the Potter brothers' homestead. To the left of the farm buildings, jacked-up cars hunkered in front of a gray cement block building, several with raised hoods. Allison had mentioned Duane and Darren worked on cars, but it appeared they did a half-assed job of it. *Not surprising.*

He gripped the steering wheel until his hands white-knuckled, recalling another time he had come here…and nearly lost his life confronting the brothers and their cousins. The night he'd uncovered their dog-fighting ring. It had sickened him then, and it sickened him now to think of the dogs that had suffered at their grimy hands. He had barely escaped, and the bullet that shattered the back window of his truck had missed his head by inches. One of the cousins had gone to jail, and the Potters were charged with animal cruelty, served a sentence, and forbidden to ever own dogs again. Doc had made sure to tell him that. But had the current sheriff followed through? He scanned the yard. No dogs in sight.

Opening the truck door, he waited, knowing the sound could be heard by a canine he didn't see. Still nothing. He slowly stepped out, pocketing the key and leaving the door un-latched to facilitate a quick getaway if needed. All his senses switched on high as he made his way to the garage. A chicken squawked and flapped across the yard. He stopped with held breath and waited for any sound of warning—a threatening growl or the click of a gun. Nothing.

At the door to the garage he paused, listening against it. A low murmur of voices drifted from within, followed by a sudden raucous whoop. Darren. Even after ten years, Shane recognized the disgusting sound. *He'd probably laughed the same way when Cousin Red pulled the trigger*.

Shane opened the door slowly, expecting at any moment for someone to give him a shove or a punch to the jaw for entering without knocking. While the Potters hadn't been known for their fighting prowess themselves, the cousins had no qualms about knocking someone on their ass. But the only thing hitting Shane was the thick, sweet smell of pot and the stale scent of sweat and unwashed bodies. He'd rather smell a pig barn.

The laughing stopped, and a smoky silence filled the room. He squinted into the murky air, and his

141

stomach settled with some relief to see only the brothers sitting in the corner on rickety barstools.

The older Potter grinned and slid off his stool to approach. "Hey, if it ain't our old buddy. What can we do for you, Shane? You wanna beer?" He held up the joint pinched between his thumb and greasy forefinger. "Or maybe some of this?"

They were nearly eye to eye. But though he outweighed Duane by probably thirty pounds, that was little comfort—as the Potters also liked to carry knives. Duane's shifty face melded with the smoke. Shane waved the vapors away and took a step back, glancing past the pothead to make sure the others weren't advancing on him. "No thanks to both. I didn't come here to socialize."

He nodded and shrugged. "Okay, so you don't want to hang with us." He squinted and then fixed him with a cold glare. "So, what do you want?"

"Just two things. I want you to leave Allison alone, and stay away from her farm."

"Don't know what the hell you're talkin' about."

"I think you do." Shane watched his reaction while keeping Darren in his peripheral vision. He didn't trust either of the Potters.

"You do?" He shook his head and turned to walk away a few steps then swiveled on one heel to come back. "You're gone for what, ten years? Then you come ridin' back in here and think you know what's goin' on. Kinda like the knight in shining armor. Ha!" His raucous laughter billowed out.

"No knight, Duane. Just a man telling you to leave someone alone." *Because if you don't, there's going to be hell to pay.* He curled his right hand into a fist, itching to land it in the guy's nose, willing to do anything to keep these two away from Allison.

"Someone who's a thief? Or maybe you don't know how she came and took something wasn't hers to take and—"

"I know, and I also know you got your own dirty deeds to hide."

"Says who?"

"Says me. You've never been clean, and you know it. Not ten years ago, and not now."

Duane came to stick his grizzled face in Shane's. The close-up view of the jerk's tobacco-stained teeth turned his stomach sour, as did the memory of the brothers' crimes of cruelty.

"We did our time." The thin lips sneered. "And all you did was run. Didn't seem you cared much for stickin' with your girl back then. You left her high and dry."

Shane stepped away. Cold truth stuck in his gut like a rock. But that didn't matter. "The difference now is I won't run, and I'm telling you again, Duane. Leave. Allison. Alone." He backed toward the door and didn't turn around until he'd stepped into the cool twilight.

Before letting the door close, he heard Duane snicker and mutter, "It ain't us who's bothering her. You remember that. Not us."

The warning kept running through his mind as he drove away. *Who else would have reason to harass Allison? Who else would stoop so low?* He hoped his little visit to the Potters would make them think twice about any further actions, but there was no certainty. The best thing he could do was keep an eye on her…without her realizing it. Something easier said than done. Accepting his protection was the last thing she wanted to do, he was sure of it, but standing between her and Lizzie and any threat to them had suddenly become the most important thing in the world to him. If only he could make her understand.

****

Allison woke with a start and glanced at the clock radio. Had Ronnie brought Lizzie home yet? She'd said to expect them before seven o'clock, but it was nearly eight. She listened for a moment for any sounds of voices drifting from downstairs. Nothing. She got up quickly and pulled on shorts and a T-shirt, tossing her hair into its usual ponytail. As she hurried down the stairs, a niggling worry pricked at her to think they weren't back yet from the shopping trip. When she found the house empty save for herself, she went to the phone and was just ready to call Ronnie's cell number when her sister-in-law's silver SUV pulled into the drive.

In a few moments, Lizzie ran up the steps, and as usual, burst into the house with the boundless energy of a nine-year-old. "Hi Mom! We had burgers at Johnny's Drive-In. The girls have roller skates on, and they bring your food on a tray! Can you believe it? How come we've never been there?"

She gave her daughter a fierce hug and tried not to let her voice give away the relief flooding through her. "Actually, we have been there, but I guess you were too small to remember. Daddy and I took you there, and you wanted to wear skates, too. You especially loved their fries."

Lizzie screwed up her face for a moment, confused. "Which daddy?"

A shot of adrenalin clutched Allison's throat. "Why your daddy, Jason, of course, silly." She glanced up and caught Ronnie's glare. "It was one of his favorite places to eat out."

Thankfully, this seemed to satisfy her daughter for the moment as she glanced about the kitchen. "How are my kitties doing? Did you feed them?"

"I did, and they're napping, but they're probably about ready for another meal. How about I fix it while you go check on them?"

"Do you want to see them, Aunt Ronnie?" Lizzie paused in the kitchen doorway. "I named them Wynkyn, Blynkyn, and Todd. They're really cute, and Shane says I'm doing very well taking care of them."

"Sure, honey, I will, but you go ahead. I'll be there in a minute. I want to talk to your mom first."

Now what? Allison grumbled silently and went to the fridge to get the kitten milk. She swallowed against a suddenly dry throat and reached for the sun tea she'd made that morning. Setting the items on the counter, she then took two glasses from the cupboard. "Would you like some? I'm sure after running around in the heat today—"

"No thanks," Ronnie cut her off. "I'm fine, but I would like to ask you about something Lizzie said today."

She poured herself a tall glass of the tea and took three long swallows to ease the constriction in her vocal chords. Sometimes, talking to Ronnie had this effect on her. "So ask."

As if gathering her thoughts for the assault, her sister-in-law checked out her new, bright orange nail polish. "Lizzie said Jason wasn't her real daddy, and

145

just now she questioned you about who went to Johnny's with her. Care to explain what that's all about?"

No, not really, but this woman would never let it go. *Might as well suck it up and tell her the truth. She's sure to find out anyway.* "Jason wasn't Lizzie's biological father."

It was as if she'd dropped a bomb in the middle of the kitchen and a rock on Ronnie's foot as her sister-in-law's mouth opened and closed like a fish gasping for water. Sheer incredulity flashed across her face, and she stammered, "What...what do you mean? How c-can that be possible?"

Allison shrugged. "It can because it is. Jason was not Lizzie's real father, but he was her father in every other way that mattered."

"Then you lied to him?"

She jerked her head up and glared. "I did *not* lie to Jason. *He* knew the truth from the beginning."

"And he married you anyway?"

"Yes." She tried to keep her tone reasonable. "And he chose to raise Lizzie as his own."

"Why? Why would he do that?" Ronnie stepped back as her voice rose to a near shriek. "I don't believe you. You're a lying b—"

Allison grabbed Ronnie's elbow and pushed the furious woman out the screen door and onto the porch. "Hush! Don't let Lizzie hear you."

"But you lied to our parents! You let them think she is their own blood. How *could* you?"

Ronnie's face was twisted with rage, and she turned away from the angry accusations. "We could because it was the only way at the time. Jason and I agreed not to tell anyone."

"Well, you ruined his life, you know." Her words were spoken with deadly quiet. "And you're the reason he died."

"How dare you!" Allison wheeled back around. "I cared for Jason. He was a good husband and a loving father." No one would ever know the affection she'd felt for him.

"But he should have gone to college! He had a football scholarship. Did he even tell you that? Our daddy begged him not to throw it away, not to get wound up with you, but he wouldn't listen. You had his head so screwed up he couldn't think straight, and all you cared about was finding a father for your illegitimate child. So, who was he, the real father? Did you even know?"

"She knew, but I didn't." Shane's deep voice cut across the still evening air. "Because if I had, I never would have left when I did." Allison met his steely blue gaze across the yard. She hadn't even heard him drive in over her sister-in-law's ranting.

He strode up to the porch and took the steps two at a time. "What Jason did, he did of his own free will. He was always a stubborn one, you know that, and he loved Allison. Just as I did. Maybe his claiming my child was his way of finally getting what he wanted."

Suddenly, tears rolled down Ronnie's face, and she fumbled in her purse for a tissue. "He had what he wanted, a chance to play football at a university, a chance to go somewhere and *be* somebody. *She* took all of it away from him. You both did."

As Shane moved closer to her, Allison gathered her wits to keep things from going bad to worse. This was not the conversation she wanted to have tonight.

"Maybe we did," Shane continued before she could. He lowered his voice, perhaps to calm Ronnie. "But it was your father's dream for him to go to college and play football, not Jason's."

"Daddy just wanted what was best for my brother."

You could have fooled me, Allison wanted to say but bit her tongue. Seemed better to let Shane handle this one.

He shook his head. "I'm sure that's true." His voice softened a little. "But it wasn't what Jason wanted."

Ronnie sniffled and blew her nose. "Then what did he want? If you're so sure you knew him so well, what did my baby brother want?"

Allison waited to hear his reply, because she'd wondered the same thing herself. What had Jason Delaney really wanted in his life?

"Freedom from your parents and their good intentions, to make his own decisions, and be his own man. He told me even before our friendship fell apart that he didn't want to go to college, at least not just yet. He needed a break from the pressure of trying to live up to everyone else's expectations."

He told me that, too, when he asked me to marry him.

But really, why *had* Jason turned away from all the chances he'd been offered? Even now, she had to wonder.

Ronnie dabbed at the mascara streaking from her eyes. "You really have a lot of nerve when you knew my brother loved football. He could have done something with his life, if only he'd listened to us."

"It was *his* choice to make, and he made it." Shane

slid his hand in front of her, as if to erase all the lost possibilities. "Nothing we can do to change it now, and blaming Allison isn't going to help."

Her sister-in-law sighed and sniffled a few more times. If she didn't know Ronnie so well, she would almost feel sorry for her, but the woman had never liked her much. Even before she and Jason had married, his sister had never missed an opportunity to annoy Allison and put her down whenever she could. It made it hard to ever have any true sympathy for this woman.

"Well, I hope you two realize someday how you destroyed my brother's life, and my family's." Clutching her tissues, she fled down the steps, and in a few moments had driven away in a cloud of dust.

Allison went to the porch swing and sank down, trying to gather her tattered nerves and scattered thoughts. Shane joined her and sat with her in silence, his foot pushing them slowly back and forth. Finally, he took her hand. "I'm sorry for all the parts I played in this, for forcing you to make hard choices, and for not being here when you needed me."

She *had* faced hard choices, but none of that could be changed now. Better they just moved ahead. "We both have things to be sorry about, but something good and beautiful did come out of it all. We have a daughter, and she is more important than anything else."

"Are the bottles ready, Mom?" Lizzie's voice sounded from the kitchen. "The kittens are hungry. *Mom!* Where are you?"

Allison met Shane's steady gaze as she gave his roughened hand a squeeze. "She's a little demanding at times, but she's our daughter, and now, since you brought them here, how would you like to help feed a kitten?"

He grinned in the way that always managed to make her heart beat a little faster. Then he leaned over and gave her a quick kiss. "Sure, *Mom*. Whatever you say."

After the kittens were once again tended to, Allison made popcorn and placed it in a big bowl on the kitchen table. For the next hour, she listened to Shane and their daughter talk about what they'd done that day. Lizzie chatting about a new store at the mall, Shane relating a funny story that involved someone's pet lizard getting loose in the clinic and running up Sandy's file cabinet. At his silly description, she and Lizzie dissolved into giggling until their sides ached. Thank goodness for laughter that relieved the earlier tension of the evening. When she finally shooed Lizzie off to bed, Allison realized how much she had missed this sort of evening. Well, not the worry and the hassle with Ronnie, but the sharing with another adult person, at the end of the day, the little things that had happened. What she didn't know she'd missed even more was when Shane drew her to him and kissed her longer and sweeter than he had on the porch. When he cradled her head against his shoulder and ran his hands through her hair she had turned loose from its ponytail. When she leaned into his tall, lean body, and his heartbeat matched her own. It was all good, and at the moment so very right. In spite of the pain they had caused each other, she was still filled with amazing contentment when she was with him.

If only it could last.

Chapter 15

Shane motioned for the jeweler to bring out the last ring in the back of the display case.

"That's an excellent choice, too, sir." The gentleman placed it next to the other two on the glass counter. "I'm sure the lady would love any one of these."

He wasn't so sure. Would Allison even consider accepting it? Was asking her to marry him crazy? Too soon? There was only one way to find out.

The diamond solitaire flashed a spark of golden fire. It reminded him of the fire that often flashed in her eyes.

"Yes, this one." He quelled any doubts this was a good idea.

"We will do free sizing, of course. Just have her come in at her convenience."

Nodding, he paid for the ring and left the hushed quiet of the jewelry store for the brash busyness of the city street. To avoid any chance of word getting out, he'd traveled fifty miles from Silver Creek to make the purchase, much as Allison had told him she'd gone three towns over to learn she was to become a mother. How strange were the twists and turns of life?

Once back in his truck, Shane flipped open the ring box. He contemplated how he would ask Allison to be his wife, and how she might answer. And what about

Lizzie's response to it all? Was he a fool to even think they would want him as a permanent fixture in their lives?

He snapped the box shut and slipped it into his shirt pocket. Starting the truck, he cranked the radio up for the drive back, hoping it would drown out the questions and doubts whirling around in his brain.

****

Allison measured out the special feed she had mixed for the two black fillies. They still suffered the ill effects of being so severely malnourished, and she made sure to give them several smaller meals a day to help them overcome their sad start in life. The night she'd brought Starlight and Stardust home from the auction, she'd not been sure they would survive, but with tender loving care and the advice of Doc Brewster, she'd been able to bring them back from the brink. Their coats were beginning to take on a glossy sheen, and you could no longer count their ribs. Caring for them had certainly drained her bank account, but it had been more than worth it.

She'd brought them into the barn early to keep the other horses from trying to horn in on the feeding.

"Hey, girls," she crooned, stopping to stroke their satiny necks and check them over for any signs they weren't continuing to thrive. "How are things going? You're mighty pretty today, you know."

They nuzzled her and blew softly on her hands when she placed the pans in their stalls.

While they munched contentedly, she went back to filling hay nets for the rest of the horses so they would be ready when she brought them in from the pasture later. Thank goodness the last few nights had been quiet ones, with no loud neighs and stamping hooves to wake her at two a.m. Yet, she hadn't slept well. Every night she'd been awakened by dreams; dreams that made her blush to remember them now. Dreams of Shane and her by the lake, and of the last time they'd been there, and the way they'd both been so desperate. How she'd wanted, needed, to talk, and he had hushed her with his kisses and whispers of how much he loved her. She'd believed him, and for a few shining moments had thought everything would be all right.

And then he'd left her.

Even in the dream, the pain and confusion over his leaving had ripped her heart in two, and her life had never been the same. In spite of his returning now, would the memories always come back to haunt her?

Can I trust him?

The question taunted her as she filled the grain buckets next. More than anything, she needed an ally in this fight to keep her business—her farm—safe, but did she dare put her faith in a man who had left her once before?

But he didn't know about Lizzie—if he had, he never would have left.

Would he?

She pushed the thoughts away and stopped to brush a hand across her forehead. After a cool spell, the weather had turned warm again. The barn was quiet, except for the buzzing of a fly at the window and the fillies crunching their grain and swishing their tails. Shortly, she would bring the other horses in, and then she could call it a day. Her body was more than ready for that. A full schedule of lessons and regular chores had left her back aching and her brain turned to mush.

Something brushed up against her legs, and she jumped a little before looking down at one of the barn cats. "Priscilla, you do like to sneak up on me, don't you?" She stooped to pet the tabby. "I've got some catnip treats I'll bring down to you and Pouncer tonight after I—"

The tabby sprang away, and the hair on the cat's neck stood up in tufts while her tail bristled like a bottle brush. She squeaked out a plaintive meow before dashing off to the hayloft.

Now what was that all about?

She shrugged and turned back to the grain bin. Cats were just weird sometimes.

"Mom! Mommy, come quick!"

Allison dropped the bucket of grain and tore out of the feed room. *Mommy.* Lizzie never called her that anymore unless she was scared or sick.

"Mommeeee! Hurry!" Her daughter's frantic cry was followed by Gypsy's frantic barking and Cayenne's shrill whinny.

At the entrance of the barn Allison searched the round pen where she had left Lizzie riding her pony. It was empty.

"Lizzie, where are you? I thought I told you to stay in the—"

The words froze in her throat. Her daughter stood beside her pony, at the edge of the lane leading into the orchard, holding desperately to the little pinto's reins. Cayenne seemed determined to break away, and the collie's barking echoed from beyond the first row of gnarled trees.

"Mommy, help!"

She didn't think she could move so fast, but in

seconds, she reached them, grabbed the reins and Lizzie's arm. Tugging at them both, she dragged the pony and her daughter back to the barn, sliding the big door shut behind them and latching it in place.

"But what about Gypsy? She ran into the orchard. Why?"

Lizzie tried to get past her, and she grabbed her again and moved in front of the door.

"I don't know. Why were you over there? What happened?" Her daughter knew better than to leave the round pen when she was alone.

Beneath Allison's hands, the slender shoulders trembled.

"I got tired and got off Cayenne and was leading him to the barn, and all of a sudden Gypsy took off, barking and growling. I went after her, to call her back, but then I heard something…a sound, like a…a…cry…or a scream." Her teary gaze fixed on her mother's face. "What is she after?"

"I don't know." Allison loosened her hold on her daughter. "But we've got to stay in here, until I do know."

"But it might hurt her, and what about the horses?"

Allison's blood chilled. If only she'd brought them all in when she fed the fillies, but it was still early.

Please, don't let any of them be injured! Please keep Gypsy safe.

"Let's put Cayenne in his stall." She tucked the reins back in her daughter's hand and urged her down the barn aisle, following behind. For the moment, she allowed the pony to go inside untacked. Feeling safe, Cayenne began to pull at his hay net.

Still shaking, Lizzie whimpered. "What are we

155

going to do? And what did I *hear* out there?"

Allison clicked the stall door shut. "What did it sound like, what you heard?" She turned to her daughter to try and reassure her, but fear shone bright in Lizzie's wet eyes.

"I-I don't know. A scream, sort of. But different. What are we going to do?" She reached out and clutched Allison's hand, sobbing softly.

"I'm not sure, honey, but it'll be okay." *It has to be okay.*

She squeezed Lizzie's hand and kept hold of it as she went back to the barn entrance to peer out the side door window. *A scream, sort of.* Could it be? Could what Shane suspected be true?

Lizzie stood at her side, sniffling. "I wish my daddy was here."

Did she mean Jason? After the confusion of the last few weeks, it would be normal for her to yearn for the man who had always kept her safe and protected. Allison had promised to do that when he'd died, and she'd managed alone for three years, but sometimes you had to admit when you needed help.

She patted the back pocket of her jeans. Thank goodness she hadn't left her phone in the house. "I want you to take Cayenne's saddle and bridle off and brush him down. Then give him his grain."

"What are you going to do?" Her daughter swiped at her eyes, leaving a streak of dirt behind.

"I'm going outside for a minute. I'll be fine. I'll call Gypsy and see if she'll come back."

"But, Mommy…"

"Do as I say. Now go."

She gave Lizzie a gentle push, and once she'd gone

back to the pony's stall, Allison slipped out the side door and glanced around to make sure the creature hadn't come closer. Seeing nothing, she slowly edged to the corner of the barn. She'd just tugged the phone from her pocket when she heard a pitiful whine.

"Gypsy? Where are you?" Heart thumping, she scanned the yard and then rushed to the place where the collie sat, head low and body trembling. She dropped down and ran shaking hands over her fur. They came away sticky with blood.

"Oh my God, no."

She searched the dog for the wounds and found them, several deep lacerations along her shoulder and near one ear.

Standing again, she scooped Gypsy into her arms, but just before she turned, she saw two emerald eyes staring at her from the shadows of the orchard. Fear like a strike of lightning numbed Allison for one second and then gave extra speed to her steps as she hastened back to the barn. Once safely inside, she met Lizzie's shocked cries.

"What happened to her? Mom, she's bleeding!"

"I know, honey, now get some towels and put them on the floor in the tack room." *I have to remain calm.*

Lizzie did as she was told, and Allison laid the dog on them. She folded one of the towels and pressed it against the worst of the wounds to staunch the bleeding. Gypsy whined and licked her hand.

"It'll be okay, girl," she promised the collie. "We're going to get you some help right now." Heart racing, she turned to Lizzie. "I need you to stay here with her. Keep this towel pressed down and don't let her get up if she tries."

"But where are you going? Don't leave us!"

"I won't, but I need to get help. I need to call Shane, and I can't always get a signal here in the tack room."

But did she have her phone? Or had she dropped it outside? Her heart sank a little until she realized she had stuck it in her front pocket. *Thank you!* And thankfully the battery wasn't on one percent as was usually the case. She hurried out to the main aisle of the barn and with shaking hands found the number he had put into her contacts and punched it in. After three rings, it went to his voicemail. Her heart pounded while she waited to leave a message.

"It's me, A-Allison." Her words tumbled out. "S-something's happened here, at the barn. Can you come, now? Please? And…hurry." She clicked off and went back to the tack room. Lizzie sat with the collie's head in her lap, holding the towel to her shoulder with one hand and gently stroking her and murmuring soothing words.

"Did you talk to Doc? I don't think she's doing too good. What did this to her? Was she attacked?" Blue eyes swam with fresh tears.

"She was." Allison dropped down beside them. "Did you see anything out there?"

"No, but I guess Gypsy did, before I heard that awful scream. I'm sorry, Mommy. I know I shouldn't leave the round pen without you, but I just wanted to call her."

Allison gave her daughter a swift hug and murmured, "It's okay, baby," before she checked the collie's breathing and how badly the wounds were bleeding. They seemed to have stopped some, but she was still not in a good way.

Hurry, Shane!

"What did I hear? What did this to Gypsy?" Lizzie hiccupped and wiped her nose on her sleeve.

She stroked her baby girl's braids to try to ease her fear. "I don't know for sure, but I am sure it's the same thing that's been scaring the horses at night, and now I've got to go bring them all in." Because whatever was stalking the farm must be desperate to come so close to people and to Gypsy.

"Mommy, no, don't go out there," Lizzie implored. "Please wait 'til Shane gets here."

"I can't wait. I can't chance any of them being attacked, too." She handed her phone to Lizzie. "If he calls back, tell him what's happened."

Her daughter took it and without further argument curled closer to the collie lying so still. "I wish Shane was here," she whispered. "Please make him be here."

At the side door again, Allison spied the can of wasp spray she kept for those intruders. Would it work against this larger one, if she had to defend herself? Better than nothing. She grabbed it and opened the door. Again, she glanced about, her stomach churning with fear. What if Green Eyes was lurking nearby? What if…?

She clamped down on the thought and made a run for it. First, she closed the two gates that would keep the horses from running off and then sprinted toward the pasture. She was relieved to see the horses all standing at the gate. Thank goodness some of her boarders were off on the summer show circuit, so there were fewer horses to bring in. Usually, she had Gypsy to help herd them, but she was on her own tonight.

"Don't give me any trouble, guys," she warned them all, but tried to keep her voice calm. "Let's just all go in for dinner like good little horsies."

When she opened the gate, they tore off for the barn with no one trying to elude her. And then, before she could get back to the sliding door, Shane's truck pulled into the drive, and he jumped out as soon as it rolled to a stop.

"What's going on?" he called out but halted his steps to the barn when Major and Duncan ran past him. "How can I help?"

"Just…help me get them inside," Allison puffed out. "They should go to their own stalls." She saw him glance at the can of spray in her hand. "I'll explain…once we're inside. But it's Gypsy that needs you. She's hurt bad. Please hurry."

Without waiting for further explanation, he slid the big door open, and the horses trotted in, each going to its own stall. More interested now in their dinner than whatever had spooked them, they were soon safely locked in and the door firmly closed.

Taking no time to catch her breath, Allison motioned to the tack room. "She's in here, with Lizzie."

He followed her in and went immediately to where the dog lay on the floor. Dropping down on his knees, he carefully took the towel from their daughter before addressing Gypsy. "What's happened to you, old girl? Got yourself in a mess of trouble looks like. Let's see if anything's broken." He ran his hands gently over the collie's body, checking her legs and ribs. She whined softly but offered him no resistance. "Did you see what did this?" he asked under his breath.

She wouldn't mention the green eyes, not with big

ears listening. "No, but there was a sound, like a scream, Lizzie said."

Watching Shane examine the wounds, Allison's heart broke for the old dog's pain. Gypsy had been with her since she was just a small puppy.

I can't stand it if she dies like this.

"Has the bleeding stopped?" She crouched down by Lizzie, praying it really wasn't so bad. "We tried to put pressure on it…"

"You did fine, and yes, it's mostly stopped. I don't feel any broken bones, but she'll need x-rays to be sure, and stitches. Plenty of those. I'll get her stabilized here, and then I'll have to take her back to the clinic. Do you have a blanket I can wrap her in?"

"Lizzie, get the one I leave in the tack box." The one she used when sitting up nights with a sick horse.

Probably glad for something to do that didn't involve holding the now blood-soaked towel, her daughter scrambled to her feet. In the moments she was gone, Allison leaned over her dog and whispered words of encouragement. "Hold on, Gypsy-girl. You've got to hold on." She swiped one hand over her eyes, hoping Shane wouldn't see the sudden rush of tears. The steadying hand he placed on her shoulder gave her a squeeze.

"I'll take care of her, Allie. I promise. I'll do everything I can. But whatever this was…" He cut off when Lizzie returned with the blue fleecy blanket and helped carefully wrap it around Gypsy.

A short time later, while Allison scanned the path to the orchard for a glimpse of any movement, he carried the injured collie to his truck and secured her in the back seat. He came back to where Allison and

Lizzie stood in the barn doorway. "Will you two be all right here? I just don't feel good leaving when we don't know what happened." Darkness had fallen, but he leveled his gaze on her in the shadows, as if trying to determine if she knew more than she'd told him. "What are you afraid of?"

Glancing past him to make sure no eyes were glowing in the dark, she avoided the question. "We— we'll be fine." A nervous chill ran through her as, palms sweating, she had a second thought. Putting her arm around her baby girl's shoulders, she felt her shiver in the night air. "I want you to go with Shane to the clinic. Take the kittens with you, because they'll have to be fed soon."

"Nooo, I won't leave you here alone." Lizzie violently shook her head. "I can't…"

She turned her daughter to face her. "You can and you will. Gypsy needs you to help watch over her tonight, and I need to stay here to watch over the horses." Over her shoulder she added, "Shane, please take her up to the house to get the kittens and their bottles and a change of clothes." The terror in those young blue eyes was nearly palpable, and it tore at Allison's heart, but she insisted, "Please, I need you to do this for me." She turned from Lizzie and met Shane's gaze, and read in it his reluctance to leave her.

"I don't know if it's a good idea, for you to stay here alone." He motioned to his truck. "Just close up the barn and come with us. I can—"

She couldn't let him know she was afraid and lifted her chin in a false act of being in charge. "I need to stay here. No arguments. Please, just go help my dog."

After a second, he held his hand out to Lizzie. "We

should go then. Gypsy needs to get to the clinic."

Their daughter gave her one more pleading look before putting her hand in Shane's. Allison watched, keeping guard, while the two climbed into the truck and drove up to the house, and didn't tear her gaze away until they were safely gone. Then heaving a huge sigh, she went back into the barn. Before closing the door firmly behind her, she glanced to where she'd found Gypsy and then to the orchard beyond, to where she'd seen the glowing eyes.

Please don't come back tonight. Please, just go away.

It would be a long night in the barn, alone with the horses, but it wasn't anything she hadn't done before.

After cleaning up the tack room, she did a stall check and found most of them dozing or at least standing quietly, watching her with their big, soulful eyes. She spoke to them all, giving out reassuring pats, and then dimmed the lights. She dragged out the folding lounge chair from the tack room and did her best to get comfortable. The night was warm, so she didn't need a blanket, but curled there in the shadowy barn, she couldn't help but shiver thinking about whatever had attacked Gypsy and been so close to Lizzie.

For the safety of them all, something had to be done to track the animal down.

Chapter 16

Shane finished washing up from surgery and sterilized the instruments he had used to stitch the collie's wounds. Sedated and with antibiotics flowing in her system, Gypsy rested in one of the recovery cages. She would survive, but she might never run as fast after the horses again.

The entire time he'd worked on her, thoughts about what could possibly have caused the wounds ran through his mind. On the ride to the clinic, Lizzie hadn't talked much, and, not wanting to traumatize her more, he'd hesitated probing his daughter for information. But he was pretty sure it was no pack of coyotes that attacked Gypsy.

I don't like what I think did it.

Except, at some point, he had to admit the truth.

Dimming the lights in the clinic, he opened the connecting door to Matthew Brewster's house and the kitchen where he'd left Lizzie feeding the kittens. Three empty bottles sat on the table, but there was no sign of her or her charges. He continued on into the living room where he found the fuzzy rascals snuggled together in their basket on the sofa beside his sound asleep daughter. Crouching down for a minute, he studied her sweet face and once again marveled at the feeling of protectiveness welled up within him. He tucked back the wisps of dark hair that had escaped her

164

long braids, hovering his hand when she sighed and murmured something in her sleep.

Slipping his arms beneath her, he lifted Lizzie from the sofa and carried her to the bedroom where he'd slept when he lived with Matthew. Since coming back, he'd bunked on the sofa, because the twin bed was too short for him now. He hadn't really spent much time in this room except to stash his duffle bags and a backpack in here. He realized now it probably hadn't been used in all the years he'd been gone and needed a good cleaning, but the bed was neatly made, something that hadn't always been true when it'd been his room.

He laid Lizzie down on top of the faded brown, corduroy bedspread and pulled off her sneakers. She had changed from her boots and riding clothes, stained with Gypsy's blood, into the shorts, sneakers, and T-shirt he had grabbed for her from a laundry basket in Allison's house. He found a clean sheet in the dresser and drew it over her, in case she was chilled during the night. There was a night-light on the bed stand, the one he'd always used because he didn't like to awaken in a dark room, even as a teenager. He switched it on. Glancing around, he wondered if he should do anything else, when his gaze rested on the high school and sports memorabilia that still adorned the walls, desk, and bookshelf. Matthew hadn't changed a thing in here since he had left on the bus ten years ago. Having lost the only home he'd ever known when his grandmother died, he had hung onto anything with meaning to him while he lived with Matthew. It was in here he'd found the miniature football he'd left on Jason's grave.

Poor Doc, probably didn't know what the heck to do with all this stuff.

He turned back to Lizzie, curled in the bed where he'd once slept. Impulsively, he leaned down and brushed a kiss across her forehead. When she murmured, "Daddy," in her sleep, his heart beat a painful rhythm. Certainly she was dreaming about Jason. Because to this young girl, he was still just Shane.

He left the door slightly ajar and went back to get the kittens that were mewing and ready to eat again. They were starting to grow into fluffy little balls of fur and looked up at him now with their baby blue eyes.

A lot like Lizzie's, he mused.

"Okay, one more feeding for you each, and then it's time for Wynkyn, Blynkyn, and Todd to sleep through the night."

Shane fixed the bottles and juggled the three kittens to get them full and happy for now. When they settled down once more, he put the basket on a chair, shrugged out of his denim shirt, loosened his belt buckle, tugged off his boots, and stretched out on the sofa. His shoulders ached and his eyes burned from lack of sleep, but he reached into his pocket for his phone. Was Allison still awake? She would want to know Lizzie and Gypsy were all right, and he needed to know she was okay. Leaving her alone tonight had stuck like a knife in his gut, and the theory he had about the attack had clogged his throat with a knot of regret the entire time he'd stitched the collie. Now, he imagined her in the barn, by herself, with the horses. His tough girl Allison would say she could handle it, but he ached to be there with her, keeping her safe. Swiping a hand across his gritty eyes, he tapped in her number.

She picked up on the second ring.

"Were you sleeping?" He kept his voice low so as not to wake Lizzie.

Her quick intake of breath caressed his ear before he heard her hushed tone. "No, how is Gypsy? And Lizzie?"

"They're fine. Well, Gypsy has some recovering ahead of her, but she'll be okay. Lizzie and the kittens are all sleeping. I put her in my old room. She was pretty tuckered out." He thought he heard a soft sob. "Hey, Allie, it was a scary situation, but she'll be all right now." He wished he could hold her and make sure she believed him. "What exactly happened out there tonight? What led to the attack on Gypsy?"

He waited for her reply, hoping she would trust him enough to say what had scared them all so badly. Then he listened while Allison relayed the incident.

"It could have been her," she choked out at the end. "Lizzie could have been attacked. Shane, what am I going to do?"

Was she actually asking for his help? He cleared his throat. "For starters, we need to call the local conservation officer, Mark Williamson. I had a talk with him the other day about some sheep attacked by coyotes in North County. We're going to tell him what's been going on at your farm."

"What if my boarders start leaving? How will I—"

"You'll start by telling them the truth and reassuring them we're doing everything we can to keep their horses safe." How would she take that?

"We? Shane, I can't…"

"Yes, you can." He spoke in his sternest voice, but dialed it back about five notches to lessen her protest. "Allie, whether you like it or not, whether you want my

167

help or not, *we* will be together on this, because from the minute you told me Lizzie is my daughter, I had the right and the responsibility to keep you both safe, and I won't take no for an answer. You need to accept that."

Her doubt and hesitation reached him even through the phone, and it hurt. If only he could kiss away her fear, though in his heart he knew it wouldn't solve their problems.

"I'll call Mark, for Lizzie's sake, and the horses." This time, her voice held resignation. "But don't let me down. I couldn't—"

"I won't. You have my solemn promise. I won't ever let you down again." He gripped the phone and brought it closer to his mouth. "Not ever again." There was silence on Allison's end, then he heard a horse stirring in the background. In his mind he saw her getting up, moving through the barn, checking each stall. "Is everything all right?"

"Yeah, just one of the girls talking to the other."

The two rescue fillies. The sound of their soft whickers traveled through the phone followed by Allison's crooning to them. Then he heard her switch on the radio, and a mellow country song drifted over the air. He had to smile. Like her grandparents, she had always liked those old songs.

Sleep tugged at him, and he suppressed a yawn. He had a full day of farm visits in the morning and clinic appointments in the afternoon. One of the stops was the Ruben Tucker place. By now, the farmers in the county knew Shane had taken over for Matthew, and he needed some rest before facing this one, but he hated to let Allison go. The aching need to keep hearing her voice seared through his veins.

"I'll come and get Lizzie in the morning after everybody's fed," she spoke again, unwittingly obliging him. "Then I can see Gypsy, and I need to stop in at the store anyway. If you have to leave before I get there, have her stay with Sandy. Hey…are you sleeping?"

He chuckled and had to quell the heat her husky voice stirred inside him. If only she were here beside him on the couch. "No, not yet, but any minute now. I love you, Allison Tyler." What would she say to that?

She hesitated. "Delaney."

"What?" So much for his declaration and the courage he'd mustered to say it.

"Delaney, remember? It's Allison Delaney."

"Right. Guess my brain's a little mushy about now." Would the ghost of Jason always stand between them? Always hold them apart? *Not if I can help it.* "But I still love you and your pluck."

Her soft laugh vibrated through him. "Pluck. Now I have pluck? Sounds like I'm a chicken."

"No, you're a strong and beautiful woman with lots of courage. Has anyone ever told you that?"

"You just did. Hey, Shane? Go to sleep. I'll see you tomorrow."

She clicked off, and he knew he would continue to hear her voice in his dreams.

****

Shane awoke to the lovely aroma of coffee brewing and bread toasting, but when he moved, every muscle in his body protested. The creaky sofa was definitely doing a number on him. He'd gotten up once during the night to check on Gypsy, and Lizzie, but otherwise had slept like a dead man. He pushed himself to sit up, trying not to groan, and found he'd been covered with the plaid blanket usually kept folded across the back of Doc's easy chair. He didn't remember doing it. He also didn't remember setting the coffee maker last night, and he sure as heck wasn't making toast in his dreams.

Swinging his legs from the lumpy cushions, he shoved back his unruly hair and stood, just in time to see Lizzie appear from the kitchen. He quickly made sure everything was zipped and in place. Damn good thing he'd left his T-shirt on, too. She blinked and glanced away for a second, then flicked the dishtowel she carried over her shoulder.

"I made you some coffee. I hope it's okay. I'm having juice, and there were English muffins, so I toasted them."

Shane brushed a hand over his whiskery face. Coffee sounded really great. "Super. I didn't know you could make coffee." He followed his daughter into the kitchen and watched as she poured him a cup. He accepted it from her and relished the first swallow of the hot brew then winked at her. "Very good. Thanks, Shortstuff."

She shrugged. "I make it for Mom sometimes in the morning while she's in the barn. She likes to have it when she comes back in. Do you like peanut butter on your English muffin? I couldn't find any jam."

"That's fine." Sitting at the dinette table, tucked into the corner of the small kitchen, he drank more coffee while Lizzie spread the peanut butter on the muffins. It was much like the mornings he remembered making breakfast for Doc and himself before he left for school. He always figured it was the least he could do for the man who'd given him a home.

When she set the plate in front of him, he noticed

the over-sized sweatshirt she'd pulled on since last night. It bore the Silver Creek high school logo on the front and his jersey number thirty-three on the back. "Cool sweatshirt."

Lizzie grinned in the way that made her nose wrinkle. "I was cold. I didn't think you'd mind."

"I don't. I doubt I can wear it anymore." Never in his life did he imagine his little girl would one day wear that sweatshirt.

She picked at the cracked, silver vinyl lettering pressed against the faded blue material and suddenly sobered. "My dad had one like this but with a different number." Her glance flashed to meet Shane's. "I mean…my other dad."

"Yeah, I know. He and I played football together at Silver Creek High. Go Mustangs!"

Lizzie's smile this time turned wistful. "I kind of remember, he took Mom and me to a game once. The Mustangs won."

"They should. They were always the best."

She sat down and started to eat her peanut butter covered muffin. Shane finished his, drank another cup of the strong coffee that was guaranteed to get him through the morning, and went to shower while she fed the ever-hungry kittens.

When he emerged twenty minutes later, freshly shaven and feeling human again in clean shirt and jeans, he found her tidying up the kitchen. She'd washed the breakfast dishes and stacked them in the drainer. So efficient.

So much like Allison.

It filled him with a rush of pride that, no thanks to him, his daughter was such a great little person.

171

Lizzie finished swiping a dishcloth across the table and draped it over the drainer. "Are you taking me home?" She followed him back to the living room where he pulled on his boots.

"Actually, your mom is picking you up. I have farm calls this morning, but Sandy will be here. You and the kittens can stay with her 'til your mom—"

He noticed the small, gray velvet box nestled in her hand and glanced to the shirt he'd shed last night and tossed over the end of the sofa. He'd tucked the ring inside the flap pocket and forgotten all about it when Allison called. He opened his mouth to say what he didn't know, but Lizzie spoke first.

"I found this on the floor. I guess maybe you dropped it."

He stared at the object in her hand. "Yep, I think you're right."

She ran her fingers over the soft velvet before holding it out to him. "Is it a ring?"

Shane stepped closer to let her place it in the palm of his hand. "It is." He flipped the top open and the diamond solitaire flashed its yellow fire, reflecting the sunlight streaming through the eastern windows.

Her blue eyes grew round. She breathed a, "Wow," and then, "It's really beautiful. Who's it for?"

Now he was stuck. It wasn't how he'd planned to do this. He'd wanted to ask Allison first, but maybe this was better. Maybe letting their daughter in on his intentions would help pave the way to Allison's heart. Well, he could hope.

He sat down on the sofa and motioned for Lizzie to do the same. She perched next to him, the sweatshirt drooping down over her knees. He cleared his throat and gathered his thoughts before speaking what might be some of the most important words of his life. "It's…the ring…is for your mom. For Allison. If she'll have it…and me."

This was about as awkward as when, at seventeen, he'd first asked Allison on a date. Who could imagine this many years later he'd be speaking to their daughter and waiting for her approval to propose to the love of his life?

"It looks like an engagement ring. You want to marry my mom?"

Shane met her surprised little face. "Yes, I do. I want to marry her very much. What do you think about that?"

Lizzie mulled it over for about five seconds. "Well, you are my real father, right?"

He nodded.

"And my mom's my real mom. Sooo, I guess it would make sense if you guys got married."

"You're okay with it?" He waited for the reply that might end the whole idea.

She wrinkled her nose again. "Sure, but does that mean you'd live with us? Or would we have to…"

He lifted one hand to halt her questions. "One thing at a time, Shortstuff. First, your mom has to say yes. Can you do me a favor, though? Can you keep it a secret for now?"

"Sure, but when are you going to ask her?" She wagged a finger at him. "You shouldn't wait too long."

Shane chuckled. "I won't. I promise, but I want it to be, you know, special for her, when I pop the question. It has to be the right time." And any alone time with Allison happened few and far between.

"I guess a proposal should be special."

"I think so. So for now, it's just between us." He motioned between them. "Nobody else can know. Can you do that?"

She plucked at a blue thread loosening from the frayed cuff of the sweatshirt. "Sure. I promise, but can I do something now?"

"What's that, Shortstuff?"

The baby blue gaze lifted to his. "Can I hug you?"

Surprise jolted through him, but it was the most natural thing in the world to hold out his arms to his daughter. She wrapped hers around his neck, and he held Lizzie close. After a moment he realized she was trembling, and her tears fell against his neck.

"Hey, what's this?" He set her away. When she tried to hide her face from him, he brushed his hand over the braids that were all askew. "It's okay. Everything's going to be okay, Lizzie. I promise you."

Man, what do I say to make this better? What does a dad say?

"Last night…it was so awful, and I was so scared. What if you hadn't come? What if—"

"But I did, and from now on, I will be there when you need me. I'll keep you and your mom safe. You can count on it. Do you believe me?" She gave a shaky sigh and nodded, wiping her face on the sweatshirt sleeve. He lifted her chin and straightened her braids. "C'mon. I've got work to do, and your mom will be here soon. So fetch your kitten pals and their gear, and we'll head up to the office. We can check on Gypsy on the way. My vet tech, Carrie, is coming in and will watch her today. I need to talk with her."

Before opening the door to the clinic, he set the

ring box on a shelf in the living room.

Just as they left the house, Lizzie clutched the kittens' basket with one arm and slipped her other hand into his. "I'm glad you came back," she said.

"So am I, Shortstuff," he admitted and winked at her. "So am I."

Chapter 17

Much as she hated to do it, Allison called Mark Williamson right after she finished barn chores. The conservation officer was no stranger. He'd graduated a few years ahead of her and Shane, and then gone on to university. He came back to the community a few years ago and was well known for his by-the-book professionalism—the last person you wanted checking out the wild story of a large cat stalking your farm, but at this point, she had no choice. Unfortunately, a downpour right before dawn had probably washed away whatever evidence the old orchard might have held.

Mark arrived shortly after noon and was now walking in the area where she'd seen the green glowing eyes. She watched him crouch down and study something on the ground before he walked on a little ways amongst the gnarled apple trees. She'd wanted to go with him, but he'd told her firmly to stay put.

Maybe it's a good idea, but it is my farm and my animals that are getting attacked.

Irritated, she tossed aside a barn rake and headed up to the house. It was strange not to have Gypsy trotting at her side. How soon could the collie come home? She had visited her when she'd picked Lizzie up at the clinic, and received a few weary doggy kisses, but recovery was a long way down the road. Her heart ached that, in trying to protect them, Gypsy had been so severely injured.

She found Lizzie on the porch swing and sat down beside her. "You look tired, honey. Did you get any sleep last night?"

Her baby girl shrugged. "Yeah, some. Shane put me in his old room, and he let me borrow his sweatshirt, the one like Dad's, with the Mustang on the front. He said they used to play football together. So…were they good friends?"

"Yes, they were." *Until I came between them.* "They had a lot of good times together."

"Do you think Shane is sad Dad is gone?"

Allison remembered the bad feelings that had pushed the two best friends apart, and her sadness in believing she was the cause. Later, after Shane left and she and Jason married, she started to understand better what had driven the division between them. Her husband's jealousy of Shane had gone far beyond them loving the same girl. With Jack Delaney constantly ruling his life, Jason had envied his best friend's freedom to make his own decisions and go his own way. She often wondered if he had really loved her at all, or just married her to get back at Shane.

"I'm sure he is." She didn't want to make either man seem bad in her daughter's eyes.

She stood with plans to start putting together some lunch when Ronnie's silver SUV pulled into the drive.

Oh good, the person I really need to see right now.

She hadn't spoken to her sister-in-law since the other night and had no desire to do so now, especially with Mark Williamson's state government truck parked by the barn. If Ronnie learned about what had happened, the whole county would soon know.

"Could you do me a favor?" Allison turned to her daughter. "Could you go in and start some eggs boiling for lunch? I thought I'd make egg salad for us." *And hopefully get rid of Ronnie before Mark finishes his investigation.*

"Sure, Mom, but how many should I make? Will Officer Williamson and Aunt Ronnie be staying, too?"

She gave a quick hard shake of her head. "I'm not planning on it, and, Lizzie? Let's not tell Aunt Ronnie about what happened last night. We wouldn't want her to worry."

When Lizzie had gone inside, Allison trekked back down to the barn, just as her sister-in-law got out of her vehicle and Mark made his way back from the orchard. Taking a deep breath, she prepared herself to deal with the both of them.

"Well, if it isn't Mark Williamson." Ronnie removed her sunglasses and smiled sweetly. "Oh, but it's *Officer* Williamson, isn't it? What brings you here? Having a problem, Allison?" She'd asked the question with an innocent air, but sarcasm lurked in her green-shadowed eyes.

"Nothing to worry about." She glanced quickly at him and hoped he could read the slight shake of her head. "The conservation department is identifying some invasive plant, and I thought I might have seen it here. Mark came out to see if that's it."

"I'm going over by the pasture. Why don't you join me in a few minutes, and you can describe the plant you think you saw."

Thank goodness he got the hint.

When he strode away, Ronnie continued to watch

him with a hungry stare. Then, as if shaking off her attraction, she turned her way. "I noticed none of the horses are in the pasture. Is it because of this strange plant Mark's looking for? Something that might make them sick?"

"No, nothing like that. I'm expecting the farrier this afternoon, and it's easier to have them all in the barn when he comes." At least it wasn't a lie and gave her a good reason to keep them inside today.

"Well, where is Lizzie? I thought she might like to go to a movie with me this afternoon."

"She's making lunch for us, but why would you want to take her to a movie?"

Ronnie put on her famous pout. "Why not? Lizzie is a sweetheart, and any woman would enjoy her company. We always have such a good time together, and she enjoys getting away from here every now and then, whether you believe it or not."

"I just thought after what I told you the other night—"

"Oh that, well, did you think it would change how I feel about her? She's still my niece, as far as I'm concerned, and I certainly don't blame her for what you and Shane did. She's just a child. Now, I'm going up to the house and tell her to get ready. If we leave in ten, we can still make it to the matinee."

Wobbling on her backless wedge sandals, her sister-in-law took off for the house before Allison could protest. When she would have started after her, Mark waved from the pasture, motioning for her to join him there. Nothing like being torn in two directions.

With a heavy sigh, she went to see what the conservation officer had to say.

****

Shane hung back from entering the hospital room where Matthew Brewster, wearing his ancient plaid robe and tattered slippers, now sat in a recliner chair. The colorful afghan Sandy had crocheted covered the old man's knees.

Gaunt eyes sank into his still pale face, but when he saw him in the doorway, he visibly perked up and waved. "Don't just stand there staring at me," he pretended to grumble. "Get in here."

He's feeling better for sure.

"Hey, Doc." He saluted as he entered the room. "Glad to see they've got you moving around, but haven't you had about enough of this place?" With nowhere else to sit, he grabbed a wheelchair from the corner and sank into it, relieved to both get off his feet and to see Matthew improving. "How soon do you think they'll spring you?"

His mentor just grunted and winced. "Hell if I know, but not soon enough." He studied Shane for a moment. "How're things going at the clinic?"

"They're fine. I was at Ruben's farm today. What a trip." He could do with never having to go back *there* again.

"Yeah, how'd he act, same old asinine self?"

"Not too excited it was Shane McBride treating his sick cows. He never had much use for me."

"Well, he needs to get over it and get used to somebody else. I'm not going back to work."

The words took a moment to sink in. Shane sat upright. "Say what?" While he'd suspected Doc's retiring could happen, hearing him actually voice it was another matter.

"You heard me. I didn't stutter." The old man fussed with the afghan, his gnarled fingers picking at the yarn.

"What I heard was, you're not going back to work…at all?" A day he'd thought would never come.

"That's right."

"Aw, come on, Doc. Aren't you being a little hasty? I know you're still not feeling the greatest, but when you've had some time—"

"I'll still feel the same, and it's time I admitted it. I'm just not what I used to be, and that isn't going to change. Fact is, I'm damn lucky to be alive." He coughed a little and grimaced.

Shane leaned toward him, wanting to touch the old man's shoulder to offer support but knowing he wouldn't like it. The only physical display of emotion Matthew Brewster had ever expressed had been when he shook Shane's hand before he boarded the bus on a rainy night ten years ago. "So, what are your plans?"

"Short term, I'm going to rehab for a few weeks. Then my niece has offered me a room at her home while I recuperate. She and her husband and kids, they're all the family I have, and I better take her up on it."

"And then?" he pressed.

"I've got a date with my fishing pole at a cabin up north. I haven't been there in a long time."

Dejected, he leaned back in the wheelchair. "You'll close the clinic?"

Matthew directed his tired gaze to him. "Guess it depends on you. Like I told you before I had the surgery, the clinic, the business, is yours, if you want it. I'm not changing my mind. So, I guess the more important question is what are you going to do about Allison?"

Shane slumped lower. "I've been thinking about that."

"Yeah, and have you come to any conclusions?"

He peered into the old man's face and swallowed hard. "I want to ask her to marry me."

If Matthew was shocked, he didn't show it, just appeared to roll the admission around in his brain for a minute. "That so? What do you think she'll say?"

"Lizzie says it's a good idea." At the raised gray eyebrow, he added, "She saw the ring I bought, and…I thought she should know my intentions."

"Well, probably is a good idea, to have your daughter's permission to marry her mom."

Damn! He knew?

That truth gave him a moment of irritation, and he chose his next words carefully. "You could have told me. All this time, and I wasn't aware I had a child with Allison, until I came back now. You know how that makes me feel?"

Lifting a gnarled hand, Doc waved away the question. "Which is all water under the bridge now. Does Lizzie know the truth?"

Pushing away the painful sense of betrayal, he nodded.

"Then what's the hold-up? Ask that girl to marry you!"

Doc started coughing, and Shane got up to fetch his cup of water while he clutched a pillow to his chest. He waited until the old man settled down again before giving voice to his own concern, the one had haunted him since the minute he bought the ring. "But what if she says no?"

What will I do then?

He'd been working on his own back in Wyoming; if he didn't return it wasn't like he'd be leaving much of a life behind. But if she had no use for him, if she still couldn't put the past behind them and make a new future, what was the sense in him staying here?

Except he was Lizzie's father, and he had every right to be in her life.

Doc sighed and leaned back in the recliner. Shane rang for a nurse and helped get him back into bed, then waited until he was nearly asleep. Not wanting to push anymore of his own problems on a sick old man, he finally headed for the door.

"I guess it all swings on what Allison says," he murmured to himself.

Later, at the clinic, he opened the door to Gypsy's cage and stroked the collie's head. She whined and managed to sit up. He checked her bandages and was pleased to see the wounds were already beginning to heal with no signs of infection.

So far, so good.

"Glad to see you're going to make it, old girl. I think maybe tomorrow you can go home. But no herding horses or tangling with other critters for a while, you hear?" When she rested her muzzle in his hands, he added, "We're going to find out what did this to you. I promise. But tonight, I'm going to see Allison, and maybe soon we'll all be one happy family. You like the idea?" The collie flicked her wet tongue over his hand. "I'll take that as a yes. Now, I've just got one more girl to win over."

After his second shower of the day, he called her,

but it went right to voicemail. He hesitated leaving a message, then just said, "Hey, good news on Gypsy. She's doing well and wants to see you. You can bring her home tomorrow." He suddenly ached to see Allison. Wanted to get this asking business over with so he knew what direction he'd take by summer's end. It would take that long to get the clinic closed down, if that's what must happen. "Call me," he added before clicking off.

****

Allison grabbed her phone from the table and stepped out of the tack room just as it quit singing its tune. Shane's name popped up, and she waited until the voicemail icon lit up before answering. She breathed a sigh of relief to hear Gypsy was doing well. Good news was certainly welcome around here. Hovering her fingers over Return Call, she wanted to hear his voice again but was reluctant to let herself need him too much.

She'd needed him last night, and he'd come right away...but would it always be that way? She'd only had herself to depend on for so long, it was hard to trust anything different. Maybe...

The phone went off again. This time it was Ronnie.

After hearing how much they'd enjoyed the movie, her sister-in-law came to the point—asking if it would be all right if she and Jerry took Lizzie out for dinner before bringing her home.

Allison asked to speak to Lizzie, who assured her she was fine and yes, she wanted to go to dinner with them.

"I'll be home in time to feed the kittens," she promised.

"Okay, honey, I'll see you a little later then. Gypsy is coming home tomorrow, so let's plan to go get her in the morning. I have lessons in the afternoon."

Even after speaking with her daughter, an odd worry still flitted about at the edge of the ten other things she needed to think about, but she pushed it away to finish up barn chores and then headed up to the house. After helping with the farrier all afternoon, she needed a hot shower.

The sun hovered above the orchard and set off a golden wash of color over the knobby old trees. Any other time she might have stopped to appreciate that brief spate of time when the daylight slipped into early evening, but the memory of green glowing eyes just beyond the round pen sent a chill rippling through her bones.

Is it still out there?

Despite Mark insisting it couldn't be, she knew what she'd seen, what had attacked her dog. To hell with his denials. The chill quickened her steps to the house.

Half an hour later, she stood in front of the fridge in her nightshirt, wondering what the heck to eat for dinner. The shelves looked a little empty. She grabbed a half container of cottage cheese. A week past expiration.

I really need to shop.

Her phone sang out—Shane again. This time she answered in time.

"Have you guys eaten yet?" he asked.

"It's just me. Lizzie's with Ronnie and Jerry, and no, I haven't."

"I have dinner combos from Tim Wong's, if you're

interested. I'm ten minutes away."

She couldn't help but smile. "You do know the way to a girl's heart."

It took her one minute to change from her nightshirt into shorts and a tank top. Another two to slap on blush, peach lip gloss, and twist her wet hair into a knot on top of her head with jabbed-in pins. By the time Shane stood at the door, she had the table set.

Entering, he juggled the combos and two containers of egg drop soup. "Here, give it to me." She took the cartons, and while dishing out the shrimp fried rice and egg rolls, it lifted her spirits he remembered how often they'd eaten this when they were kids. In a moment of contentment, she put the soup into her fancy blue willow mugs, and before they sat down, glanced up at him and grinned. "This was always my favorite dinner."

"And mine. Never have found anybody who makes it like Tim Wong."

"In all your travels?" She meant it as a joke but sensed it pricked a sore spot when his lips pressed tight together. "Sit," she ordered to cover the awkward moment and poured him a glass of iced tea.

When she joined him, she found eating dinner with Shane brought a calm to the otherwise hectic day. Though they didn't talk much, Allison began to think it was almost like the old days again.

Once the food was gone, she broke open her fortune cookie first. "Hmmm, 'Life will soon take an interesting turn.' I wonder what *that* means?" As if her life hadn't taken enough strange turns lately. "What does yours say?"

Shane drew the tiny slip of paper from his cookie.

"'Seek happiness where the heart lies.'" He watched her across the table. "I already know where my heart lies. No doubt about it."

To avoid the disturbing touch of his steady blue gaze, she jumped up and began to clear the dishes. When she came to gather his, Shane took her hand and pulled her gently onto his lap. He tucked stray wisps of hair back from her face and then leaned up and kissed her for a long, slow minute.

"Mmmm, peaches," he murmured.

He placed her hand on his chest, and the rapid but steady thump-thump-thump of his heart vibrated against her palm, sending a zing of powerful awareness through her body and setting her own heart wild.

"It's true, you know."

"Wh-what is?" She couldn't stop her voice from trembling.

"My heart, Allie, it's here, with you and Lizzie. I know our past is shaky, and maybe we both still have trust issues, but my heart has always been here, and it always will be."

"I…want to believe you." She leaned her forehead against his, and he kissed the tip of her nose. "It's been hard, all these years. I wanted to let you know, so many times, but I didn't know how, and then I thought…maybe it wouldn't even matter."

"It would have mattered. It matters now. I hope you believe me."

She nodded and patted her hand on his chest before getting up and taking some of the dishes to the sink, putting distance between them. *I guess I'm just not ready yet to trust so easily.*

"You haven't asked me what happened today," she

said to change the subject. "I called Mark Williamson, about what's been going on and about Gypsy getting attacked."

"Did he come out?"

"Yes, and he looked around for about an hour. He's pretty sure it's coyotes. Because of the rain, he couldn't find any evidence or tracks, but they've caused problems at other farms this summer. Attacking sheep and a couple of dogs, killing chickens."

"That's a little different than going after horses. Did you tell him about the larger paw print in the pasture?"

"He shrugged it off, said it couldn't have been what we thought." She glanced at him, knowing he wouldn't like Mark's verdict. "According to the Fish and Game Department, there are no cougars in this part of Michigan, at least not this far south. That's their official statement."

Shane shook his head. "Well, I've seen how the other dogs were attacked, and I beg to differ with him, because the method was totally different. And it sure as hell wasn't a coyote track in your pasture. Maybe I need to stop in and have a word with Officer Williamson, man-to-man, and show him the picture on my phone."

"No, please just let it go." *I need to handle this on my own. I can't let you take over for me.* Because, what if he still did leave? She turned to loading the dishwasher. "I can't risk—"

"What you can't risk is another animal, or worse yet, you or Lizzie getting hurt." He got up from the table and brought the rest of the dishes to the sink. Setting them on the countertop, he tried to turn her to face him, but she resisted. "You can't pretend it won't happen again, because it will, it's just a matter of when."

The fear of that, and the memory of those green eyes shining in the dark, almost made her give in to him, but years of learning to depend on herself made her pull away. "Shane, I can handle it, so you can drop this 'man-to-man' stuff. I'm perfectly capable of taking care of *my* farm and *my* daughter. I've done it this long. Why should now be any different?" She almost regretted the words the moment they left her mouth, but allowing him to take control would only make her more vulnerable if he left again.

If? More like when.

A stunned silence followed. When he spoke, Shane's voice held no warmth. "She's my daughter, too." He turned on his heel to walk away, pausing before he opened the door. "You can pick Gypsy up in the morning, or I can bring her home when I'm done for the day. It's up to you. You'll need to keep her quiet for a week or so yet, 'til I can remove the stitches."

Quick regret sagged her shoulders as Allison turned from the sink. "Shane, I didn't mean—" *Please don't go.*

He held up a silencing hand. "Maybe not, but whatever you do mean, you need to figure it out, because now I know Lizzie is my child, I intend to be a father to her. If you didn't want me to do that, you should never have told me."

The hollow sound of the closing door echoed the fact nothing she could say at the moment would bring him back.

Any more than I can bring back everybody who left

me.

She had managed to go on through all those losses, and it was why she had to stay strong, stand on her own, and trust only herself. Yet, at the thought Shane might never come back, her stomach sank.

What if this time, he really is gone forever?

Chapter 18

When Allison took Lizzie to pick up Gypsy the next morning, Shane had already left for the day.

"He had a lot of barn calls to make," Sandy said. "Some horses down in the South County area are showing signs of encephalitis, and he needed to check them out ASAP. He was gone before seven, but Gypsy is doing well, and you can take her home. Carrie will bring her out and give you instructions for her care."

Allison bit her lip and handed the leash to Carrie. She had hoped he would be here, so she could…could what? Offer an apology? Admit she was bullheaded? But she feared a mere, *I'm sorry,* wouldn't fix what was wrong between them.

She waited until the recent tech school graduate went into the kennel before turning back to Sandy. "Can we put this on my account until the first of the month? I know I still have a balance, and I'll pay it up when the board checks come in July. Things are just a little tight right now." She hated owing Doc Brewster, but the extra care for Pride, and then the tire she'd had to replace, had put a definite crimp in her budget.

"Sure, hon, that's fine," the kind receptionist assured her. "Doc knows you're good for the money. By the way, have you been up to see him lately? He's talking they may let him out here soon, but he's got a long row to hoe before he can come back to work."

"I'm sure." Allison sighed and tamped down guilt because she hadn't been back to see Doc. Life had become just too crazy lately.

Carrie led Gypsy out, and the collie went right to Lizzie, leaned against her and wagged her feathery tail. The vet tech handed the leash to her and talked over the two printed sheets of directions with Allison. She gave Gypsy a parting pat on the head. "You stay away from those old coyotes now. They're nothing to mess with."

Lizzie's glance jumped to Allison's. "Was it...?"

"We don't know for sure," she answered quickly, "but probably." No need to get into a discussion here about what had taken place at her farm.

Before anymore could be said, she hustled her daughter and dog out into her vehicle. She lifted Gypsy onto the blanketed back seat and secured her. In a few moments, they were on the highway back home.

"I don't think it was a coyote," Lizzie finally said. "I've heard them yip before, and this...didn't."

Allison couldn't argue with her, nor did she want to encourage the young mind to keep thinking about the terror of two nights ago. "I know, and Officer Williamson is looking into it. Let's hope he has a better answer." Except he'd given his answer, and it was the easiest one, not what she herself believed.

At home, she settled Gypsy in a crate in the house to keep her from moving around too much, and then students began to arrive for the afternoon group lesson. Jenny's mother dropped her off, and the high school girl set to work helping the kids saddle up the horses.

To Allison's relief, the lessons went off without a hitch and the horses all behaved themselves, in spite of having been kept inside the past two days. But when

Jenny would have let them out to pasture for the rest of the afternoon, Allison had to stop her.

"I'd like them to go back in their stalls. I…have plans this evening, and I'll feed them early." It was as good excuse as any, even if it wasn't really true.

"Uh-oh, you must have a date with the hot vet," her part-timer teased. "I heard he's taking over Doc Brewster's practice for good. Bet you're happy about that," she added as she led a suddenly antsy Major to the barn.

The sorrel wasn't happy about not getting his usual run in the pasture, and Allison knew this couldn't go on for much longer.

"I'm sure I don't know what you're talking about." She led two of the other equally unhappy horses inside. "Doc Brewster is doing well, and knowing him, he'll probably be back to work by end of summer." *And then will Shane leave?*

"Well, my mom is good friends with Sandy, and she thinks Doc Brewster is going to retire. Do you think he will? I mean, it would be really cool if your boyfriend took over and—"

"Not my boyfriend," Allison stated. Especially not after last night. He hadn't phoned her at all today. Would he call tonight?

She turned to putting the horses in their respective stalls. When finished, Jenny had already left the barn and was outside talking to one of the moms, Betsy Finnegan. The teenager shook her head and shrugged then pointed toward where Allison stood.

Now what?

The Finnegans had boarded their horse here for nearly two years, and their daughter, Bethanne, took lessons twice a week. Their child could be a little bossy, and Betsy catered to her every whim, but they were dependable and always paid their board on time.

Allison could tell as Betsy approached she was clearly upset about something. "Hi, Betsy, what's up?" She tried to keep her voice upbeat.

The woman pushed back her coppery hair and shifted her oversized designer purse on her shoulder. "Well, Bethanne is having a birthday party sleepover this Friday night, and Lizzie is invited, but I have to ask you about something I've heard."

"Of course." Her pulse took a sudden leap.

The well-kept woman hesitated and chewed her bottom lip. "I was talking to Sylvia at Jackson's General, and she mentioned you've had problems out here with coyotes bothering the horses. Is that true, and has anything happened to endanger anyone?"

How on earth did Sylvia know what was happening here? Mentally, she ticked off the people who knew. Shane, Mark Williamson, Sandy, and the vet tech. She'd not mentioned it to anyone else. But someone had, and of course Sylvia would have been only too happy to pass on what she knew.

"I'm not sure who Sylvia has talked to, but there is nothing dangerous going on here. We had an incident the other night, but the horses are all fine. It's all under control."

The redhead didn't appear convinced. "Hmm. Well, I certainly hope so. We would hate for anything to happen to Bethanne's Apollo. You know we have hopes for them on the show circuit next year. Perhaps you should consider getting someone out here to trap the animals causing the problem? Or just shoot them."

Allison flinched at either solution. "Shooting around the horses isn't an option, but I do have the conservation officer checking into it, so you needn't worry about Apollo. You know my first concern is for the safety of all the horses and the children who come here."

"I'm sure that's true, and we trust you, but we might have to think about moving to a different boarding barn if anything else happens."

"It won't." She glanced to where two of the other mothers were still talking, and she could see them shaking their heads. Had they all heard something?

After studying Allison for a moment, maybe gauging how upset she was by all this, Betsy waved a manicured hand. "Anyway, like I said, I really came over to invite Lizzie to Bethanne's sleepover this weekend. We'll start about six on Friday. They'll be watching movies and eating pizza. I hope she can come. I'm even happy to pick her up for you."

It was just the sort of thing she had wanted for her daughter, some normal girl-type activities. "Of course she can come. Sounds like a fun time for the girls. Thanks for inviting her."

"It'll be good for Lizzie. Don't forget, have her bring a sleeping bag and pillow."

Allison nodded and was relieved when Betsy and the other mothers left for the day. How much they'd discussed what might have happened here at the barn she could only guess, but knowing how news good or bad traveled, it was only a matter of time before a lot more folks would hear some version of the truth. And yet, she could not bring herself to tell them the truth.

****

Shane packed up the equipment he had used at the last barn call of the day and started for home. Inoculating the horses in South County and treating a couple of sick cows and a colicky horse had kept him busy all afternoon, and he'd had little time to think about the conversation with Allison the night before. But once he got on the highway, his last words to her came back to haunt him, and he could have kicked himself for being so curt. She had every right to feel the way she did. Circumstances had been hard for her, and yet she'd made the best of it and carved out a life for herself and Lizzie. Did he have the right to come into it now and demand she change just for him?

In spite of the surprise of discovering he was a father, he wanted to *be* that father, more than anything he'd wanted in a long time. And he wanted Allison to be his wife. Could he still convince her they could be a family?

Only one way to know, and he made up his mind on the drive back to the clinic not to wait any longer to find out.

When he pulled into the drive at Allison's Farm, a peaceful and serene scene greeted him. The sun would soon set and golden light spilled across the pastures, orchard, barn, and farmhouse. It reminded him of the first time he'd seen the farm, when he'd come to apply for a job, a desperate kid from the city in need of a home and a reason to make something worthwhile of himself. He'd found all that and so much more, only to lose it for what he thought would be forever. Now, here he was back again and determined this time not to lose the only thing that had ever really mattered to him.

He found her sitting on the porch swing, her gaze

focused on the gnarled apple trees and the path into the woods. With one sneakered foot, she pushed herself slowly back and forth and looked for all the world like a child lost in her thoughts.

Shane paused at the foot of the steps and cleared his throat. She brought her gaze back from wherever it had wandered and settled it on him. A sad smile touched her lips, and it tugged at his heart just as her smile always did.

"You're here."

"Am I welcome?"

She shifted over on the swing and made room for him.

Without hesitating, he went up the steps and sat down next to her, careful to still keep a few inches between them. "I thought I'd stop in and see how Gypsy is doing. Has she gotten around much today?" A safe topic.

"Lizzie had her on the leash a little while ago, and they walked around the yard a bit. She ate a good supper."

He nodded and rested his hands on his knees, wondering how to tell her what was in his heart. To his surprise, she turned his face to hers and kissed him, her hand curving along his jaw and slipping around the back of his head to pull him closer. His thoughts spun for the moment. Did she know how much he loved her?

She ended the kiss with a sigh and rested her head on his shoulder. Relieved, he drew her closer and pressed his face into her hair.

Lizzie found them that way and clicked her tongue in make-believe disapproval. "All right, you guys. What's going on out here?"

197

Allison smiled and pushed away from him. "I was just taking a nap. Is dinner ready yet?"

Their daughter snapped the dishtowel she held and flung it over her shoulder. "It is. Mac and cheese and fresh green beans from the garden. I just picked them this morning. Will you be eating with us?"

She pinned him with what he was now recognizing as her "Lizzie look."

Shane dipped his head to peer into Allison's face. "Will I?" *Are we okay now?*

"If you like." Her cheeks flushed pink. "I think mac and cheese was always one of your favorites, and it is Grandma Ellie's recipe, not from a box."

"Then what are we waiting for?" He rose, and taking her hand, pulled Allison up after him. She leaned into him a little, and he so wanted to kiss her again.

Later.

"I'll set another place." Lizzie held the screen door for them, motioning her mother in first, and when he walked past her, his daughter gave him a nudge and mouthed the words, *Did you ask her?*

He quickly shook his head.

"When?" This time she whispered.

"Soon," he side-whispered back.

Allison stopped ahead of them. "What's going on with you two?"

Silence hung in the air, and Shane went to pull out a chair for her then winked at Lizzie. "Just saying how much I love mac and cheese."

Allison glanced suspiciously between them, then, with a shrug, sat down.

After an enjoyable family dinner, he helped clear the dishes and spent some time checking Gypsy's injuries. The collie made no protest and seemed to know his gentle hands had saved her a few nights before. Thank goodness he'd been here. Another loss would have been devastating for Allison.

Not long after, he sat with her on the sofa while their daughter fed the kittens. Like fat little fur balls, they tumbled across the floor and pounced on each other in play.

"Wynkyn is the fastest. He doesn't want to stay in the basket anymore." Lizzie snatched him from scooting underneath a bookcase. "Blynkyn is shy, and Todd is always happy." She sat on the sofa and cuddled the three fluffy babies. "I'm glad you brought them to me to take care of. Just think what might have happened to them if you hadn't."

Pride filled his chest. "You've done a great job, too. Look how much they've grown already." He tickled Wynkyn's tummy, and the kitten nibbled his finger. "You should think about being a vet someday."

She seemed to contemplate this. "If I did, maybe we could work together."

"I would like that, Shortstuff," Her sweet little face, so intent, gave him another rush of emotion, one he could only figure was fatherly love as he thought about what the future might bring. "I would like that a lot."

When she took the kittens up to her room with her, Shane turned to Allison. "I was at the hospital to see Doc the other day. He's doing well, but he's decided not to return to work. He's retiring."

That bit of news knitted her brows. "I guess that's not surprising, after what he's been through, but what will happen to the clinic?"

He paused. Did he tell her now?

Go for it!

"He's offered it to me."

She contemplated that a moment. "Are you sure it's what you want?"

"I guess that depends."

"On?"

You. But this isn't the moment. It has to be just right.

He leaned back on the sofa and chose his words carefully. "I guess we need to talk, but not right now. Not here."

She tipped her head in question, and he leaned closer. "I think we should go out. Just the two of us. A nice dinner. After all that's happened here recently, you deserve a night out and a little R and R."

She laughed softly. "R and R sounds lovely, but as you well know, there is never any rest around here, let alone recreation."

"Well, I think tomorrow night would be the perfect time to start a new tradition. Just you and me and some alone time. Maybe we can talk your pal Jenny into staying with Lizzie."

She laughed. "Actually, you seem to have planned it just right. Lizzie has a sleepover at Bethanne Finnegan's house tomorrow night. It's a first for her."

He tried to place the name. "Finnegans. Did I ever know them?"

She shook her head. "They moved here a few years ago. Bethanne is in Lizzie's class at school. I'm hoping it will be good for her to go to a party for a change instead of hanging out with me and the horses."

Shane plucked at her ponytail and wound the

honey-colored strands around his fingers. Still as soft as the silk he remembered. He drew her close and kissed her for a long time while he imagined so much more.

"So, will you go out with me?" he finally asked against her lips.

"Sounds like you're asking me on a date."

Her fingers played a soft tune at the back of his neck, and he suppressed the shiver of pleasure that threatened to ripple through him. "I am. We haven't been on a date in a long time. I think we have a lot of catching up to do."

And I have something very important to ask you.

Chapter 19

Allison dumped grain into the last feed pan and waited for Jenny to fill the water buckets. The horses all munched contentedly, which was music to her ears. It meant they were calm, and so far, there had been no more unwanted excitement. Hopefully, it would stay that way while she was gone tonight.

"All done." Jenny began to roll up the hose. "Is there anything else you need me to do?"

She glanced in the tack room, which needed a good straightening. Never one to have a sloppy barn, she realized she'd let things go lately, but there wasn't time, and Lizzie had already been picked up for Bethanne's party. Tomorrow for sure she would spend several hours putting it all right.

"I think we're done for today. I'm sure you have plans for a Friday night and would like to get home." She pulled an envelope out of her back pocket that contained Jenny's pay for the week. Money might be tight, but she would always compensate the girl for the work she did. "Thanks for staying later and for all your help."

Jenny brushed her hands on her jeans and took the envelope eagerly. "I do have plans. I'm going to a movie with friends and to hang out at Jeremy's after."

Ah, the latest interest. The teenager seemed to have a new boyfriend every other week or so.

"What about you?" Jenny took her phone from her pocket to check for messages. "With Lizzie gone for the night, you should go out for a change, or something."

"I am doing something." She tried to sound nonchalant. "I'm going out for dinner. In fact, I have exactly an hour to get ready."

Thin brunette brows went up an inch. "You are? I mean, hey that's great. Is it with Doc McBride?"

She didn't want to admit it and just murmured, "Maybe."

Jenny grinned. "I knew you guys were an item, and he really is a hottie, for an older guy. Well, you have a good time, and if you need me to come in the morning to help out I can."

"Um, that's okay. I can handle it. You can take the weekend off."

"Gee, thanks. Should I come on Monday afternoon then?"

"Sounds good."

She watched the girl run out of the barn, a little envious of Jenny's youthful exuberance and energy. For herself, a nap suddenly sounded really good right about now, and yet a thrill of anticipation ran through her when she thought of going out with Shane tonight. Something she had been certain would never happen again.

Checking on all the horses one more time, she closed the barn and went up to the house.

An hour later, Allison stood in front of the full-length mirror in her grandparents' old room and surveyed her attempts to look pretty. The pink flowered skirt and white embroidered peasant blouse were out of style compared to the svelte dresses she saw other women wear, but she'd been hard pressed to come up with anything else.

I guess I need to shop for some new clothes or start sewing again.

Except paying bills came first, and there was little left for indulgences, as there never was. She sighed and went to her closet in search of a pair of sandals.

By the time Shane knocked at the door, she had swept her hair into a quick twist and fastened it with several of Grandma Ellie's sparkly combs, applied her peach-flavored lip gloss, and grabbed a summer shawl.

Since he'd arrived back home in Michigan, she had only seen him in his working clothes; the sight of him in dark gray slacks, a blue western shirt, and bolo tie made her do a double take. All he needed was a Stetson, and he would be the perfect cowboy. When she just stared at him he flushed.

"Sorry, these are the only dress clothes I brought with me. A little old-fashioned, I guess."

He looked like every hero she'd ever imagined riding off into the sunset with, and her heart skipped several beats. Her Shane really had turned into quite the handsome man.

"No more than mine." She picked at her flowered skirt. "I'm really behind the times."

He stepped into the kitchen and stood right in front of her. "You are fabulous," he said in a low voice, kissed her cheek, then handed her a bouquet of daisies, her favorite flower.

She promptly melted. "You remembered." How many times had he brought her daisies in those long ago years?

"There isn't much I've forgotten." He drew her

into his arms. "Like how you always were delicate as a daisy, and yet tough."

His lips skimmed her temple and a frisson of sudden desire shivered through her.

"And you always tasted of peaches." He ran his tongue over her lips before taking over her mouth.

Allison's knees went weak, and she clutched the bouquet with one hand and his arm with the other. Sooner than she wanted, the kiss ended.

"I think…we need to go…now," she breathed against his smoothly shaven chin.

"Mmm, I think…maybe you're right." He set her away from him but took her hand in his. "C'mon, Allison Tyler Delaney. Let's go have a good time."

****

The Emerald Lake Inn had been the site of their senior prom, and Allison would always recall how they had danced outside on the patio that soft spring night. Apple blossoms had been in bloom, and the promise of a future together shone brightly along with the sparkling lights rimming the dark satin water. How soon it had all come to an end. But they were here together tonight, by life's strange twists of fate, and to her, it seemed as though it was meant to be.

We're older, but are we any wiser? Can we still have a future together?

Dinner passed in a haze, and when Shane led her out onto the patio, it seemed as natural as anything in the world to slip into his arms and move to the music of a song that brought back sweet memories. He had always been an incredible slow dancer; he said it was because he came from Detroit. Against her cheek, he sang the words, and they swayed together in the shadowy mellowness of the summer night. Before the song ended, Allison finally accepted she had lost her heart all over again to the man she had never stopped loving.

When they left an hour later, she was surprised when Shane drove to the south end of the lake. He held her hand as they walked along the shore, then found a bench to sit on and watch the moon rise.

"It always stayed with me," he said, his deep blue gaze settling on her.

"The way mosquitoes were always so thick here by the lake?" She swatted one away from her face and then flushed at the earnest look in his eyes.

"The way the moonlight reflected on the lake here and in your hair."

The low timbre of his voice reached out to entice her, and it was so hard not to let it draw her into his spell.

Still, she shook her head. "But I don't remember you always being so romantic nor so poetic. In fact, if my memory serves me right, you were only interested in one thing."

His mouth slanted in a sheepish grin. "I was a teenage guy and head over heels for you. I've learned a lot about life, especially since coming home and finding you and Lizzie. Do you believe me?"

Twisting the fringe on her shawl around her fingers, she considered how she did feel. "I want to, more than anything, but I have to admit, I'm afraid."

"Afraid of me?" He seemed taken aback.

"Afraid you'll eventually go away. Like everybody else in my life who meant anything to me. My parents, Grandma Ellie, Pop, you, and Jason. All gone. I was left with no one to depend on but me. Can you understand why I'm afraid to believe and to trust again?" She steadied her gaze on him. How could she make him know what it was like to feel so abandoned? But then, maybe he did know. As a boy, he'd been abandoned, too.

Shane reached for her hand and lifted it to his lips to kiss the back of her fingers. "I'm here now, and I'm not going anywhere. You can believe that."

A cool breeze drifted in from the lake, and she trembled in the damp evening air. "I want to. I really do."

He reached into his pocket, and in the next moment, Shane knelt down on the ground beside her. "Then believe, Allison. Believe…and marry me. Be with me forever."

On a gasp, her breath caught in her throat. Never in a million years had she expected this. Was it really happening? Or was she only dreaming, conjuring up a fantasy in her mind? Any second now would she wake up and find herself alone?

This can't be true. And yet…

"Let me be everything I ever wanted to be to you, and to our child. Let me have a chance."

He held up a ring that shone like golden fire in the moonlight. Taking her trembling left hand, he slipped the ring on the finger where she had once worn a wedding band. She'd taken that ring off three years ago. How strange to have another replace it, and to have Shane put it there. The diamond winked back at her, as if trying to convince her this was all true.

Still holding her hand, Shane turned it over and kissed the palm and then stood and pulled her up with him and kissed her again. At the taste of his warm lips, Allison let her doubt and uncertainty fade away. Maybe she only needed to have someone to rely on, someone who would always be at her side, but as always, when Shane was kissing her, she didn't have much sensible thought going on in her head.

After a few wonderful moments, the whine of another mosquito brought her to her senses. "Maybe we should go before we turn into their dinner," she murmured.

Shane only chuckled and tucked her hand in his as they walked back to his truck. Inside, he didn't look at her and hesitated turning on the motor. "You didn't answer me."

She wanted to shout yes, but one last doubt held her back. "Is it only because of Lizzie? I understand if that's true, but is our having a child a good enough reason to get married? Will it hold us together?"

She studied his profile and waited for an answer. There needed to be more than that between them, but for now, maybe, it was enough. But when he faced her, she read the truth in his honest expression, and it warmed her heart.

"It will, but the better reason is I love *you*. I have from the day you opened the door to a kid from the city who needed a new life. And that is the best reason I can think of for you to marry me. Of course, if you loved me, too…"

Now his eyes held the question, and she knew she had to answer.

"I do." Allison touched the ring on her finger. "And I will."

On the drive back to her house, she held his words

close and prayed they would always stay true, that they would have their second chance.

At the door to her kitchen, she lifted her face to Shane's and stood on tiptoe to kiss him. There was so much she wanted to say, but the time for talking had passed. She could only show him what she felt for him, what she had always felt, was still as strong as ever.

Ending the kiss, she placed her left hand against his chest. "I need to take Gypsy out, but please don't leave."

"Let me do it."

He went to get the collie's leash. For a few minutes, he walked Gypsy around the yard while she did her business, then brought her back in to the dog pillow Allison had set up in the corner of the kitchen. Gypsy thumped her tail, as if in thanks. He stayed crouched there a few moments, petting the collie and the kittens before he rose.

"Allison, I—"

An eerie sound drifted through the night, and Gypsy whined. Shane turned toward the still opened door, listening. Several seconds passed and it didn't repeat, but he started for the door anyway.

"Don't you dare go out there." A rush of fear for what could happen to him made her call him back. "Whatever it is can't get in the barn, and as long as the horses aren't going crazy, it will be okay."

Please don't put yourself in danger.

"You sound so sure." He slanted her a strange look.

"I…just feel it, but you can't go out there and take chances. Not after you've just asked me to marry you. You just…can't." She hated the desperation in her voice, but did he realize what she was saying? That suddenly his safety meant more to her than almost anything else.

He came back and stood very close. "I did ask you, didn't I? Which means I promise to protect you and everything you hold dear. Everything."

"Then don't leave tonight. Stay with me." Did she really say that? Three little words that said so much. How would he reply? She lifted her gaze to his and saw uncertainty.

He searched her face. "Are you sure?"

For her answer, Allison closed the kitchen door and locked it. Taking his hand, she led him up the stairs, into her room, and sat with him on the edge of her bed...and waited. His fingers entwined with hers, but otherwise he didn't touch her. A moment of doubt rippled through her. Should she make the first move?

He still hesitated, but finally said, "I need to tell you, I'm not prepared to protect you, but I'm okay. My...health is good. Are you on...?"

She wanted to laugh. He'd never worried about that before. "I'm not, but...if we're going to get married, does it matter?" Worry over another pregnancy was never necessary after Lizzie.

But how do I explain the way it was with Jason and me?

When Shane reached up to pull the combs from her hair, she leaned her cheek into his hand for a moment and relished the roughness of his thumb against her skin. She shook out her hair, and when it drifted down over her shoulders, he ran his fingers through it. He always liked to do that. It pleased her to know he still did, and she let him trail them along her neck to her shoulder and down her arm to linger at the sensitive spot just above her elbow. He drew soft sensuous circles there and lower on the inside of her wrist. She couldn't suppress a quick intake of breath.

"Is this okay?" he asked.

She nodded and closed her eyes. "It's just been a long time, you know? Jason and I…we…"

"Hush, you don't have to tell me." He leaned over and sweetly kissed her. "And if you still don't want to do this…"

Allison opened her eyes. "I do! With you. Only with you, but you need to know…there was only ever you." *There*, she'd said it. How would he react?

He knitted his brows, as if perplexed. "But you and Jason were married for six years. Are you telling me…?"

She swallowed hard, remembering her confusion and eventual resignation to the way Jason had acted. Admitting the truth was like prying loose a deeply held secret. "We slept together, for the first few years, but nothing ever happened. At first, he said it was because of the pregnancy, and I was okay with that. I didn't really want to…but even after, when he tried, he…couldn't. I don't know why. Maybe it was something about me, or he couldn't accept I was with you first, but we never…consummated our marriage." An old-fashioned term, but how else could she say it? "I didn't understand it then…and I still don't."

Shane nodded and drew her against him. "I guess we'll never know what was inside Jason's head, and it really doesn't matter. I'll always be thankful he took care of you and was a father to Lizzie, but whatever was wrong, I'm pretty sure it was Jason's problem and not anything you did."

"I cared about him. I wanted for us to have a normal life together, and I wanted to love him, but I couldn't, not like that. Maybe he knew, and it destroyed whatever love he had for me." Leaning into his shoulder, she needed to say this without seeing his scrutiny. "I was so consumed with guilt over his death. We needed money. Pop was gone, and we were having trouble making ends meet. I had rescued two more horses, and my business giving lessons was just getting off the ground. Jason worked for his dad, but he took a second job with a tree trimming service. There was this terrible spring storm with lots of downed trees. I remember he was excited for the extra hours, and had been out for days clearing away the branches for the power company. Then one night, they came from the sheriff's department and told me there'd been an accident. A tree they were cutting fell...on Jason..." She broke off, still remembering the horror of seeing the deputies on her doorstep and knowing something had gone terribly wrong.

Shane rubbed his hand up and down her arm in reassurance. "So, that's why Ronnie and her family blame you for Jason dying. But you know it's not your fault. I loved Jason like the brother I never had, but he acted a little crazy at times. More apt it was something he did, or didn't do, that caused the accident. Or maybe it was just an accident."

As much as she wanted to believe that, what had happened to Jason still haunted her. She sighed and leaned into Shane's strength. "But I've always felt somehow responsible."

If not for me, he wouldn't have gone out to work such a dangerous job.

"You don't need to think that way anymore. All of it's in the past, and we have to learn to leave it there. We have a future to think about, and it starts here."

He kissed her again, and Allison let the problems of the past and present slip away just as the peasant blouse and the pink flowered skirt soon did. She turned down the white crocheted bedspread and slid between the cool sheets. When Shane joined her, it was like coming home again after way too many years.

"My teenage assistant says you're pretty hot, for an older guy," she teased and ran her hands over his hard arms and across his chest, remembering the time he had broken a rib falling from one of her horses. He still had a little dent. She pressed a kiss there. "She's been after me to date you."

"Did you tell her we were going out tonight?" He kissed her chin and then her neck.

She had to suppress a giggle when he touched a ticklish spot. "Not in so many words, but she guessed." How quickly would everyone hear about her date tonight? "You know it won't be long before people are talking." But seriously, did she care anymore?

Shane pressed her back into the pillows and hovered above her. The heat of his body seared through her as he dipped his head and murmured against her lips, "Then let them talk."

His kisses were as sweet as she ever remembered, and the magic his hands could work took her to the levels she'd imagined in her dreams. But when he touched the places that had changed since the last time they'd been together, self-conscious embarrassment made her cheeks heat, and she stopped his exploration.

"I'm not seventeen," she whispered.

"Neither am I." His finger gently traced the faded lines across her stomach.

"Stretch marks. They never went away, in spite of all the lotion I used. Not…very romantic, are they?"

"I'd say they're badges of honor, honestly earned." He pressed his lips to each of them.

In that tender gesture, Allison found she could let go of the lonely years and embrace all that was now and real.

Through the open windows, the sounds of the night and the soft chirpings and leaf stirrings lulled her as she moved together with Shane in a summer symphony. Soon her sighs matched his, and as her soul lifted to the height of rediscovery, she knew they were still a perfect match in perfect rhythm. The years apart fell away so they no longer mattered, and she let her body relearn his.

Far into the night, she remembered secrets she'd only ever known with him and learned new ones that brought her to a tender trust in the one man she'd always loved.

When she finally curled against his side with his arms around her, she watched his chest rise and fall and listened to his deep, even breathing. Before she fell asleep, she was thankful she had only ever given herself to Shane McBride.

Chapter 20

Allison didn't want to open her eyes. The dream had been so lovely, so real, and once her eyes opened it would be over. The warmth of Shane's body still lay on her skin, and her own body hummed from the night. So many times dreams like this one had awakened her in the lonely hours, but none had brought this sense of fulfillment, this utter…

There was water running. The shower? Reaching out to the pillow beside her own, she ran her hand over the hollow and caught the familiar woodsy scent that had always been his. She opened her eyes and sat up, flushed when she saw the clothes strewn at the foot of the bed.

Oh my…

A few moments later, Shane walked into the room, toweling his hair. He had another around his waist, and Allison blinked to make sure he didn't disappear. He didn't, simply pulled the towel from his head and grinned.

"Hey, rise and shine. The day is calling." He came over to her side of the bed and bent down to kiss her cheek. "Where did I hear that before?"

"From Pop," she whispered, remembering how her grandfather had called her every morning, and apparently called Shane, too, on the few occasions Pop had allowed him to spend the night in the barn. "I thought…" She peered into his face.

"What?"

"I just had a dream. That you'd come back and we…"

"No dream." He leaned in closer, tilted her chin up, and gave her a quick kiss. "At least not for me it wasn't. It was much better."

She sighed, but still pulled the sheet up to her neck, suddenly feeling self-conscious and unsure.

As if he knew, Shane went to get his clothes lying crumpled on the floor. "I'll get coffee started." He shook out the wrinkles before pulling on his T-shirt and pants. "And I can make a pretty mean omelet." He turned and winked at her. "I'll be downstairs."

Through the double windows, she saw the sky turning pink with early morning light. Any minute now she would hear the first stirrings from the barn.

"I have horses to feed and Gypsy to take out and the kittens…"

"And me to help you," he said as he left the room.

Allison sat for a moment, gathering her wits, grateful he had given her the privacy she was used to. She touched the ring on her finger and remembered his question, and her answer, of the night before. Had it been the right answer? Would it work out this time? Life for both of them had changed in just a matter of days, a matter of hours, and she had to hang onto the hope this time that it would all be right.

When she joined Shane in the kitchen, breakfast waited on the table, Gypsy lay in the corner with a dog biscuit, and the kittens were scrambling over a pan of softened kibble. He stood at the counter pouring coffee, and she wondered how any man could look so damn sexy in wrinkled dress pants and a white T-shirt?

"I have to get down to the barn." She tried to hurry past him, but he corralled her with an arm around her waist.

"You have to eat first, and then we'll *both* go to the barn." He steered her to a chair and handed her a coffee mug. "I don't have to be at the clinic 'til ten."

"You can't do barn work in those clothes."

"I keep a change of jeans and a shirt in the truck. You never know what you'll run into on farm calls."

"I have to pick up Lizzie." She sipped at the coffee he'd made just the way she liked it. "And students are coming for lessons at eleven."

Shane shrugged and sat down across from her. "Life goes on." He reached over and took her left hand and rubbed his thumb over the ring. "But last night…last night was incredible."

His smile this time was wistful, in a way she hadn't seen in many long years, or maybe never.

"Now, eat up. We have work to do."

Fifteen minutes later, she had just put the dishes in the sink and gone for her barn boots when she heard a vehicle pull into the drive. From her corner, Gypsy growled low in her throat. It was too early for students, and Jenny had the day off.

Allison jammed her feet into the rubber boots and went out to the porch. The rusted out sedan made her stomach lurch and acid burn in her throat.

"What the hell do they want?" Shane spoke from close behind her.

"Hard to say, but whatever it is won't be good."

Bolstered by having him at her back and a sudden new sense of power pumping in her veins, she went down the steps to meet the Potter brothers at their vehicle.

"Well, well, what do we have here?" As usual, Duane spoke first. "Payin' a vet call a little early, aren't ya, Shane? Or maybe you made one of them overnight visits." He snickered and leaned out his window to shoot a stream of tobacco into the grass. It landed just to the left of where she stood. "You're lookin' mighty pretty this morning, Allison. Guess them overnight visits agree with you."

Before she could stop him, Shane stepped around her and strode up to the rattletrap car, his fists clenched. Fear clutched her heart at the glower on his face.

"You shut your mouth, Duane, or I'll shut it for you," he ground out.

She knew how bad he wanted to land one in the middle of the elder brother's grimy face. Much as she would like to see him do it, it was the last thing she needed to happen here. "Chill out guys," she demanded and stared at the Potters. "What do you want?"

Duane squinted his eyes at Shane, and the old animosity between the men loomed large as ever. "Darren and me just come to give you a hand. That's all."

She propped her hands on her hips and glared at him. "And why would you think I need or want *your* help?"

"Wellll, we heard you've had a little trouble here at the farm, and we just thought we could get rid of some pests." His whiney voice grated against the mellow morning air.

"I don't know what you're talking about," Allison snapped. "There is no trouble here, and I'd appreciate it if you'd just leave."

Darren leaned across the sedan's raggedy front seat to stare out his brother's window. "So there ain't no coyotes hangin' 'round causin' problems?"

"No there aren't, and I'll tell you again to get off my property."

Her disgust with them flaring, she moved closer to their car. Shane grabbed her arm to stop her, and she jerked away, but not before she saw the two rifles lying across the car's backseat. A shiver of fear shot more adrenaline through her, and she quickly took two steps back. Like the night she had caught them poaching the deer, she wanted the two lowlifes to get the punishment they deserved, but they couldn't be trusted any more than she could trust a hornet not to sting her.

"We got a right to know. We just want to protect what's rightfully ours," Duane said.

"You have no right to anything on my property."

"You know it ain't true. 'Course, you probably just don't want Shane here to know what you done. Come right to our place when we weren't home and took what wasn't yours to take."

"And I'd do it again in a minute." She waved her arm toward the road. "Now, get out of here, unless you want me to let the sheriff know you guys are out here with guns, threatening to shoot up my place. Convicted felons in possession of firearms."

The two brothers eyed her for another few seconds, then Duane slid the sedan in reverse and backed down the drive. At the edge of the road, he turned around and peeled out, leaving no doubt an inch of rubber on the pavement.

Once they were gone, relief flooded through

Allison, leaving her whole body drained and shaking. She put her hands over her face and struggled to compose herself. How many more times would she have to deal with the Potters? Or would she never be rid of them?

When Shane touched her shoulders, she turned and leaned into him.

"Are you okay?" He folded his arms around her.

"I will be in a minute." The warmth and strength of his embrace shored her up again and reminded Allison she wasn't alone in this. "Maybe I should tell the sheriff about Duane and Darren, too, but what will happen if I do? I've already got parents questioning me about trouble here. How will I convince them their children are safe if they think I'm a thief, and that I have anything to do with the Potters?"

Shane stroked her hair and then held her away and tipped her face up. "If they care at all about an animal, they'll know you did what you did for all the right reasons. As for those jerks, you've got plenty on them to keep them at bay, and they know it."

"But you know they can't be trusted, besides—"

"And besides, I'm here now, and it will be a cold day in hell before I let them come near you or your farm again."

His hard kiss that followed made her believe for the moment that everything would be all right.

Once they'd fed the horses and turned them out in the small pasture nearest the barn, Shane offered, "How about I go pick up Lizzie at the Finnegan's. I can take her over to the clinic with me. I'll only be there a few hours today."

Allison parked the wheelbarrow and glanced at the

big clock on the barn wall. She'd barely have time to go and get back before her lesson group arrived. But what would the Finnegans, or anyone else for that matter, think if Shane arrived to take Lizzie home?

"Guess they're all going to know sooner or later, and I'm hoping it's sooner."

He, of course, could read her mind.

Shane came over and brushed some wisps of hay from her hair. "Or do you plan to keep me hanging on, Allison Delaney?"

She wasn't prepared to give him an answer yet as to how soon they would marry. The night before still seemed like a dream…except the ring on her finger was very real. She relented, and after watching him leave, turned to get ready for her students.

****

The Finnegans lived in a new development that had sprung up in the last five years. Shane remembered the land had once been a huge cherry orchard. He drove his truck past streets named Robin's Way, Sparrow Drive, and Mockingbird Lane. Neatly trimmed yards with perfect flower beds and curving driveways led up to large brick and stone houses with three car garages.

"More house than anybody needs," he muttered while searching for Goldfinch Path. Nothing like Allison's homey and comfortable farmhouse…or the rambling ranch houses in Wyoming.

He hadn't thought much of Wyoming in the past few weeks, not since he'd learned he had a daughter and was needed here, but this morning, he had a sudden yearning for the wide open range and the towering mountains he'd come to know and love. When he'd first gone west, it had been a huge adjustment for a guy used to the city, and then to small town life. But he'd grown to love it, and he missed it now, the feeling of freedom to be who he was and to breathe air that felt new every day. Would he feel the yearning the rest of his life? Would he always long for those sun-warmed canyons and the whispering winds through the lodgepole pines? Maybe he could convince Allison to love it, too, and start life over, as he had.

But no, her heart was, would always be, here. He couldn't ask that of her, and as long as she lived here, his heart would be with her.

He pulled into the Finnegan's driveway and parked behind a late model sports car. Just as he got out, the front door opened and five girls and their mothers emerged from a vast entry way. The girls giggled and poked at each other while their mothers carried their backpacks and sleeping bags. The women stopped talking when they saw Shane striding up the brick walkway.

With their stylish summer bobbed hairstyles, trim capris, and designer sandals, they were all very fashionable but a far cry from the woman he had just left working in her barn. In truth, he much preferred the one in jeans and T-shirt with her honey-brown hair pulled back in a ponytail, especially the way she had looked last night when she'd lost all abandon with him.

He quickly shook that thought away to focus on the here and now.

Shane recognized several of the women from the new boarding stable south of town but didn't recall their names, except for the one who had brought her poodle in to the clinic a few days ago. "Mrs. Clemons." He nodded to the petite blonde, then to the others.

"Beautiful morning, isn't it?"

The women exchanged glances, and Sally Clemons shook her head in puzzlement. "Dr. McBride, what on earth brings you here? No problems with our horses, I hope."

"Nope, far as I know they're all doing just fine. I'm here to pick up Lizzie. Is she ready?"

Another "look" zinged among them, and no one spoke when Lizzie stepped out the door, hugging her hastily rolled sleeping bag with one arm and her pillow in the other while her backpack hung off her thin shoulders. She struggled to keep from dropping the sleeping bag, and Shane heard one of the other girls snicker.

When he saw the flash of embarrassment turning Lizzie's cheeks pink, he stepped forward. "Hey, let me give you a hand." He grabbed the sleeping bag before it slipped to the ground and met her wide-eyed surprise.

"Shane! Why are you here? Where's my mom?" She glanced past him as if waiting for Allison to appear.

"She had a class to teach this morning, so I offered to pick you up. Hope that's okay."

Her mouth quivered for a second, and she hauled the backpack up her shoulder. "Sure. But can we go now?"

Without saying goodbye to the other girls, she headed for the truck. He thanked the woman he took to be Mrs. Finnegan and followed his daughter. She scrunched down in the corner and stared out the window as they drove away.

A couple of miles down the road she hadn't said a word, so he asked. "Did you have a good time?"

Lizzie shrugged. "I guess."

"You don't sound too sure of that. Something happen?" His first impression of the other girls was a tight little group who didn't accept just anyone into their circle. Apparently, some things never changed.

When she still didn't answer, he focused on the road ahead. "Of course, if you'd rather not talk about it, it's okay. I just thought maybe…"

"It wasn't…I mean, I guess I…don't fit in. Mom…shouldn't have made me go." Her voiced held a small tremor.

"She just thought you would enjoy getting away from the farm for a bit. She worries and wants you to have friends." *Poor kid. Must have been a miserable night.*

"I have friends! Cayenne and all the other horses, *they're* my friends, and at least they don't make fun of me…and they're never mean."

The hint of tears in her voice made him want to turn the truck around and go right back to give those girls and their too-perfect moms a piece of his mind, but it wouldn't solve this problem and might only make it worse. What could he say to let Lizzie know he understood?

At a stop sign, he waited before driving on. "Yeah, that's one good thing about horses, they do make pretty good friends. But we still need people."

"Well, I have Mom…and you. I have you, don't I?" The pleading eyes of his little girl made his heart turn over.

"You bet, Shortstuff." He reached over to brush away the single tear sliding down her cheek. "You bet you do. Now, how about you give me a hand at the clinic? It's never too soon to start getting ready for veterinary school, you know."

She grinned, and he supposed this was what it meant to be a father. Trying to fix the little things as well as the big, and just letting his child know he loved her.

Chapter 21

Allison set the pitcher of lemonade in the fridge and turned to survey the table she'd set with Grandma Ellie's china. Adorned with delicate pink rose garlands, the treasured set of dishes had been handed down for three generations, and she had always loved her grandmother using them for special occasions. She hadn't taken the dishes out of the china cabinet since Grandma Ellie was gone, but this occasion was about as special as it could get. Tonight, they would tell Lizzie about the engagement, and to use the dishes on this evening was like a blessing from her grandparents.

Standing at the window, she gazed down at the ring that winked and sparkled at her in the afternoon sunlight. How strange and yet so totally right for it to be there.

What would they think of it, her grandparents, the two people who had raised her and taught her to believe and have faith, in herself and in what she could do and accomplish? Who had dried her tears when her favorite horse died and held her hand after an emergency appendectomy?

She thought back to the morning she'd found out Shane was gone. Pop had been the one to tell her and later had found her in the barn, weeping bitterly. With Grandma Ellie already passed, they'd only had each other. He hadn't known quite what to say to comfort his teenage granddaughter, but she knew he understood how deep the pain went in her heart. He knew how much she loved Shane, so he simply sat with her and let her cry.

Yet several weeks later, when she and Jason announced they were getting married, Pop didn't ask any questions. Did he also know the truth? Or did he just accept the reasoning whispered at the time—that she had married Jason on the rebound?

Her phone sang out, and she tracked the sound to the living room.

"How are things going?" Shane's voice came over the cell. "Everything all right?"

"Everything's fine. When are you and Lizzie coming home?" Home! Did the word mean as much to him as it did to her? Did it mean the same thing?

"On our way in just a few. Closing up the clinic now. What about din?"

"It's ready. Nothing fancy, just spaghetti and meatballs." Did he remember it was the first meal she'd cooked for him and Pop, after Grandma Ellie passed?

"Sounds great. See you soon."

He rang off, and she wondered if this was the beginning. From now on, would she welcome Shane home after work? Would he pick Lizzie up from school sometimes? Take her to the library? Would dinner be the focal point of their day, when they sat together as a family and shared their lives?

Rubbing cold hands up and down her arms, she went back to the kitchen, but after a bit realized she'd been staring out the window trying to quell the apprehension those questions presented. As much as she wanted to cherish the possibilities of a new life with

Shane, the thought of change was scary, and trust, because she hadn't been quite truthful. Everything wasn't fine. She still had reservations, still wondered if Wyoming called to him, feared he would tire of all this and go back to the plains and mountains he'd come to know and love these past ten years. She couldn't blame him if he did, if he chose the life he'd made there over the place that had caused a lot of change for him. Yet, he'd once told her it had also given him a sense of stability he'd never known and shown him love. Would it prove to be enough?

Allison began to turn away, to check the sauce bubbling on the stove, but before taking a step she heard the call of distress from the pasture. A shrill whinny that begged for help.

Stardust!

She knew the filly's cry, and her breath stilled in her chest. Gypsy rose from her bed and growled, ready as ever to spring into action, in spite of her still-healing injuries.

"No, you stay." She put out a hand to halt her steps to the door. Without thinking twice, she went upstairs to the closet in her grandparents' room. Behind an old overcoat stood the .410 Jason had insisted she learn how to shoot. Her hand closed over the cold barrel, and she shivered. She hated guns, hadn't touched this one since the day Jason had taken her to a shooting range and given her the lessons she didn't want to learn. Did she still remember how to shoot it? Or even load it?

Another whinny split the late afternoon and pierced her heart. She pulled the shotgun from the closet and turned to the top drawer of Pop's chest. The box of shells still lurked beneath a stack of handkerchiefs. Her fingers shook as she slipped one into the chamber. She raced with the shotgun down the stairs and pushed past Gypsy to get out the door. Holding it next to her side, she hastened to the pasture where all the horses seemed to have gathered at one end. All but Stardust.

The black filly circled in the center of the pasture, stopping to paw the ground and shake her head. Allison could feel her fear even from where she stood. How strange she hadn't run with the rest of the herd. What would keep her from her sister's side?

Then she saw the lithe, crouching body with tawny fur and long, twitching tail. Huge paws dug deadly claws into the ground and prepared the big cat to launch.

Taking a deep breath around her pounding heart, Allison raised the .410 to her shoulder and settled it in the hollow. She tried to think back to the moments when Jason had stood behind her and steadied her arms, and she heard his voice in her ear.

"Don't wait, Allie. He's going to spring."

Not Jason's, but Shane's voice. He moved in quietly and stood at her shoulder.

"I can't," she murmured.

"Then give it to me."

The cat moved. Stardust shrieked. Allison's breathing stopped, and she squeezed the trigger.

The shell hit short of its mark but splotches of dirt kicked up in the pasture, and the filly fled, joining the herd in less than three seconds.

The cat was gone.

Allison's hands shook as she lowered the shotgun and handed it to Shane as she tried to locate the beast.

"He took off into the woods, but he'll come back.

229

We need to call Mark again. They have to do something, now this has happened."

"Mommy?"

Hearing Lizzie's tremulous voice behind her, she spun to take her daughter into her arms. She stayed silent for a moment, pressing the small face against her breasts. This was more than she could take, and her own shoulders shook.

"Are you okay?" Lizzie spoke, her voice muffled.

Allison steeled herself to calm her pounding heart. "Yes, but I need to check the horses now and get them inside." She released her baby girl and set her away. "You can help by taking Cayenne to his stall."

Shane's calm demeanor as they brought the horses into the barn kept Allison focused as much as it kept the spooked animals from setting off on a wild run to the barn. She knew as flight animals, they wanted to do just that—flee.

And I want to do the same. What on earth will happen next around here? She shuddered to think.

Later, when the horses were all safe in their stalls and pulling hay from their nets, Allison let Shane close up the barn, and she and Lizzie trudged to the house, all the while keeping an eye out for the cougar to return.

Her daughter grabbed her hand. "What was it? It…is it a big cat?"

Allison let out a breath slowly. "It is."

"But…"

"I know, it doesn't seem real," she tried to steady her voice, "and yet we saw it, and now something must be done."

"Will we have to…kill it?"

Tender-hearted Lizzie hated that idea as much as

she did.

When they stood on the porch, Allison stared out to the orchard and to the woods beyond. How was all this happening? Something so out of the realm of possibility and yet…

She met Lizzie's questioning gaze. "I hope not but maybe. If it's the only answer."

"Did you try to kill it when you shot?"

She hugged her baby girl again. "If I did, I'm not very good at it. I guess…I really just wanted to scare it off, but I would do anything to keep us safe here. Anything."

"So would I."

Stepping up on the porch, Shane stood beside her and put one arm around Allison, while Lizzie clutched his other hand. "*Are* you okay?"

He gazed into her eyes, and she saw in his a promise to always be here for them, no matter what. It eased the fear and uncertainty that still dwelled in her heart.

"With you here, I am," she admitted. She touched his face, knowing she spoke the truth now.

The moment was interrupted when Lizzie let go of Shane's hand and grabbed hers, startling her into glancing down.

"You asked her?" Their daughter stared at the ring, then turned her blue gaze up to Allison. "And you said yes?"

She glanced back to Shane and saw him wink at Lizzie.

"She did, and we're going to get married very soon. That is, if we have your approval."

How ironic we're asking our daughter's

opinion…and yet how fitting.

An excited Lizzie bounced up and down. "Yay! You do! You knew that."

Hmmm. What's going on here? Allison narrowed her brows at Shane. "You did? Wait a minute. Did you two already talk about thi—"

Lizzie giggled when Shane kissed Allison and stopped her question.

For the moment, the terror of the day slipped away, but she didn't feel at ease until a bit later when she had dinner on the table, and they were sitting down together.

"Gosh, Mom, I don't think we've ever used these dishes. They're so pretty."

"They're very special, used for only special occasions. My grandma got them from her mother for a wedding gift."

Lizzie glanced between the two of them and grinned. "Guess this is pretty special, if you guys are getting married. I never knew Grandma Ellie, but I bet she'd like it we're using her dishes."

"I like to think so." Allison's heart brimmed with renewed hope the three of them would be a family. Yet, beneath her newfound happiness, a shiver of fear still flickered.

The cat. What if it comes back? What will we do about it?

****

When Lizzie had gone off to bed, the kittens in tow, Shane drew Allison down to sit beside him on the sofa. While he wanted to believe everything would work out, there were some things that still needed to be said before he made a final commitment to his new family. He took a deep breath and let it out slowly. "We need to talk."

She gave him a wary glance. "If it's about what I did today…"

"It's about what I did, ten years ago, when I left you."

She pulled her legs up underneath her and leaned toward him. "We've been over it enough times, and it's okay. I understand why you left. It was just as much my fault that I didn't tell you."

"Yeah, but why I stayed away so long, there was another reason." His stomach clenched as he tried to find the right words

She frowned. "I'm not sure I understand what you're saying."

"I'm not sure I can explain." He turned away and let his gaze travel around the room. With its homey touches, it reflected everything Allison loved and valued, and that he wanted to also love, but a bit of the truth he had learned about himself over the years still lingered in his soul. "The time I lived here, with you and your family and with Doc, I was really just a dumb kid who didn't have a clue what he truly wanted in life. When I left it was hard, and I missed everyone, especially you. But as time went on and everything happened as it did, I started to know myself better, who I was and what mattered. And I started to like the fact I didn't have to live up to anyone's expectations or live down a reputation, real or imagined. I could be me and…I liked that."

"Is it part of the reason you stayed away then?"

"It was. That, and the fact I found out you were married so thought you didn't want me anymore." He brought his gaze back to hers and leaned into the sofa.

She sighed. "Do you want to go back there? To Wyoming?"

Yes. No. How did he make her understand? He put his arm around her shoulders. His gentle tug asked her to fit herself against him, and she obliged.

"Only if you went with me, but I know that's a lot to ask…so I'm not asking. But maybe someday we'll go, you, me, and Lizzie."

"But what about the horses?"

He heard the fear in her voice and quickly assured her. "They'd go with us. We'd find a way, but that's in the someday. In the now, we have to deal with what happened here today…and last night."

Allison lifted her face up to him, and her eyes were swimming, melting his heart.

"How?" Her voice trembled, barely above a whisper.

"By not waiting. I want to be here with you and Lizzie, to keep you safe and help you and love you." He kissed her long and slow but held himself back from letting it go further. "Let's get married soon, Allie. Very soon. There's no reason to wait. I want to sleep here with you every night and wake up with you every morning. We've wasted so much time. Let's not waste anymore."

She sank into him, nestling her head against his shoulder, and it was as if the world had been handed to him, a second chance to have what he'd always wanted, and he was determined this time not to blow it.

"I want to get married here," she said. "At the farm. It just seems right, because it's where we first met."

"Then let's do it. How about in two weeks?"

She lifted her head from his shoulder. "Really?"

"I found out from Sandy today Doc Brewster is moving to his niece's home in three weeks. I'd…like him here for our day. We can pull it together. I know Lizzie will be okay with it."

"About that. How did she know? She pinned him again with the question. "Have you two been conniving?"

He only smiled and once again silenced her questions with his kiss.

****

Three days later, Shane ran into Mark Williamson when they both stopped at a highway rest area. At the sight of the conservation officer, a streak of irritation shot through him. The calls Allison had placed to the local Fish and Game Department had not been answered. He had even stopped to see Mark himself, between yesterday's clinic appointments, only to find him out of the office. The fact they were not taking the situation seriously angered him. How could they not have sent someone to check out Allison's report now that she had witnessed the cat herself? He was sorely tempted to jump the guy's case, but once again, words his grandmother often said came back to him. *You catch more flies with honey than vinegar.* So maybe a pleasant attitude would gain him more than an angry one.

He did a quick scan of the officer, noting his usually well-groomed appearance had taken a serious dive. Mark's pants had water stains, and his wrinkled shirt stuck to his body.

"You have a rough night, too?" Shane tore open a

235

candy bar he'd bought from the vending machine and debated how much he should say about the incident in Allison's pasture.

"Looking into reports of illegal trapping. Those guys like to go out and check their lines after dark."

It didn't sound fun to Shane. Maybe dealing with a cranky mare in labor was an easier way to spend a night after all.

Mark went to the coffee machine and reached into his gray shirt pocket for a dollar bill. He came up with only a five. "Damn. Not sure this coffee is worth five dollars. Last time the machine didn't give me any change."

"Here, I've got one." Shane pulled a crinkled bill from his jeans pocket and handed it to the officer. "It might smell like a horse, but I doubt the machine cares."

"Thanks, I'll catch you next time." He smoothed out the bill against his dark green uniform pants and stuck it in the pay slot.

"Consider it on the house." Shane shoved the rest of the candy bar in his mouth and sipped on his coffee to wash it down. He knew the guy's job was probably a pain at times, but he wasn't going to let him or his department off the hook this easily. Try as they might to deny the cat's existence, they needed to acknowledge the truth. "You know, there is something you can do for me."

Mark stretched what must be a kink in his neck, while the coffee cup filled. "Yeah, what would that be?"

He kept his voice non-accusatory. "You know those coyotes you said were hanging around Allison

Delaney's place and attacked her dog? When I stitched her up, the wounds just didn't look like anything coyotes could make, and then, when the critter showed up again, I'll be damned if it didn't look like a mountain lion."

Mark's hand stilled as he reached for the steaming coffee. "You don't say?"

"I do say."

A nerve twitched in the officer's shadowed jaw. He gave a nervous laugh. "You sure it's not just a little female hysteria? You know how women are about their horses."

Jerk. Shane set his coffee down on the top of a trash can and pulled out his phone. Opening the photo app, he found the picture he'd taken of the paw print in Allison's pasture and held it up. "I actually took this a while ago at her place. Does it look like any coyote print you've ever seen?" He waited for the officer's reaction.

Mark rubbed his stubbly chin. "Can't say it does."

"Yeah, I didn't think so either. I've wanted to talk to you about it, but Allison, she's pretty stubborn about wanting to take care of things herself. So when that cat showed up in her pasture again and threatened her horses, she took the matter into her own hands and shot at it. I stood there and watched it happen."

Mark's eyebrows shot up an inch. "It's illegal to shoot an animal that's protected as endangered."

"Tell that to Allison when one of her horses is threatened. She already almost lost her dog. It could have been her *child*."

Mark finally took his coffee from the machine and heaved a tired sigh. "So, what would you have me do?

We let it out there's a cougar stalking somebody's farm and folks are liable to panic and—"

"Look, I'm not asking you to publish it on the front page of the *Silver Creek News*, but can you at least acknowledge it's a reality and offer some solution?"

The officer blew on the coffee and grimaced when he took a swallow. "Stuff tastes like swill," he muttered. "Okay, I'll check it out and have a talk with my superior. See what he suggests. Maybe we can have another look around Ms. Delaney's woods."

Considering this guy's attitude, and the reaction he'd gotten from the one in the Fish and Game Department's office, Shane didn't hold out a lot of hope for anything happening soon. But at least he'd spoken his mind.

Before he left the rest stop, he asked one more thing from Mark Williamson. "When you talk to Allison, I'd appreciate it if you wouldn't mention this conversation to her. You're investigating again because she called, not because you saw me. Like I said, she's a stubborn and independent woman, and she's used to taking care of things on her own."

"I did get that impression," Mark admitted. "I take it you two are…"

"We are, but that doesn't mean she lets me handle her business, and I doubt that'll change when we get married."

Mark tossed the half-empty Styrofoam cup in the trash container and checked his watch. "Married, huh? Well, good luck with that."

Shane nodded to him as they left the building. Yeah, luck was what he would need if Allison ever found out he'd had the "man-to-man" talk with Mark.

****

Allison sat with Lizzie on the porch, browsing through the wedding magazine she had brought home the day before. Excitedly, her baby girl peered at the pages of flowers and cakes and summer brides. "I think we should do something like this." She turned the magazine so they both could see the beautifully decorated table. "Only we can use our own flowers. The daisies will still be blooming and Grandma Ellie's roses. The pink ones would be especially pretty."

"She'd like that, and so would I."

Allison thought of the fabric she still needed to buy to sew her dress and one for Lizzie for the big day, and the gazillion other things she needed to do.

Why did I ever agree to getting married in two weeks? It would never be enough time.

"This is really crazy. How will we—" Her phone rang just then.

"I'd be so pleased if you'd let me bake the wedding cake for you," Thelma Jackson gushed before Allison could even say hello.

Apparently, word had already travelled.

"Murray and I are just thrilled for you and Shane, and if there's anything else we can do to help, you let me know."

"I really appreciate it." She thought a moment and then added, "There actually is something. Would you be my matron of honor?" After all the kindnesses Thelma had shown them in the past few years, she couldn't think of anyone she wanted more to witness her marriage to Shane.

On the other end, the older woman gasped and then laughed. "Are you sure you want me? It's not like I'm the youngest nor the fanciest gal around here."

"But you are one of the sweetest, and you've done so much for Lizzie and me since…well, since everyone's been gone. I'd really love it if you would do this. It'd mean a lot."

Thelma agreed and said she would email pictures of cakes so she and Shane could choose the one they wanted before just as quickly hanging up.

"Well, that's one less thing to worry about," she murmured and went back to perusing flower arrangements, glad Lizzie had learned about it when she'd entered flowers in the fair. "But we'd better go into town tomorrow and look at dress patterns. I won't have time to do anything too complicated, but I'm sure I can sew up something simple."

They were talking about wearing a wreath of daisies in her hair when the silver SUV pulled into the drive. Her stomach clenched as Ronnie stepped out and made her way to the porch, stumbling a little on the uneven dirt in her usual wedge sandals. She hadn't spoken to her in days. Why was she here now?

Thank goodness Wynkyn chose that moment to get stuck climbing the screen door, and Allison sent Lizzie inside to rescue the adventurous kitten. "Why don't you check their dishes, too? They might need some food." She hoped to stall her daughter's return, in case Ronnie was in a mood.

Quickly, she snatched the magazine and stuck it behind her. "Hi there." Allison pasted on a smile and waved her to sit down. "How's it going?"

Ronnie settled in the chair Lizzie had vacated. "Oh, okay, except I find it a little strange everyone else seems to know but you couldn't tell me."

"Knows what?"

"What's going on with you and Shane."

Fire burned in her throat, but she cleared it and tried to sound nonchalant. "I don't know what you mean."

"Don't play coy with me." Ronnie wagged one manicured finger at her. "Are you or are you not marrying him?"

She heaved a sigh. *Might as well be straight about it all.*

Allison brought out the magazine again and set it back on the table. "We're getting married a week from this coming Saturday."

Ronnie picked at her pale green nail polish. "Seems a little rushed, but I guess since you've known each other for so long, what does it matter? I just wish *you* could have let me know. I had to hear it from Sylvia at the feed store."

She wanted to ask why Ronnie was at the feed store but just said, "I'm sorry. Guess I didn't think I made your list of favorite people anymore. However, you and Jerry are certainly invited, if you'd like to come. We're having it here at the farm, and I'm asking only a few people. We just want it really quiet and simple."

"Well, you know we'll be here." She paused a moment, fingernails tapping on top of the magazine, then her expression lit up with an eager smile. "I've got an idea! Why don't we take Lizzie camping with us? Jerry took our travel trailer to the state park for the summer. He and Lizzy can go fishing, and there's a beach. It'll be a great little vacation for her, and you and Shane can spend some time alone. Unless you already have a honeymoon planned? In that case, she can stay longer—"

"No, no honeymoon," Allison cut into her excited rambling. "I can't get away from the farm, and he's taking over Doc Brewster's practice permanently. So we'll just be staying here." She wasn't so sure she liked the thought of her baby going away with Ronnie for more than a few hours, but it *was* very generous of her considering, and Lizzie always had a good time with her exuberant aunt. "I'm sure she'd love to go for a day or so, and…thank you, Ronnie, for trying to understand. I know it's hard to accept the truth about all this, but—"

"It's all best left in the past at this point. No sense in going on about it, and besides, it's not Lizzie's fault." Ronnie picked up the magazine and began to flip through it.

"What's not my fault?" Lizzie pushed open the screen door and came out, carrying a plate of the peanut butter cookies she'd baked earlier.

"Nothing, honey," Allison took one of the cookies and leaned over to kiss the imp's cheek. "Nothing at all."

She spent the next half hour paging through the magazine with the two of them; her sister-in-law even ended up offering to help Lizzie with the flower arrangements. While she still wanted to harbor her dislike for Ronnie, Allison found herself relenting and accepting the offer.

She's right. We can't dwell on the past, and it's better to keep the relationship open than let bad feelings eat away at us.

Ronnie left with the promise to pick up some extra vases, and Allison ignored the niggling little worry scratching at the corner of her mind that her sister-in-law was a bit too encouraging.

Chapter 22

Shane sent Sandy home and was ready to close up the clinic early when Allison called him later that afternoon. He immediately heard the tremor in her voice. Had the cat returned?

"No, but something is off with a few of the horses. I don't think it's colic but...I can't tell for sure, and the strange thing is, it's Tank and Melody. They never have any issues. I don't know—"

"I'll be right there." In two minutes, he was in his truck and heading to Allison's Farm. Once there he hurried to the pasture where he could see her standing beside the visibly distressed mare. Melody's head hung down and sweat dampened her flanks. Not far away, Tank, the sturdy dun, appeared to be in the same condition. "When did you notice this?" He ran his hands over the mare's trembling withers and down her front legs, lifting first one hoof and then the other.

"Just when I came out to bring them into the barn. The others appear to be all right...so far. I got them inside, but wanted to wait for you before I did anything further with Tank and Melody."

"First thing we need to do is get them out of here and someplace where I can start treating them."

"For what? What do you think happened?"

Shane cast his gaze around the pasture and spotted something unusual near the far end. He motioned for her to follow him. A small pile of hay was scattered about, with a few pinkish flowers mixed among the alfalfa.

"This is odd." She peered at the hay. "I never feed the horses out here."

He squatted down to scoop up some in his hands and study it, then brushed his palms together before squinting up at her. "I think they've been poisoned."

Her eyes grew large. "But how? I check this pasture regularly for any toxic weeds…and I certainly didn't put out this hay with the weird flowers in it."

"But somebody did." Shane stood, scrubbing his hands on his jeans. If what he suspected was true, there was no time to waste. Motioning for her to follow, he hastened back to the two horses now having respiratory problems. "Let's try to get them closer to the barn." He helped Allison lead them to the round pen. When he'd given each horse a more thorough exam, he went to his truck for the activated charcoal he hoped would lessen the effect of the poison, and an injection to stabilize their heart rates. It might be a longshot, but he was pretty certain the pink flowers were oleander blossoms.

They can do some serious damage. I need to work fast here. If he lost these two patients, Allison would be devastated.

Thankfully, the treatment began to work and the two horses calmed down, their breathing becoming less distressed.

While he continued to monitor them, Allison leaned against the fence and watched as Melody and Tank stood together in the round pen, offering comfort to each other. "This is crazy. How could this have happened?" she muttered.

"I think it's pretty obvious. Somebody dumped the hay in the pasture, and it appears to have oleander blossoms in it. It's not very common around here, but not to say somebody couldn't buy it at a nursery." He studied her reaction to this before adding, "You know this wasn't an accident."

"But who would do it? And why?" Then, answering herself, she added, "They're not going to leave me alone, are they? Not 'til something terrible happens here." She rubbed a hand over her forehead.

"Nothing terrible is going to happen." *Not if I can help it anyway.* He went to stand beside her and drew her against his side. "I won't let it. I'll take some of the hay back to the clinic and have it checked out to make sure." Fury that the Potters could have done this set his blood to boiling, but he had to let it simmer for now and take care of the matter at hand.

Allison turned her face up to him, and it let him know just how badly this latest incident frightened her. Her mouth quivered, and he wanted so badly to kiss it, but that wouldn't solve anything right now. They needed to think clearly, and letting emotions get in the way would just muddle things worse.

He hugged her closer and kissed the top of her head. "We're going to see this through together, Allie, and we'll put a stop to it, once and for all."

Come hell or high water, Duane and Darren won't continue with their tricks any longer.

****

By morning, Melody and Tank were nearly back to normal, and after clearing the pasture of any remaining tainted hay, Allison allowed the rest of the horses to go out. "But I feel like I need to stand guard over them all day," she rued. "What's going to happen next?"

Shane downed the coffee she'd brought to the barn for him. He'd spent the night there, keeping watch over the two, and she could see by his reddened eyes he hadn't slept much. In her mind, he couldn't have done more to prove how much he loved her.

"I hope nothing today. I'm due at the clinic in an hour. I'm pretty sure Melody and her boyfriend will be all right. Just keep an eye on them, and call my cell if there's any change."

Before he could leave, Allison slipped her hand into his and drew him close. "I guess it's a good thing I'm marrying my horses' vet, because we seem to be running up an awfully big bill here." She stood on tiptoe and kissed him quickly. In the early morning light, she brushed her cheek against his roughened jaw. "You don't know what it means to me. How can I ever thank you?"

"I can think of a few ways," he murmured in her ear, "but guess I'll just have to wait. We're going to make it, Allie. You have my word on that."

****

The light from O'Malley's Bar and Grill cast an orange glow over the sidewalk. Shane kept an eye on it from where he stood inside the shadowy doorway of the hardware store across the street. *"They're here most Friday nights,"* he remembered Harry saying. And sure enough a few minutes ago, Duane and Darren had pulled up in the rusted sedan and parked on the main street. He watched them get out and toss their cigarettes before going into the bar.

After waiting a few more minutes, he entered the bar and glanced quickly about, assessing the situation.

The place was hopping tonight with locals as well as people who came to stay out at the lake. The aroma of burgers and fish frying reminded him he hadn't eaten since this morning, but tonight, he had one thing on his mind—to settle a score once and for all.

And try not to land in jail, or worse, doing it.

The Potters stood at the end of the bar. He elbowed his way in and asked the bartender for a draft. Harry was busy delivering baskets of food, limping back and forth. He didn't want to cause trouble for the old guy and knew he should take this outside, but how would he lure the two sleaze balls out there?

Keeping his straw cowboy hat tipped down low on his forehead, he fixed his gaze back on the brothers while he drank the beer, eventually tossing some bills on the counter when he'd finished. Luckily, Duane and Darren chose the same moment to gravitate to the back room's pool table. He waited about three minutes and made his way toward them.

Checking out who else surrounded the table and who hunkered at the video games, Shane made sure Cousin Red or any of the other Potters weren't also lurking about. The brothers stood off to the side, still dressed in their greasy garage clothes but apparently not caring about their appearance. They both carried beer mugs and paid no attention when someone jostled them and the foamy liquid slopped over the sides. Duane threw back his head and laughed at something one of the pool players said while Darren flipped the guy off. Shane had the feeling if he didn't move fast somebody else would beat him to showing the two out the back door.

He slid past the red-haired waitress with her tray

lofted above her head and ran up against a group of guys who, in their designer jeans and boat shoes, were definitely out-of-towners. They fit in about like he did. Tipping his hat to them when they eyed him, he nodded toward the restrooms, and they let him by.

The younger Potter saw him coming, and his mouth grew slack with recognition. Before he could poke his brother, Shane sidled up, reached around him, and took the beer mug from his hand to set it on a nearby round table.

"What the hell?" The jerk stumbled but wheeled around. His brown eyes grew black with hate. "What do you think you're doin', McBride? We ain't botherin' you any."

"Oh, but you are," he assured him and started pushing him toward the door. "And I need to talk to you about it. Outside." Darren tried to step in, but he knocked him aside with one swipe of his hand. "Stay out of it. This is between me and your brother."

Thankfully, the back door of the bar opened out. He shoved the animal abuser through it and into the alley. The shorter man almost went down but regained his balance when he reached him.

Duane lifted his hands as if in surrender. "You outta your mind, McBride?"

"Not yet, but I may be soon." He kept his distance, not believing the jerk would give up so easily. "We need to talk."

Thin lips curled over a weak chin. "Just what is it we need to talk about?" he sneered. "Or maybe you need some advice."

Shane snorted. "What advice would I need from you?"

"I hear you and Allison are gettin' hitched soon." He spit tobacco into the alley.

"Why is that any of your concern?" *And how dare you even mention her name.*

A sly smile creased the grimy face. "Thought you might need to know how to keep your relationship with her from goin' south this time. She's a mighty pretty woman, and I'm not sure you're man enough to keep her happy."

His blood started to boil. "What's between my future wife and me is none of your damn business, but here's what is." He poked a finger in the puny chest. "You need to keep the hell away from her and her horses."

The creep squinted at him. "And your kid?"

Like he'd been sucker-punched, Shane exhaled a sharp breath. Had the whole damn world known but him?

"Yeah, we all figured she was yours. She sure as heck wasn't Jason's. You thought he wanted your girl? Ha! Not by a long shot."

"Would you stop talking out your ass and—"

"You never figured it out?" Duane ran on, "Jason liked boys. But he was afraid of his daddy, so maybe he thought marryin' Allison in her time of need was one way to try and get himself straight. Don't know how it worked out, seein' how they didn't have any more kids."

The sudden truth shining a light on a lot of things blind-sided Shane for a split second, just enough time to let his guard down and for Duane to land a fist to his gut.

The air knocked out of him, he went down,

skidding across the gritty pavement as something sharp dug into his knee. The next second, the fist met his face. Blinding pain shot through his jaw and seared like white fire into his cheek as his head snapped back and the straw cowboy hat went flying. Behind his eyes, stars lit up the night as a second blow jolted his body against the black gravel of the street, his hands stinging as they slid through shards of broken glass.

His bells ringing, Shane shook his head to clear the flashing lights and tried to get up, only to get a clip to his jaw. Another split his lip, and a trickle of warmth slid down his chin. Struggling to open his eyes, he saw Duane had backed away, but what was that sound? Had the back door opened? From the corner of his puffing eye, he spotted Darren, then…

Click!

The year he'd spent in juvenile hall had taught Shane a few tricks. Had taught him to recognize that sound, and he flung himself away just in time to avoid the nasty little knife Darren wielded. It sang through the air and missed him by inches. He rolled to the left through a pile of soggy trash and somehow managed to get back on his feet, his brain still spinning.

Images came back to him in a rush, the way these two had treated the dogs he and Doc had cared for ten years ago, the way they'd laughed about it, and how they'd let their cousin do the shooting at him that night. The way they'd leered at Allison and the grief they'd caused her. It was more than anyone needed to stand, and he wasn't standing for it anymore.

Darren jumped, and the knife came close enough to slice through Shane's shirt, but not enough to hold him back from bringing a clenched fist up to send the knife flying and the other down on his attacker's surprised head. When the younger Potter sprawled in the alley, he spun around in time to grab his brother by the neck and pin him up against the brick building.

The door swung open, shedding more light and sound on the alley.

"Don't do it! He's not worth it."

"Stay away, Harry," he growled and pressed his thumbs into the scrawny throat.

"Screw you," Duane rasped out.

He pushed harder. When the black eyes bulged and a gasp for air squeaked out, the need for vengeance surged through him.

"Let up on him, or I'm calling the sheriff," the bar owner warned and hobbled closer.

Shane stared into Duane Potter's eyes and saw a flicker of fear begin to grow.

Good.

Ever so slightly, he eased pressure on the man's windpipe but kept his grip tight. "No more." He tasted the blood running into his mouth. "Harry's right. You're not worth losing my family again, but know this. *No. More.* If you so much as set foot on that farm, so much as breathe the same air as my wife and child, you best look over your shoulder, because I *will* be there to finish this."

He shoved the wheezing man away from him and watched in satisfaction while he stumbled over to where his brother still sat on the ground shaking his head. Feeling woozy himself, he went to pick up the knife and click it closed, then handed it to Harry.

"Sorry to have caused this trouble."

The old man shook his head but took the knife and

slipped it into his shirt pocket. He gingerly touched Shane's jaw. "You best get on home and let Allison take care of that. It's not pretty."

He nodded and started to go back inside, but one last memory of the past reared its ugly head, the one of the Potters drunk and cheering alongside the pit with the fighting dogs the night he'd discovered the ring. Without saying a word, he went to where Duane stood now and landed his fist straight into his nose. He thought he heard a crunch, and a sense of deep satisfaction burned in his blood.

Just as he started to leave, one of the out-of-towners handed him his hat. "Hey man, best fight we've seen in a while." The guy gave a thumbs up.

Jamming his hat on his splitting head, he walked away. Every bone in his body ached right now, but it was all worth it.

For sure they'll leave Allison alone now. He was certain of it.

Chapter 23

"I cannot believe this. You, in a knife fight, a common bar brawl." Allison pulled out a chair at the kitchen table and sat him down. "What were you *thinking*?" Shane had shown up on the porch, clearly still reeling, and her first reaction had been to want to clock him one herself.

"Well...for starters...it wasn't in the bar." He formed the words slowly. "It was...an alley brawl, and second...I wasn't thinking."

She took his chin in her hand and turned his head to study the bruises, and black eye, and split lip swelling as she watched it. Then she saw the blood trickling from the back of his hand and the crimson stain on his shirt. Turning his hands over, she noted the grit and a glass shard sticking up.

This is more than I can handle. "Maybe we should take you to the ER. This doesn't look good."

"Nah, just...fix me up like you would one of your horses. I'll be fine."

"If you were one of my horses, I'd be calling the vet," she scolded. "Oh wait, *you* are the vet."

He tried to grin but winced instead. "Just get the peroxide and a couple of bandages," he mumbled.

She went for the first-aid kit that had become rather popular of late. With a peroxide soaked cotton ball, she dabbed at the corner of his mouth first and almost laughed when he used a word she'd never heard him say before. His hand bore a small slice; he said it was from when he'd knocked the knife away from Darren.

A knife! He could have been killed!

She cleaned it up and removed the glass shard with tweezers and plastered it all with antibiotic cream and the wide bandages. Then she demanded he shed his shirt.

"This is retribution for making me show you the bruises on my leg," she muttered and bent to the thin cut that zig-zagged in a broken line across his belly, just above his belt. She didn't like the looks of it and soaked another cotton ball to dab at it.

He swore again.

"I'm sorry," she breathed, suddenly thinking of what might have happened to him…and all because of her. "You shouldn't have done this. It wasn't necessary."

Grimacing, he grabbed her hands and pulled her back up to face him. "It was, and it was worth more than a few cuts. They won't bother us again."

"How do you know?"

He wiggled his jaw to loosen it up and eased her onto his lap. "Because I made sure of it."

"How can you be so sure?" She rested her arms on his shoulders and pressed her forehead against his. "How can we trust them?"

"Well, all I can say is I warned them, and not in a gentle way. I don't think Duane and Darren will come looking for any more trouble."

Allison sighed and touched her lips to his forehead. "You've always been my hero, Shane McBride. Did you know?" Had she ever told him?

"Afraid I haven't always been a very good one, but if you want, you can show me your appreciation."

She dared to ask, "How?"

"You can kiss me…" He raised one hand and touched his split and swollen lip. "Here."

Oh Shane. What will I ever do with you? But softly, she did as he asked.

With a raspy, "Ow," he moved his finger to the other side. "And over here."

She kissed where indicated, and then he turned and met her lips full on. It was a barely-there kiss, but oh so tender, and Allison's heart suddenly filled to brimming. How had she ever lived without him?

How will I live with him?

"Where's Lizzie?" he asked, moving his knees to bring her closer.

"In her room." She shifted on his lap to avoid the cut and in doing so gave him access to slipping his hand up inside her T-shirt. He stroked along her stomach and then moved farther while pressing feather-light kisses along her cheek and down to the small pulse pounding in her throat, all the while murmuring soft "ows" each time his lips moved. Wherever he touched her, her skin quivered until she knew this had to stop.

"I don't think this is a good idea," she gasped and stopped his hand from traveling to the hooks on her bra.

"Best cure I know of…ow."

"Shane, you have to let me see that cut on your stomach. It's—"

"You can kiss it, too," he offered.

"Not a chance." She scooted off his lap and out of reach, just as Lizzie entered the kitchen with her arms full of kittens and Gypsy close behind.

Allison quickly straightened her clothes as the collie ambled up to Shane and laid her muzzle on his knee. Apparently, he was her hero, too.

The smile Lizzie first flashed him dissolved in an instant. "Da—ad, I mean Shane! What happened?" She deposited the kittens in their bed in the corner and approached him with her blue eyes wide. "You're hurt. Who did this to you?"

Shane looked to Allison for help, but she backed off. "You better tell her." Once again, this was his call, and she wasn't going to cover for him.

He pulled his shirt back on and did his best to button up and cover the jagged wound. "I'm sorry you had to see this, Shortstuff. I just took care of some bad guys."

"Looks more like they took care of you," her ever-honest daughter countered. "I hope they look as bad."

"Lizzie!" Allison started at the remark.

"Well, it's true, I hope they do." She touched the red welt on his cheek. "Was it the Potter brothers?"

He glanced at Allison. Perhaps in silent surprise that Lizzie knew who did this, too?

"Yes, and someday I'll explain it all to you, but right now, it's not important you understand." He covered her small hand with his own. "I just want you to know you and your mom are safe now I'm here. I'll make sure of it."

Lizzie took a moment to absorb it all then turned to her mother. "We better get him fixed up, or he won't look so good for the wedding."

As usual, their daughter was right.

****

Allison put the last stitch in the hem of the dress

and pulled it through the machine Grandma Ellie had taught her to sew on when she was not much older than Lizzie. Now there was only a little hand sewing left to do. Together, they'd chosen the patterns and material for both their dresses, and she'd worked on them every night this week, barely getting to bed before she needed to get up again. But at least planning for the wedding helped keep her mind off the threats to her farm—the incident in the pasture…and the big cat.

There'd been no other sign of the predator. No other nights with restless horses kicking in their stalls.

Maybe my bad shot scared it off for good.

She had to hope because Mark Williamson hadn't been around to investigate the report she'd called in. The man could be such a jerk.

Forcing those thoughts away, she turned the dress right side out and shook it. Her baby girl would be so cute in the buttercup yellow and cream confection.

"I'm going to wear my best boots with it," Lizzie had declared when they picked out the pattern. "I think it'll look really cool. You should, too, Mom."

"We'll see," Allison had mused. "I'm not sure they'll go with my dress."

Her simple ivory lace and pale peach sheath hung on the dressmaker's form, waiting for her to hem it tonight…if she could keep her eyes open. She wasn't sure about wearing boots with it, but the flowered wreath her daughter promised to fashion for her hair would be just perfect.

Too bad Mom and Dad can't come home this one time. A swift stab of pain brought tears to her eyes.

When she called their condo, the housekeeper had told her they were on a month-long cruise on the

Danube, and then going to the Mediterranean to celebrate their thirty-fifth anniversary.

She swiped at her eyes and pushed away the disappointment, deciding these were the last tears she'd shed for the parents who couldn't be bothered with their own child.

Allison was just getting up to slide the yellow dress on a hanger when she heard Shane's footsteps in the hall. As they neared the sewing room, she jumped to the doorway to keep him from coming inside and collided with his tall frame.

"Whoa, hey, what's the deal?" He grabbed her arms to steady them both.

"You can't see my dress!" She kept him from moving through the door, inched him out, and closed it behind her. "It's a secret."

"Secret, huh? So, is that why you've been burning the midnight oil?" He had set up a cot in the barn and spent most nights there this past week. In spite of the longing kisses he gave her every night, he refused to sleep in the house again until they were properly wed, "out of respect for our daughter," but wanted to stay close for safety's sake. It made her love him even more, and just knowing he was close by had given her peace of mind.

"Maybe, but are you spying on me?" She gave him a teasing, sidelong glance.

"Just in hopes of catching a glimpse of your silhouette in the window." He dipped his head and stole a kiss before she could protest.

Allison gave up and wrapped her arms around his middle. "It doesn't seem possible," she murmured.

"What doesn't?"

His hands stroking down the curve of her back set off little shocks of awareness.

"In just a few more days we'll be together, forever and always." She still had to pinch herself sometimes to make sure she wasn't dreaming it all.

"And always," he added, then pulled her arms from around him, and taking her by the hand, tugged her toward the living room where he sat her down on the couch and took his place beside her, but didn't touch her again.

She knew by now this meant there was something important he had to say and drew her legs up beneath her in her best listening pose. "What's up?"

Shane leaned forward a little and clasped his hands together in front of him, a nervous gesture she recognized. Whatever he needed to talk about made him uncomfortable.

"There's something I think you should know, something I just found out but should have realized a long time ago."

"About us?" Her heart beat a painful thump.

He faced her. "In a way, but mainly a truth I hope will give you some closure. Us some closure."

"I don't understand."

"It's about Jason, and how he…how he really was. I guess we just never realized."

What on earth is he talking about? His clenched hands and set jaw had her worried. "Shane, would you please just tell me what it is?"

He closed his eyes, as if thinking before he spoke. "When you told me you and Jason never…that you slept together but you never made love, I had a hard time believing it, because I always thought he was in love with you, too, and maybe he was, in his own way."

"I guess if he was I didn't live up to his expectations, because I'm not lying when I tell you nothing ever happened between us. Not before Lizzie was born nor after." Something she'd learned to live with the years they were married, and yet she'd never understood. "But like you said, that's all in the past. So why does it even matter?"

His steady blue gaze met hers. "Because I want you to know it was never about you, Allison. It was about Jason, and how he felt…about me." He shifted uneasily. "Jason had more to hide from his family than not wanting to go to college and play football. They never would have accepted him for who he really was. Do you know what I'm saying?"

Allison studied him as memories surfaced. Uncertainty when Jason offered to marry her, the gratitude for his caring, but then relief when she'd never had to share what she'd only ever shared with Shane. How she hadn't wanted to try and figure it out when he'd turned his back to her; how he'd barely ever kissed her. Sinking every emotion into caring for her daughter and the horses, and how she'd been glad when Jason didn't seem to want any more from her than dinner on the table and her presence at the Delaney holiday parties. At first, she had questioned and blamed herself. Then she had just been relieved.

She nodded slowly. It all made sense now, though not any easier to understand…for either of them by the way Shane glanced away from her, as if reluctant to say anymore, to speak the truth in plain words.

"I—I honestly never knew," she admitted. *Although, I always knew there was something he would never talk about.* "Poor Jason, to think he had to live a lie and never got to be himself."

Tears welled in her eyes, and she couldn't help but remember that, in spite of his never showing her any intimate affection, he was only ever kind and protective of her and Lizzie. The day her daughter had been born, Jason stayed with her throughout it all.

"I can only hope we gave him some measure of happiness in those years we were together."

Shane sighed, and hands on his knees, pushed himself up from the couch. "I've got some early barn calls in the morning, so I best get some sleep."

Allison ached to reach out and hold him, because she sensed his personal turmoil in all this. "You can stay here." She motioned to the couch. "It'll be okay."

He turned, and just for a moment, leaned down to touch her face. The cuts by his mouth were almost healed, and the bruises were fading away, and she wanted to kiss them all again.

"I think we need this one night to process all this, and then to put it in the past where it belongs before we start our new life together." He ran his hand over her hair before he straightened.

She nodded and before he left the room said softly, "Thank you for telling me. I love you."

Later, curled in her bed alone, she couldn't stop thinking about shattered friendships and lives changed forever, and how they'd all suffered.

If only we'd known the truth, how different things might have turned out.

****

After doing one more barn check for the night, Shane stretched out on the lounge chair in the tack room. Clasping his hands behind his head, he thought about the conversation with Allison. How could she not have known about Jason? She'd lived with him for six years. Yet, by her own admission, she'd been okay with the arrangement she and Jason had come to and never questioned it, because it had served her as well as it did him. For that reason, maybe she'd never let herself wonder why it was only friendship they shared. Because to know more would have been to jeopardize the arrangement. Was that Jason's purpose as well?

Was that why he had never let himself see the truth, either?

He could only wonder now if there had been signs. Things he'd shut out, because the truth wasn't something he wanted to know.

Now he did know the truth, it didn't matter anymore. Jason was gone. Life went on, and the life he'd always wanted with Allison was about to become a reality. That was his future.

But in his heart, he knew he would never forget what lay in the past.

Chapter 24

It was nearly perfect. The day. The flowers. The late afternoon sun shining across the pastures and the old orchard of Allison's Farm. Most of all, the man waiting for her at the rose arbor, just below the walkway Lizzie and Ronnie had strewn with fragrant petals.

I wish you and Pop were here, Grandma Ellie. Then I would have a dream come true.

Thoughts of her grandparents had filled her mind this morning, and as she hesitated but a moment before going down the walk, a tiny, painful lump formed in her throat. She swallowed it down, but tears still brimmed in her eyes.

"We're here, Allie. We've always been here. Now go, meet your young man and live a happy life."

Where the thought came from she wasn't sure, but it calmed her as if she'd received a warm hug from the two people she had so loved.

A pair of mourning doves cooed from the willow tree, and Allison's hands trembled as she clutched her bouquet of daisies and baby's breath.

"Are you okay, Mom?" Lizzie stood at her side and touched her arm. "Is something wrong?"

She smiled down at her sweet daughter in her handmade, yellow dress and cowboy boots. "I am just fine, and everything is perfect."

The three musicians Ronnie's husband, Jerry, had employed for the day struck up the first few chords of "The Wedding Song," a tune that had been one of her grandmother's favorites. She waited while Thelma and Lizzie walked ahead of her and then set out to start her new life. When Shane put out his hand to her, she took it, catching the wink Matthew Brewster, the best man, sent her way. Doc stood next to Thelma now, leaning on his cane but not bothering to hide a big grin.

She handed her bouquet to Lizzie in order to join hands with Shane. Before she knew it, they'd spoken their vows, exchanged rings, and made their promises, and the preacher pronounced them husband and wife.

"You may kiss your bride, Dr. McBride."

One of the horses—Allison was pretty sure it was Starlight—whinnied loudly from her view in the nearby pasture and was quickly joined by several others.

"Do you think we have their approval?" Shane murmured against her lips.

"I think so." Smiling, she leaned into him and his heart beat sure and strong against her own. "Around here, you know that's everything."

Lizzie hugged them both and grasped them each by a hand. To the sound of everyone's applause, and with a full heart, Allison left the arbor with the two people she loved most in the world.

The next few hours passed in a blur. Thankfully, Jenny took pictures, and Sandy and Ronnie handled the caterer set up on the porch.

"How did you manage to plan all this?" She turned to Shane, who was shaking Jerry's hand. "I didn't expect it." He just winked at her.

Later, after Murray made the last toast, Jenny,

Lizzie, and Thelma cut and served the three-tiered, ivory and peach cake. To their cheers, Allison tossed her daisy bouquet, and Carrie, the vet tech, caught it while the musicians played a final song.

As everyone began to wander home, Allison followed Lizzie upstairs while her daughter changed and got her bags for the camping trip.

"Are you sure you want to go with Aunt Ronnie and Uncle Jerry?" She helped stuff a few more books in the backpack. "If you'd rather stay home, it's okay—"

"Aunt Ronnie said you and Shane need some time alone." Lizzie grabbed her teddy bear and her pillow. "I'll be fine, but you'll look after the kittens, right?"

"Yep. They're not so much trouble now they can eat kibble. I'll try to keep them out of mischief, though." She sat on the edge of Lizzie's bed and drew her baby girl into her arms for a hug. "Thank you for everything you did to help today, fixing the flowers and serving the cake. It was lovely." Hard to believe it was over already, that she and Shane were married, and they were a family now. She pressed her face into her little girl's hair and held back a few tears.

Lizzie let her hold her for a minute but broke away sooner than Allison wanted to let her go.

"I'm glad you and Shane got married, Mom. It'll be nice having him here all the time." She turned to pick up her bags. "I better get back downstairs. Aunt Ronnie said they're all ready to go, so we can get to the park before it's too late."

A sudden twinge of doubt about the whole idea pricked at Allison.

Change your mind, Lizzie.

It was probably just anxiety from all the changes

lately—even her little girl was growing up. But still, on the way to the stairs she ducked into her bedroom to snatch her phone from the dresser. Luckily, she'd charged it last night and hadn't used the device all day.

"Here, I want you to take this with you." She unzipped a pocket on the backpack and shoved it inside. "Shane's number is entered and of course our house number. If for any reason you want to call me, you can." On second thought, she stuffed the charge cord into the pocket and zipped it closed. "Or just text me. Okay?"

"I will, but you're being silly. You and Shane are going to be too kissy kissy to worry about me."

Allison chuckled, but before she could say anymore, Lizzie gave her a quick hug, hurried down the stairs, and climbed into Ronnie and Jerry's silver SUV. She watched Shane stop at the car window and speak with them a moment before they drove off.

Her daughter's small hand waved as they pulled from the drive, and she waved back. A lump swelled in her throat, but she knew it was just the high emotions of the day finally catching up to her.

****

Shane finished taking down the last of the folding tables and slid them into the back of Murray Jackson's truck. Thelma had sent leftover cake home with the last departing guests and was now finished cleaning up. She removed her frilly apron and came up to him.

"Everything's done, and I put the top layer of the cake in the freezer. You can tell Allison."

He slammed the tailgate of the truck shut. "The top layer. For what?"

"Your first anniversary, silly. You're supposed to

eat it on your first anniversary." She looked past him toward the house. "Your bride appears a little peaked. She's had a busy week, and I think you need to go be with her now."

Exactly what he wanted to do.

Allison stood on the porch watching the last of the day's sunlight fade over the old orchard. Gypsy stood beside her, ever watchful with his wife's hand resting on the collie's head.

Is she happy?

The question twisted his stomach into a knot. Crazy, but the one thing he had always wanted had suddenly come true, and now here he was afraid…that they'd rushed into this…that maybe she didn't really…

She turned his way, and her gaze seemed a little wistful. But then she smiled, and the knot in his stomach dissolved. He knew she still worried about the big cat making another appearance, as did he, but thank goodness there'd been no more sighting in the past two weeks, or anymore strange happenings at the farm, and all had gone well today.

"Thanks so much for everything." He turned to shake Murray's hand again and drop a kiss on Thelma's flushed cheek. "We couldn't have done this without your help."

"How about us?" Jenny spoke up as she and her friend, Jeremy, brushed hay from their hands and clothes. "The horses are fed and tucked in the barn for the night. They should all be happy as clams."

"Thanks to you guys, too." Shane winked at Jenny who promptly blushed. "You're the best."

He waited until they'd all pulled their vehicles onto the road, then taking a deep breath, he headed up to the house and his new wife on the porch.

She still wore the lacey dress, though she was barefoot, and the flower wreath had side-slipped into the soft curls tumbling from the loose topknot she'd fastened earlier. She was so soft and beautiful and enticing. But her lips pressed together tightly when he joined her. Thelma was right. His wife did look a little tired. His instinct was to swoop her up and carry her inside and make them both forget all the worries and heartaches of the last ten years, but there was time. For right now, he knew the thing she needed most was a chance to unwind.

"Let's sit for a while." He took her hand and pulled her toward the swing, the place where, years ago, they'd shared their first kiss.

Allison pushed it slowly back and forth while crickets chirped, and a soft evening breeze brought them the scent of rose petals now lying in the dew-damp grass.

"Doc is recuperating well. I'm so glad he was able to be here for you." She rested her head on his shoulder. "It was nice, the way everybody helped out and made it so special today. Lizzie's flowers were beautiful, and the cake was lovely and—"

"Ah, before I forget, Thelma said to tell you the top layer is in the freezer. We're supposed to eat it next year, on our first anniversary." *Not sure why we want to do that, but whatever.*

Allison snuggled closer and sighed. "Dear Thelma. She remembers everything."

A night bird twittered in the oak tree as her fingers trailed down his arm where he'd pushed up his shirtsleeves. His pulse quickened. She tipped her head back, and the touch of her gaze warmed his skin.

"What do you think it will be like a year from now? What will we be like? Where will we be?"

Shane kept her hand from moving back up his arm and laced his fingers through hers to hold it still. "I would like to think we'll be right here, sitting in this old swing, and listening to all the sounds that make Allison's Farm such a special place."

"It's the most I could hope for."

He couldn't wait any longer and turned his face to hers, their lips just a breath away from touching. "As long as I'm with you, Allie, it doesn't matter where I am. We just never need to be apart…not ever again."

He kissed her then, and all the lonely nights he'd ever spent in his life drifted far into the past.

When the sun was only a dim glow over the orchard and a breeze had carried away the last of the day's warmth, Allison yawned and shivered against him. He needed to get his bride inside before she fell asleep in the swing.

Keeping a hold of her hand, he drew her along with him and opened the screen door, turning to the collie. "You coming, too?"

Gypsy wagged her plumy tail and hurried to her pillow in the corner of the kitchen where the three kittens were already snuggled together. When he closed the door, Shane knew he was finally home.

In the living room, Allison turned on the old-fashioned stereo Pop and Grandma Ellie had once played, and she hummed as the classic country songs she had grown up listening to wrapped their melodies around her. Removing the flower wreath from her hair, she set it on the bureau that displayed all the pictures of her life. Soon the wedding photo of her and Shane and Lizzie would join them.

She touched the one of Lizzie with her crooked front tooth. "I hope she's okay," she murmured.

The comforting weight of Shane's hands came to rest on her shoulders.

"I'm sure she's in dreamland about now, but if you want, we'll go get her tomorrow."

She loved him all the more for saying that and turned to him. "Really? You won't mind?"

He touched her hair where the curls had fallen on her shoulders. "I love her, too, and I want her here, with us. But tonight, tonight is ours."

She smiled and raised her arms to encircle his neck. Closing the small space between them, she moved slowly with him around the room, relishing his warmth against her while the music played. Moment by moment, she fell into a world where only the two of them existed.

I want to remember every moment of this night, every kiss, every touch, every whisper.

Had she murmured it aloud? Or was it the connection she and Shane had always shared? So that he knew what she wanted without her asking. So that she felt cherished and loved as only Shane could love her.

"Let's go upstairs." She turned off the stereo and led him to the steps.

It took a while to reach her room, what with stopping every step or two to kiss and laugh about some silly remark. Once there, it didn't take so long for Shane to unzip the peach and ivory lace dress and slip it from her shoulders. It puddled at her feet, soon joined by the satiny slip, her "something old" to wear.

The pearl snaps of Shane's western shirt gave way easily beneath her fingers, though her hands shook a little as she tugged it free from his belt. How was it possible she was nervous? She knew him so well...and yet this was somehow different tonight.

"Let me finish." He turned away to take off his shirt.

She took the moment to drape the dress she'd worked all week to finish across a chair in the corner.

My wedding dress!

She hadn't worn one when she married Jason. The long-held dream, the one she'd put aside years ago, had finally come true.

The warmth of Shane's strong arms encircled her from behind, and he nuzzled the back of her neck. Her knees almost betrayed her, but he slipped one arm beneath them and lifted her as if she weighed nothing. When he put her down gently on the bed, he turned away long enough to open the nearby window a little wider, to let in the warm breeze stirring in the late July night. Then he slipped in beside her, and Allison sighed.

"Will o' the wisp," she murmured and slid her hands over his broad shoulders. "It's like that."

"What is?"

He began a chain of feather-light kisses that started at her collarbone and trailed down to her breasts. The brush of his whiskers against her suddenly hot skin sent waves of desire surging everywhere.

"This is." She tangled her fingers in his dark hair he'd let grow a little too long of late. "Something you're not quite sure is there. Something so fragile, so elusive you're afraid if you look away, it will be gone."

"It won't be, Allie. Not ever again. That's my vow."

Her breath caught in her throat, and she arched against him. Soon her soft gasps met his, and then words no longer were important. Only his touch, lifting her to the place she could only fly with him, only the secret whispers following the ascent, and then the sinking back down into a golden cloud that rivaled the will o' the wisp in its glow.

****

Shane listened to Allison's soft breaths, each one tickling across his chest. She slept deeply now, and all trace of worry and stress were missing from her flushed pink face. He kissed her forehead, and without waking, she snuggled closer, one hand sliding across his middle and settling in possessively beneath his arm. Finally, he could hold her and let himself relax.

He'd never imagined his life could turn out so perfect and so right. Oh, he'd known since the day he'd stepped onto the Tyler's porch, and she'd opened the door, that Allison was the one, and even after all these years, it was still true. The separation hadn't changed any of the feeling, but the years apart had given them other ways to grow. Now, here they were, together and still in love as ever. Like a priceless gift, they'd been given a second chance, and he would do everything within his power to keep it this way. Everything. *Anything*.

Chapter 25

Mommy!

Allison started awake, her heart beating like she'd run a mile.

Lizzie?

Where had the sound come from? She listened to hear it again. Nothing. Dreaming. She had to be dreaming.

Shane lay beside her, his arm stretched protectively across her. He wasn't a dream. She could still feel the places where his whiskers had rubbed against her skin. Her heartbeat slowed, and she almost nestled back down into his warmth when a flash of certainty that something was wrong brought her fully awake.

Carefully, she slid away from him and the bed with its tossed sheets and coverlet trailing on the floor. Goosebumps raised up on her arms when the curtains drifted out into the room. She shivered and went to the window, pausing before she closed it. What had awakened her? Why this strange sense of unease?

Could the big cat have returned?

She listened for the horses, but no whinnies drifted up from the barn. Somewhere miles away lightning flickered, and a rumble of thunder rolled in the night. Perhaps that's what she'd heard. Just a summer storm. She tried to assure herself with that thought.

Nevertheless, a chill raced up her spine and spiked

along her shoulder blades. She searched in her dresser drawer for a nightshirt, pulling it on before she went to the other two windows in the room. Another flash of lightning streaked across the night sky, this time closer, and the following thunder vibrated the room.

Eyes straining to watch shadows flit across the yard and shimmy up the barn, she rubbed her forehead. *What's bothering me?* She listened for the horses, but the only sound she heard was rain pattering on the roof, and the only shadows were from the long willow fronds and the solid oak's branches. No creature moved out there tonight, and yet something had awakened her with such a resounding jolt. She crossed her arms against a peculiar chill that had nothing to do with the cool air creeping about the room.

Behind her, Shane stirred in the bed. "Allie? Honey, what is it?"

She turned from the window. "I don't know. I just woke up, and thought I heard something."

"The horses?" The bed creaked as he started to get up. "Maybe I should go check—"

"No, it's not them." She was certain of that. "It all seems quiet out there."

Thunder rumbled again, closer still. "Probably just the storm." He lay back down, his voice still husky from sleep. "Come on back to bed."

Was it only the storm? She couldn't say, but just as she turned to join him it was there again.

Mommy!

The sound, the voice, in her head.

"It's Lizzie," she said softly, then, as her stomach jolted, she cried louder, "Oh my God, Shane! We have to go! We have to go now!" She began to grab clothes, underwear, jeans, and a shirt, struggling to get the nightshirt off while her heart raced.

This time, Shane leaped from the bed and grabbed her by the arms. "What are you talking about? What about Lizzie?"

Allison pulled away and fumbled with tugging on her jeans. "She needs us. Something's wrong." In her mind now, there was no question.

He ran a hand through his rumpled hair. "I don't understand, how do you know?"

"I shouldn't have let her go. I knew it didn't feel right. I've known for a while. Why didn't I listen?" She yanked a shirt over her head and shoved her bare feet into some old clogs. She had to get out, had to find her baby. Didn't he understand?

Shane's hand shot out and kept her from leaving the room. "Listen to who? Allison, stop!"

She glared up at him, furious he was just standing there, and desperate to make him understand. "I don't know. I just know something told me Lizzie's going tonight was a bad idea. But I didn't listen, Shane. I didn't listen and now…something's wrong. I know it."

His hands stilled on her as he searched her face, and then he released her and reached for his clothes. As they left the bedroom, Shane's phone sang out. He pulled it from his jeans pocket.

"Is it a call?" In the stairway, she glanced back at him, dread washing through her veins. No call at two in the morning was ever good.

His mouth tensed. "A text." He showed her the screen.

Her eyes focused on the simple message.

—*Scared Mommy! Plse come get me*—

Her legs wilted at the plea. Her baby girl was somewhere…scared. The notion of that tore at her, and she almost crumpled with fear for her safety.

Shane held her up as she quickly typed a reply.

"Come on, Allie. We'll find her." He guided her down the steps and through the darkened house to the kitchen. Jagged flashes of lightning lit up the room. "Maybe it's just the storm scaring Lizzie."

Allison shook her head furiously at him. "She's never afraid of storms. She always sleeps right through them." She grabbed the phone to punch in Ronnie's cell number. It went immediately to voicemail. Her stomach sank.

He snatched her rain poncho from its hook by the door and pulled it over her head. "Probably iffy signal out at the park."

Small comfort. She pushed past him and tore open the kitchen door. Behind her, Gypsy whined, and Shane gave her the quick command to stay.

Dashing out into the night, she found it had turned from a sweet summer dream into a savage torrent, much like her life. Sheets of rain driven by gusts of wind slammed against her, as her heart slammed in her chest. She was soaked before reaching the truck. Shane pulled the driver's door open, and rather than run to the other side, she scooted across the front seat.

Once inside, she had to clench her teeth to keep them from chattering. Water poured off the poncho's hood. When Shane joined her, his hair was plastered to his head. He slicked it back with one hand and shoved the key in the ignition with the other. The truck engine roared to life.

"They were going to the state park. Which one?

This county or—"

"Yes, this county! Please, we have to hurry." She clutched his phone in her hand, praying for another text message. Had Lizzie somehow gotten lost in the park? But why would she go outside? She must be terrified...*especially if she's thinking a big cat might stalk her.* The thought stuck a knife of fresh fear in her pounding heart. *If I thought facing the cougar was terrifying, this is a million times worse.*

Shane jerked the truck into gear, and they pulled from the driveway onto the road as lightning lit up the sky again. "What do you think is wrong? Why is Lizzie afraid?"

Allison stared out into the crow-black night, watching how the wind whipped the trees, trying to push the image of the cougar—and her daughter wandering alone in the woods—from her rattled mind. "I...don't know. Maybe Ronnie left her alone. Or...or maybe it's the Potters. Maybe they went to the park and got her. Maybe they hurt Ronnie and Jerry. They hate all of us." It was a wild idea, but all sense of normality seemed lost. All that mattered was finding her baby girl. She pressed her face to the window and hung on desperately to her sanity.

Shane stepped on the gas, holding tight to the steering wheel and praying the truck didn't hydro-plane on the rain-swept pavement. The state park was twenty miles west, closer to Lake Michigan. Did he remember how to get there? He and Matthew had gone a few times to fish in the creek that wound through it, and once he'd gone with Jason on a hike.

Help me get through to Lizzie now, he asked the friend who had cared for his daughter like his own.

Help us find her!

Water dripped from his wet hair into his eyes. He swiped it away, concentrating on maneuvering around some downed branches in the road while every scenario of what could have happened played out in his mind. Would Ronnie leave Lizzie alone? He'd wring her neck if she did. Could the Potters have done this? Did their hatred for him go so deep they would harm a child? He'd thought the incident in the alley had ended it all…but he couldn't think about the Potters now. He could only drive into the fierce night.

"M-maybe we should go by the Potters' house first, s-see if the car is there." Allison's voice shook. "If it's gone…" She couldn't finish and wrapped her arms around her body, shivering beneath the poncho.

Shane cranked up the truck's heat and tried to be logical. "How would they know where she's at? Would they really go up against Jerry and Ronnie?"

She paused, then said, "Maybe they followed them. Maybe after your fight with them the Potters know this is the only way to get back at both of us."

Does she blame me?

He gripped the wheel harder and gave the truck more gas. When they reached the crossroad, he hesitated. To turn toward the east would take them to the Potter's house but add at least twenty minutes to the way to the park. If he went straight to the park, without knowing the whereabouts of Duane and Darren, they might lose precious time.

In two seconds, he had the truck driving east. They reached the brothers' house just as the first wave of the storm abated. He heard Allison groan at the sight of the decrepit buildings, and eased the truck into the muddy drive. Was the rusted sedan there? Yes, it sat next to the cement building.

"You stay here." He threw the gearshift into park and leaped out, sprinting for the house's screen door that sagged from its hinges. Pounding on it, he yelled out Duane's name. A few seconds later a light came on, and he could hear the man stumbling and cursing.

Potter glared out the window, and when he yanked open the door, his face twisted in anger. "McBride! What in hell do you want? It's two-thirty in the damn morning!" A bandage still covered his broken nose, and, in stained sweatpants and T-shirt, he looked more rough than usual.

"I know what time it is," Shane ground out, "but you need to tell me where my daughter is. If you've done anything to hurt her, I swear I'll kill you both!"

"You're crazy. I don't know what you're talking about."

He attempted to shut the door in his face, but Shane stuck his foot in the way and stepped in closer. Naked fear flared in the dark eyes.

"I'm tellin' you, man, I don't know nothing about your kid. Why're you askin' me where's she's at anyway?"

For some insane reason, Shane believed him. He stepped back down. "We got a text message from her saying she's scared and wants us to come get her."

"And you don't know where she's at?" Duane scratched his head. "Kinda your own stupid fault then, ain't it?"

"She's…with Ronnie," he murmured and ran a hand through his slicked back hair. "Ronnie and Jerry took her camping in the park."

"That crazy bitch? *She's* who's watchin' your kid? Then you better get your butt out there and find her before—"

A deep fear he'd never known in his life formed in the pit of his stomach and clawed its way upward, along with sudden terrifying memories...of Ronnie's anger when, years ago, he'd pushed her away and she'd come at him and dug at his arms with those nails...of his own certainty even then that she was unbalanced...of the way she'd doted on her brother and blamed Allison for Jason's death. In a moment of clarity, it all added up and he knew Duane was right.

Shane lit out for the truck. Allison watched him with wide questioning eyes when he jumped back inside.

"What did he say?"

He started the truck and threw it into gear. "Lizzie's not here, and we need to get to the campground." *Before something happens we'll all regret.*

The next half an hour dragged by with few words passing between them...and no new texts. He knew Allison was terrified and nothing he could say would help. Only finding Lizzie would take away her fear.

Water rushed over the road into Big Pine State Park. Shane didn't have a choice but to slow the truck to a crawl as he drove in, feeling the water lapping against the tires.

"Creek must have gone over." He knew how fast it could happen—he'd once seen a dry bed turn into a rushing torrent in a matter of minutes. "Luckily the campsites are on higher ground." Which didn't mean they, too, couldn't flood.

He drove them deeper into the park until they found the campground. Many of the campers were packing up and getting ready to leave before the next storm hit.

Allison sat forward and scanned each site they passed. "I don't even know what their trailer looks like." She pressed her face against the truck window and stifled a sob. "How could I let Lizzie go? Why didn't I trust it was a bad idea?"

He reached across the seat and put a hand on her quaking shoulder. "Let's hope they're here and everything is fine. Maybe it really was just the storm scaring her or a bad dream." But in his heart, he feared it was more than that, too.

"There! Look!" Allison pointed to a campsite just ahead of them. "Is that Jerry, out walking around?"

He recognized the heavyset man, who just hours ago had laughed at their wedding and shaken his hand. Now he appeared to stumble toward the road, holding onto his head. Shane swung the truck into the nearest opening.

As soon as he stopped, Allison jumped out and ran. When she reached Jerry, she grabbed him by the arms and shook him. "Where is she? Where is Lizzie?" she shouted above the wind that had started to pick up again and blew through the pines.

Jerry stared at her and then at Shane as he approached. "What are you two doing here? What's going on?"

The blank look in the older man's eyes told him Jerry wasn't quite with it. He took his elbow to steer him back toward the trailer at the rear of the campsite. The silver SUV wasn't there.

Allison followed, throwing out questions one after the other. "Where is she, Jerry? Where is my daughter? Lizzie texted me she was afraid. Why? What is going on?"

Shane opened the door to the trailer and let Jerry go inside first. He turned swiftly to Allison. "Did you see his eyes? Something's wrong with him. I'll look around inside, and you just watch him."

"But I need him to tell me where my daughter is!"

Her eyes blazed, and even in the dark he saw the gold fire in them.

"*Our* daughter," he reminded her and let her go inside ahead of him. In the trailer, he pushed Jerry into a chair at the dinette table. "Stay put," he ordered and strode to the bedroom at the back. It was empty, but clothes lay on the bed in disarray, some hanging out of the built-in drawers. Another small bedroom held bunkbeds that hadn't been slept in. There was nothing of Lizzie's in here.

Had their daughter even been here tonight?

He scanned the room for anything, anything to give him a clue. There was nothing.

Back at the dinette, Jerry held his head in his hands and moaned.

"He won't tell me anything. I think he's drunk." Allison went to peer out the tiny window above the sink. "We need to just go out and look for her."

Shane held up a hand for her to wait and crouched next to the older man. "Hey, Jerry? Hey, man, what happened here? Where are Ronnie and Lizzie?"

"I…don't know," he muttered. "I must have fallen asleep early, right after we got here. Lizzie…I remember she wanted a snack. Ronnie fixed her something and made us drinks. Then I...must have blacked out. But I only had the one..."

"You don't know when they left?"

"I woke up when the wind started, but I was so groggy. I looked outside but couldn't see anything with all the rain. I don't know when they left or...or why. Damn, my head hurts."

"Look at me." Shane stood and tipped the man's head back, studying his bloodshot eyes for a second. Then he picked up a short glass from the table. A whitish puddle still sat in the bottom of it. He glanced around the tiny kitchen and spotted a brown prescription bottle sitting on the counter. Reaching past Jerry, he snatched it up and read the label. A common but strong painkiller. He shook the bottle; only two pills remained. "I think you've been drugged, and with the booze, it's no wonder your head hurts, but you'll be okay once it wears off."

"But...I don't understand." Jerry rubbed at his eyes. "Did Ronnie do this? Why would she?"

"Good question. For the same reason she's done a lot of crazy stuff, like poisoning the horses?" Shane met Allison's stunned gaze, silently conveying a truth he hated to accept but which now made too much sense to ignore.

She stared at him in disbelief, but then her expression changed as all the pieces started to come together, and fear flared in her eyes.

"Because she thinks it's my fault Jason died?" Turning to Jerry, she spoke in a trembling voice. "Because she will hurt me any way she can? Because she's always thought I'm a terrible mother and wants my child? Take your pick." She swiped a hand across her face, then jumped when the trailer creaked against the wind's assault.

The rain started again. Car doors slammed and campers shouted as they evacuated the park.

"We need to get out of here before the road is impassable." Shane took the man's arm and pulled him up. "C'mon Jerry, you better come with us. You can help us figure out where she'd take Lizzie."

"I told you, I don't know where she's gone. I don't know why—" The older man sagged a little when Shane started for the door.

"Well, we need to figure it out pretty quick, or should I call the state police and ask them to issue an Amber Alert?" He took his phone from Allison's hand. "Maybe that's just what I should do." His thumb pressed the first number for emergency.

"N-no," Jerry moaned, shaking his head. "She'd never hurt Lizzie. She's always wanted a child. Ronnie's just…"

"Just what? Jealous? A little crazy?" He pressed the second number just as a flash of lightning and crack of thunder joined together to shake the trailer.

"There's no time!" Allison snatched the phone back from him. "Let's just go. I'll call them from the truck."

Shane hauled the older man to the door and opened it into the wind that once more lashed the trees and howled overhead. A small pine went down just a few feet away from the truck but thankfully didn't block the road out. Outside, he pushed Jerry into the back seat and waited until Allison slid across the front. She was shaking again, and Jerry groaned from behind him.

He squeezed his eyes shut for a moment and

hesitated turning the truck key. What should he do? Where did they begin to search for Lizzie?

His phone sang out, and he snapped his head up. Allison leaned over so he could read the text, too.

—*Ringer off so she can't hear. Where r u? Plse, hurry. I'm scared*—

"I'm going to answer her." Her trembling fingers tapped out a reply.

—*We r coming but don't know where to look. Where do u think u r?*—

A few painful seconds passed.

—*So dark. Think going north? At gas station. Connor's Quik Mart. She's coming back. Hurry*—

Shane threw a glance at Jerry in the rearview mirror. "Connor's Quik Mart—any clue where that is?"

The heavyset man leaned forward a little, still holding his head. "We...stayed at a cottage last summer, about seventy-five miles north, off Hwy. 31 on Mirror Lake, town of the same name. I remember passing the gas station on the way."

"Why would she go there?" Shane started the truck and painfully eased it through the flooded campground and around other campers trying to leave.

"She liked it, and I thought we were doing okay, but there...was..."

"Was what? Speak up, Jerry," Allison practically yelled.

"Someone. A man. We...almost separated then but she promised me she wouldn't see him again. But...she did. I found out Ronnie went back without me in the fall."

"And you think that's where she's headed now?"

"Ronnie doesn't know I found out about her

meeting him again, but the gas station isn't far from the lake." Jerry sighed and leaned back. "I love her and didn't want to lose her."

Shane ignored his muttered ramblings. From the corner of his eye, he saw Allison tap in 9-1-1.

"It keeps dropping the call." Desperation laced her voice. "Now it says 'no service.' Stupid phone."

Once on the highway, he glanced at her as she tried again to no avail. Her fear and anguish were palpable, and he had to force himself to keep his focus on the road ahead.

So this was it. They were on their own to find Lizzie. He figured they were at least an hour behind Ronnie, if she indeed was heading for Mirror Lake.

He could only pray she didn't leave again once she got there.

A quick glance to Allison found her staring out the truck window.

"How could I have let Lizzie go with Ronnie all those times?" she murmured on a sob. "I only wanted her to have the things I couldn't give her. I wanted her to have a better life. But how…?"

"Don't do this to yourself, Allie." It was all he could say to try and calm her. "We will find her. I promise you." It was as solemn a vow as he'd spoken hours earlier.

Chapter 26

Shane pulled into the gas station that loomed up out of the early morning mist. The storms had moved on, but thick fog had enveloped the two-lane highway for the last ten miles, and visibility deteriorated the farther north they went. To the east, a bare trace of dawn glimmered on the horizon, and he hoped the sun would quickly burn off the fog that crept along the ground. A dim light glowed from inside the building. Would the attendant be of any help?

In the backseat, Jerry snored, no doubt still feeling the effects of the drug.

Allison had already clicked open the truck door. "I'm going inside."

"I'm going with you." He knew there was no dissuading her. She'd kept it together this past hour when there'd been no more texts, and he could only follow her as she ran into Connor's Quik Mart.

The guy at the counter was twenty tops with just the beginnings of a mustache. He nodded to them while he stocked a shelf. "You folks are out and about early. Going fishing?"

"Too foggy." Shane squinted his gritty eyes to see the kid's name tag. "But are we close to Mirror Lake?" He made out the name. "Kevin. It's important."

"Yep, sure are. Just keep going down here about five miles." The clerk pointed toward the highway.

"Turn left on Mirror Road. It'll take you right to the lake, another three, four miles."

"Did you see a little girl?" Allison insisted, pushing past Shane to get in the kid's face. "I know they were here. She's about this tall." She held a shaking hand up to her side. "Dark hair, blue eyes. Tell me!"

The kid took refuge behind the counter, but she followed. Shane quickly slid behind it and gripped her shoulder. "It's okay, we're not here to hurt you," he assured the clerk. "We just need to know if a woman and a girl came in here, say around three-thirty?"

Kevin chewed his lip then shook his head. "No kid came in, but a woman did. She filled up, got coffee and a juice."

"Was she driving a silver SUV?"

He thought again, and Shane took a step closer to help him remember.

Kevin moved to the register. "Yeah, maybe. Why do you want to know?"

His patience waned. "What was she driving?"

"It was raining and pretty dark. I really didn't pay much attention." The clerk reached beneath the counter for what Shane suspected might be an alarm button. When he would have grabbed the kid to stop him, Allison put a cautious hand on his arm.

"Please," she all but whispered, begging now. "She has our daughter, and we need to find her."

Kevin met her steady gaze and relented. "Yeah, okay. I really didn't pay much attention, but I think she was driving a light-colored SUV. Only reason I did notice was because it had a taillight out."

"Thank you." She nodded toward the back and then turned and hurried to the ladies' room.

Shane filled three coffees and went back to the register. He pushed a twenty-dollar bill across the glass-topped counter. "Keep the change."

Allison came back, snagged one of the Styrofoam cups, and headed for the truck.

Shane followed with the other two coffees. Inside the cab, he handed one to Jerry, who had roused and was looking around with bleary eyes. He took the cup offered and popped off the lid to blow on it.

"They were here," Shane informed him. "So, does this guy Ronnie was seeing have a place on Mirror Lake?"

Jerry breathed in the steam from the coffee and coughed. "Across the lake from the cottage where we stayed. On the high side. It's pretty steep going up there."

"And you think that's where she's headed."

"She always liked it up here." Jerry hiccupped. "Thought it'd be a good place to raise kids."

Shane blew on his own coffee and kept an eye on Allison as she set hers in the cup holder and checked his phone for messages. Her hands shook in obvious frustration at Jerry's words.

"Can we please just go?" She stared out the window again at the dense fog.

Taking a small gulp of the hot liquid, he was thankful for the caffeine's jolt to his body but then stuck the cup in the holder, started the truck, and pulled back out on the highway, fishtailing on the wet pavement.

"We wanted a family," Jerry rambled, his voice raspy, "but every time Ronnie got pregnant, she lost the baby. She blamed me."

"I'm not sure I understand. How is that your fault?" Or was it just a part of Ronnie's instability?

"Her doctor recommended us to a specialist for high-risk pregnancies, but when she made the appointment, I wouldn't go. I...just got tired of going through all that with her, you know? Seeing her get so excited, only to be devastated. I said it was time to quit trying. I thought staying at the lake would help us just be happy with each other."

Shane reached for his coffee and took another swig. "Instead, she had an affair?"

"She wanted to get back at me, I guess." Jerry hesitated. "What will you do when we find them?"

Shane glanced at him in the rearview mirror. "I don't know. What will *you* do?"

"She's my wife. I can't let her go."

"But she kidnapped our daughter! She could have left Lizzie out of the seedy mess she created!" Allison turned to face her brother-in-law. "She didn't have to drag us into it."

"I'm so s-sorry." Jerry sounded on the verge of tears. "If I'd known she was going to pull something like this, I would never have brought them up to the park. Ronnie's got her problems, but she's always loved Lizzie like her own. She'd never hurt her."

"Just scare her half to death." Allison turned back around. "There! There's Mirror Road." She pointed to the street sign barely visible through the mist.

The two-lane, paved road gave way to one made of dirt and gravel. They soon climbed into the hills that dominated the area, and the fog-filled woods closed in on them. The dirt was soft and slippery from the heavy rain, and even the truck's wide tires had a hard time getting a purchase. A couple of times it started to slide, and Shane gripped the steering wheel tighter.

A sound chimed in the near quiet cab, and glancing over he saw a message light up the phone in Allison's hand.

"So dark...please hurry...hurts," she read, then gasped. "Lizzie's hurt! Oh dear God, where is she? We're coming! Hang tight, baby, we're almost there."

His heart racing, Shane stepped on the gas. *Where are you, Shortstuff?* He tromped on the pedal again, and the truck leaped forward.

Jerry spoke up, as if remembering something. "Watch out up ahead here, there's a switchback. You almost can't see it, and in the dark it's easy to go down the wrong way into the ravine."

Shane slowed just in time to avoid driving off the side of the hill, but the truck's tires slid in the soft dirt and pulled them toward the edge. He steered the vehicle to the right, and it came to rest in the middle of the road.

"I hear it again." Allison's whispered. "In my head. But no new message has come through. How can it..." She clutched the silent phone. "She's here," she murmured and then spoke louder, "Lizzie's here!" She jumped from the truck and ran like a scared deer.

Where was she going? Though he now fully trusted her mother's intuition, he feared she might disappear into the fog.

Flinging open his door, Shane tore after her, catching her just before she went over the edge of the ravine. "What are you doing? You can't just—" He stopped them at the brink and stared down the hill still wrapped in gray, at the line of small, bent trees and flattened brush.

A thin stream of pale daylight forced its way into the woods, and for an instant, the mist lifted to reveal a ghost, something nearly swallowed up by the trees, something that just as quickly disappeared…except for a faint blink…blink…blink of a single red light…like a red will o' the wisp calling to them from what seemed like the end of the world.

His chest tightened painfully.

"Wait." He slipped but ran back to the truck, returning with a high beam flashlight.

He laced his fingers with Allison's and helped her as, together, they went over the edge into the ravine. Briar bushes tore at his clothes. Allison went down on a knee, but he pulled her up. Her sharp breaths matched his own, making him flashback to the rush he'd felt just hours ago. Only now, he rushed with her to something even more precious, something he knew neither of them could live without. Their child. The one he'd made with her ten years ago, who needed him desperately, and who he promised to protect.

The silver SUV, propelled by momentum off the switchback, had plowed through the dense undergrowth of forest and come to rest at the edge of marshland. Not much farther and it would have surely sunk in the scummy water, never to be found.

His stomach lurched at the thought.

The vehicle was still perched precariously, leaning sideways against the trunk of an oak tree that had long-ago lost its battle with the swamp and might at any moment give up the fight. Shane beamed the flashlight over the battered mass. They inched closer and reached the passenger side door. Holding his breath, he peered over his wife's head as she scrambled to look inside. Ronnie lay slumped over the steering wheel against the deployed airbag. The passenger seat was empty. Allison gasped as he shined the light into the back seat…where a small hand sneaked up to lay against the window.

Thank God.

Relief flooded his body, but his pulse thrummed in his ears as he reached for the door handle and it didn't give. They heard a soft cry.

"Lizzie? Lizzie honey, we're here," Allison assured her. "We're here, and we'll have you out in no time. Just stay calm, okay?"

His baby girl sat up on her knees and pressed her face to the window. "It's stuck! I tried to get it open, and I couldn't," she called out. Then she started to cry. "I couldn't open the door, and Aunt Ronnie…she's—"

"It'll be all right," Allison promised. "Just hang on." She turned back to him with a terrified plea in her eyes. *Save our child!*

Shane made his way to the other side of the SUV and surveyed the damage. Afraid to jostle it too much, he tried that door and it gave just a bit. He tried once more, but it wouldn't budge. Then he heard the tree start to creak.

"We've got to get them out!" Allison's voice bordered on panic mode. "What can we do?"

He stepped back and looked around for something, anything he could use to break a window. The mist started to lift, and pale light seeped into the ravine just enough to reveal broken limbs and a few small rocks. He picked up one rock and went to the window where Lizzie peered out at them, tears streaming down her face.

From above them, Jerry called out, "What's happening? Are they down there?"

"They're trapped, we can't open the doors!" Allison shouted and once more laid her hand against the window where their terrified daughter pressed hers.

Jerry crashed down the hillside, calling Ronnie's name. In seconds, he lunged for the SUV.

"Get back," Shane warned, yanking him away. "I'm going to break a window so we can get them out. I can't tell what shape Ronnie's in. We'll have to get her help, but we can't wait for them to get here." He approached the window where Lizzie waited. "Can you hear me, Shortstuff?"

She wiped her nose on her sleeve and nodded.

"I need for you to move to the other side, then I want you to close your eyes and cover your face with something. Do you have your jacket or a blanket?"

She leaned down and ran her hands around and came up with a plaid car blanket.

"Good! That'll work. Now move slowly, over to the other side, and cover your face."

"I'm scared." Her voice was muffled but she did as instructed.

"That's my brave girl. Now crouch down a little and don't be scared. I'm coming in after you in just a minute."

Shane glanced at Allison and saw the light that shone in her eyes, reflecting all her love and trust in him. She said he'd always been her hero. He didn't want to be a hero, not for anybody, but he didn't have a choice.

Please God, let me be worthy of their love and trust.

Heaving the stone back in his grip, he brought it forward with all the strength he possessed…and then some. Once, twice, three times, and the glass spider-webbed and fell away. His hand and the rock went through the window, jagged edges scraping against his arm. "Help me get the glass out."

Allison already pulled at what remained in the frame while Jerry stood back and moaned.

"Here, give me your rain poncho." He held out his hand to her.

When she'd ripped it off, he set it over the broken glass still sticking up in the window frame and leaned through the opening. The vehicle creaked and groaned. Lizzie cried out.

"It's okay now, Shortstuff." He spoke quietly. "I'll take you out of here. Just come to me."

She pulled the blanket from her face and put out her hands to him.

"Slowly now, just inch your way over here."

In a moment she reached him. "Daddy," she sobbed and grabbed his arms. He'd never known anything as sweet as when he pulled her small body against him and slowly eased her through the window.

Thank you, he breathed.

Then they both collapsed on the wet muddy ground. Holding his child to his chest, he bowed his head over hers and thanked God and all the angels above that she was safe.

"I knew you'd come for me, Daddy. I knew you would." She tightened her embrace around him.

For a second Shane let the precious word sink into his brain. *Daddy.* "I think Mom wants to see you." His voice was husky as he pushed tangled hair from her tear-stained face. "She's the one who heard you and told me we needed to come."

Lizzie reached for Allison who swept her up and hugged her close.

Shane pulled himself up and faced the trembling Jerry. "I'm going to crawl through the window and see if I can open the front passenger door from inside. I'll have to get Ronnie's seat belt off before we can bring her out."

"What if we shouldn't move her? Maybe we should wait for help to come." Jerry wrung his hands and then raked them through his thinning hair. "We might hurt her worse."

"I don't think we can wait." The tree creaked louder, and the front end of the SUV slid closer to the drop into the swamp. "Allison, take Lizzie and see if you can get a signal on my phone. Maybe it'll work up there. Call 9-1-1." While they scrambled out of the ravine, he turned again to the broken window. "Come around this side," he told Jerry. "Help me get through here, and when I'm ready, you pull on the door while I push from inside."

Once he had crawled into the vehicle and onto the front seat next to Ronnie, he brushed aside the remains of the airbags and pressed two fingers to her throat. To his relief, a thready pulse fluttered against them. She stirred and whimpered a name.

"Just hush, we're going to have you out of here." He managed to speak gently to the woman, who in just a few hours had caused him and Allison a lifetime of fear. "First, I have to get the seat belt off you."

When he did, Shane checked to make sure her legs weren't caught anywhere. She whimpered again, this time he made out the name Jerry. Well, at least she was asking for her husband and not some jerk she'd hooked up with last year.

Letting her lean against the seat, he put a shoulder to the car door, ramming it while Jerry pulled from the outside. After two attempts it creaked open. He slid an arm behind her and eased Ronnie away from the steering wheel toward the door, and together they moved her from the car and far enough away to lay her down and wait for help to arrive.

He left Jerry sitting on the wet hillside, cradling Ronnie's head and murmuring unintelligible words to her as Shane climbed from the ravine to check on his family.

****

Allison was relieved when, after several hours of getting observed and examined at a local hospital, Lizzie was released with only a few bumps and bruises to show for the terrifying experience, and was allowed to go home. Her baby girl slept all the way, while she sat with her in the back seat, clasping her small hands and humming softly to her. Her own body ached from the night's efforts, but her heart was full of gratitude they were all together. It was near dinner time when Shane pulled the truck into the driveway. She followed two steps behind him as he carried Lizzie into the house and up to her room.

Careful not to awaken her, he laid her down on her bed, brushing a kiss on her forehead before he stepped back. "I'll check on the horses while you tuck her in."

Allison heard a catch in his voice and reached out before he could leave, catching his hand and bringing it up to press her lips against the scratches from the briars in the ravine. "Thank you for believing me," she whispered. "And for bringing our daughter home."

Our family is going to be fine now. I know you'll always be here with us, and we'll be just fine.

Later, with Gypsy at her heels, she slipped down to the barn herself while he kept watch over their sleeping daughter. Bless Jenny, when she'd texted the teenager earlier in the day, she and a few of her friends had once more come to the rescue and cared for the horses. Every equine face gazed at Allison now as if to say, *"Where have you been today?"*

She spent a few minutes with each one to reassure herself as much as them that they were okay.

"Will life ever go back to normal around here?"

She paused to rub Starlight's inquisitive nose and thought about how her life had changed, and whatever had been normal before was no longer true.

"I guess we'll have to find a new normal. Just as you and Stardust, and all of you did when you first came here." Allison gazed down the aisle of the barn, at the curious faces staring at her over their stall doors. As always, she had a lot to learn from them about resilience…and trust.

Shane met her on the porch with a cup of chamomile tea. "I figured you didn't need coffee but something more soothing." He put it in her hands and nodded toward their favorite place. "Let's sit for a while."

"Is Lizzie—"

"Safe and still sound asleep."

She sank onto the swing and let out a long sigh. How could it be less than a day ago they had sat here, coming to grips with the reality of being newly married? After the events of the night, it seemed far in the past.

He sat beside her, and she touched the bandages that covered long scrapes on his arms where he'd reached through the broken window to free Lizzie from the car. When he lifted his arm to put it around her, she saw him wince. No doubt his shoulder was sore from slamming it against the car door.

"Seems you're always getting beat up on my account." She lifted her gaze to his and noticed the fatigue in his face, the shadows in his eyes. He'd been afraid, too, but he'd held it together for her and just as he'd promised, he had brought Lizzie home. Tears of love and gratitude brimmed in her eyes, and she rested her head against his shoulder so he wouldn't see them. "She called you Daddy."

"She...did." His voice broke, and he didn't say anymore.

Allison drank her tea and gave him time for that to sink in. After a few minutes she asked, "What do you think will happen to Ronnie?"

"Guess that depends if you want to press charges. Ronnie was behind most of what's happened this summer, you know. She put the Potters up to cutting the tire, but she left the poisoned hay in the pasture on her own. Pretty sure she drove around the pasture and prowled by the barn, scaring the horses, too. Jerry told me she admitted it all in the ambulance on the way to the hospital. Maybe she was afraid she was going to die. The only thing we can't pin on her is the cougar stalking." He paused a moment, as if contemplating that, then in a wry voice added, "Though, if she would've known about it, she might have had second thoughts on snooping around in the dark out here. Too bad she didn't get a good scare."

Would have served her right. "I guess I always knew Ronnie hated me, I just never knew how much." But instead of anger, sadness welled inside her. *We could have been friends, if only...* "What hurts most of all is she pretended to care, about Lizzie and me, and foolishly I trusted her."

"Could be she hoped to prove it was unsafe for Lizzie to live here to try and get custody of her."

"She should have known I'd never let that happen. Not *ever*." Just the thought of it made her shudder.

"Guess when that didn't work she went to Plan B. Believe me, Ronnie's always had problems. But about bringing charges against her—"

"I won't, as long as she gets help and stays away from us. I hope she and Jerry can both get help." She met his concerned gaze and reached up to touch his face, resting her hand there. He didn't agree with her. She could tell by the set of his jaw and the look in his eyes, but he wouldn't argue.

By now, he knows that's a useless endeavor.

"I feel safe that you're here," she whispered. "And that will always be true."

They were a family now, and her heart overflowed with contentment.

****

A week later, Mark Williamson and a wildlife biologist scoured the orchard and nearby woods again, searching for signs of a big cat in the vicinity. Although she had hoped there would be a trace of the creature, Allison really wasn't surprised when they found nothing.

"Understand, I'm not denying what you saw. We just can't verify it without solid evidence," Mark told her while she cleaned stalls.

"Of course you can't." She leaned on the barn rake and blew a loose strand of hair from her face. Those storms had most likely washed away any evidence of prints long ago. Today, however, the summer afternoon had grown warm, and the two men were both sweating from their efforts in the woods. "Thank you for at least looking."

The conservation officer took off his hat and swiped his shirtsleeve over his face. "We might consider putting a trail cam out here, if you don't mind. That could give us the proof we need."

"I have no objection." But there was another reason she wanted to tell him not to bother.

Since the wedding, more than one change had taken place at Allison's Farm, and there'd been no more restlessness among the animals or sleepless nights—unless she counted the ones when her husband kept her awake, making up for what he called lost time.

When Allison sat with Shane later that evening on the porch swing, she told him what Mark had said.

"At least he's finally taking this seriously. I wonder what changed his mind?" He leisurely toyed with her hair where she'd let it loose to fall around her shoulders.

"It's a little late, I'd say. Anyway, I don't think they'll see anything." She gave him a sideways glance to see his reaction.

Shane turned her toward him and studied her face. "And you know this how?"

Intuition—something she was going to trust far

more now.

She took his hand in hers and placed it over her heart. "I just feel it, here. Do you believe me?"

For his answer, he leaned in and kissed her.

When the sun left a swash of brilliant pink and yellow in the sky and crickets chirped their nightly chorus, she went into the house with him. In the corner of the kitchen, Gypsy and the kittens curled together on their pillow. Upstairs, Lizzie clutched her teddy bear and slept.

Opening the windows, Allison sat there for a moment, but saw nothing but familiar shadows fall across the yard as she listened to the sounds that would always give her a peaceful feeling. A quiet barn, mourning doves cooing their evening farewell…and a loved one's voice beckoning to her. She turned, but just before she went to Shane, a thought whispered through her mind.

Like a will o' the wisp it's moved on, and all is well.

Lucy Naylor Kubash

Author's Note

Coyotes blamed for attacks on horses, but owners disagree. They claim it was a cougar.

A writer never knows what will create a spark that starts a story growing. Some years ago, similar headlines in our local newspaper drew my attention, and I began to follow the many articles that appeared concerning numerous reports of large cats being seen in our area. A controversy grew surrounding the strange sightings, as to whether or not cougars once again existed in Michigan's Lower Peninsula. The last wild cougars were supposedly wiped out here in 1906, and this was nearly one hundred years later. Yet, in spite of the countless testimonials and some DNA evidence, state biologists continued to deny that a breeding population of cougars existed in Lower Michigan in the 21st century.

The dispute, as well as the absence of absolute proof of their existence, made me start to ask the eternal question, what if? What if a woman lived alone with her daughter on her grandparents' farm? What if something attacked one of her horses? What if she feared not only for their safety but the success of her business that is her livelihood? What if the one man she never thought she'd see again suddenly came back into her life? What if she had to trust him?

The answer to those questions became this story, *Will O' the Wisp*. But the answer to the question of wild cougars in west Michigan is still elusive. The local sightings stopped, and no one has reported seeing any big cats for a while. But still, you have to wonder…

A word about the author…

Lucy Naylor Kubash has had a lifelong love of reading and has been writing for as long as she can remember. She is published in short fiction and novel-length contemporary romance, as well as nonfiction, having written a column called the Pet Corner for nearly 15 years. She is a longtime member of Romance Writers of America and her local chapter, Mid-Michigan RWA.

She loves anything to do with the American West and especially traveling there whenever possible. When not writing she likes to spend time with her family and pets.

www.lucynaylorkubash.com

Thank you for purchasing
this publication of The Wild Rose Press, Inc.

For questions or more information
contact us at
info@thewildrosepress.com.

The Wild Rose Press, Inc.
www.thewildrosepress.com

To visit with authors of
The Wild Rose Press, Inc.
join our yahoo loop at
http://groups.yahoo.com/group/thewildrosepress/